DEDICATION

To Gigi and Nina for the inspiration to be a strong woman and a writer. Your guidance into the Arts has led me to my lifelong passion. Now your favorite pastimes can live on through me.

ACKNOWLEDGMENTS

A big thank you to all of my readers. Without you, my writing would just be words printed on a page, but you allow my stories to breathe life.

Lisa Brown, my hugely talented editor. Thank you for being at the receiving end of my excitement, fear, tears and questions for this book. You always intricately sew my thoughts together, helping me create the best version of my story.

Barb Shuler and Emily Maynard, my sounding board and my support. Your encouragement and motivation have become an asset during my writing journey, and I don't know what I would do without you. Thank you for polishing *A Heart of Time* with your exceptional eye for detail.

Linda and Sassy Savvy Fabulous, thank you for your instrumental help in getting my book out there. I'm grateful you took a chance on me and I'm looking forward to working with you more in the future.

My beta readers: Lori, Mignon, Christina, Heather, and Carla—you are my lifeline. Being honest with critique is never easy but I know you all love me enough to give it to me straight.

Twisted Drifters, you make being an author feel like a privilege, and I thank you for your continuous support.

Book reviewers, you illuminate authors' books and your support is what makes this industry evolve and grow. Thank you for continuously sacrificing your time.

Lori, my sister, my always first reader...sorry you had to read this while you were pregnant but I love you for sticking with it and for always being by my side. Love you!

Mom, Dad, Mark, and Ev, Grandma and Papa, thank you for your continued love and support with my books. Your motivation means the world to me.

Boys—Bryce and Brayden—some day when you're old enough to read this book, you'll see the love your mommy and daddy have for each other through the words I have written here. You are both gifted and I hope you never forget that.

Josh, with our road into parenthood the second time around, this story my nightmare in those moments. It woke me up many nights knowing how close you were to becoming the character in this I've written what I've feared the most and I'm grateful every that our family is together and perfect. Thank you for being solid rock and the best husband I could have ever asked for.

PROLOGUE

"SHH," I TELL Her. "Just trust me."

I lift Ellie up, helping her over the wrought iron gate, listening for the slight thud on the other side of the darkness. "Come on!" I hoist myself up and over to the other side where she is waiting for me. Taking her hand, I lead us down the moss covered steps we have walked up and down hundreds of times over the course of our lives. "It's so dark in here at night," she says, breathlessly.

"Are you scared?" I ask, tickling my fingers against her side.

She playfully elbows me in the gut, followed by a sarcastic scoff. "No, dummy. But, what if there are animals or something?"

"I'll protect you," I tell her, wrapping my arm tightly around her shoulders.

"What would I do without you?" she laments. "My knight and shining Hunter."

With no response necessary, I place a quick kiss on her temple and continue down the steps. As soon as we reach the flat ground, I pull my flashlight out of my back pocket and illuminate the path leading to a bench and group of thick oaks. Fear seems to have seeped away and Ellie has now fallen into a fit of quiet giggles. "Ell," I tell her, bringing her up to the closest tree.

"Yeah?" she says through her continued laughter.

I point the flashlight to the ground and grab the sharpest rock I can find. "I'm about to do something totally lame," I tell her.

"Don't even tell me you're going to carve our names into the tree," she says in a way that tells me she loves this idea—corny and lame, or not. I place the flashlight down on the bench and loop my arms loosely around her neck. With a break in the branches, a slight glow from the moon is illuminating her face. She smiles that smile, the one that has always been just for me since we were five years old. With the crickets chirping around us and the slight chill in the May air, I kiss her, the girl who has always been mine.

When our lips part, I take her hand and slip the rock between her fingers. With my hand squeezed tightly around hers, I press it up against the tree, tersely dragging the rock in straight lines, etching our names into the soft bark before encircling it with a heart. "If anyone on the football team hears about this…"

"Our secret forever," she whispers into my ear.

"You know what isn't a secret?" I listen for a response, a cue for me to continue what I'm about to say, but there is only silence. "I am so in love with you, Ellie. I have loved you as my best friend all of these years, but now, getting ready to graduate high school and head off into the big bad world, I need you to know how much I really love you. It's the kind of love that makes a guy want to carve his girl's name into a tree. It's the kind of love that I hope never goes away."

"I am yours forever, Hunter. And this will always be our tree."

CHAPTER ONE

DECEMBER 26TH
- SEVEN YEARS LATER -

"I CAN'T BELIEVE we're finally going to be parents," Ellie says, still breathing heavily from her last contraction. While I run around the house like a loose chicken, she's clutching the armrest of the sofa so tightly her knuckles are turning white.

Overnight bag...got it. Baby bag...check. What else? "There was something else. What am I forgetting?"

"The baby's blanket. The one I knitted," she yells from the living room. Ellie spent the last seven months knitting a tiny, pink blanket. She didn't know how to knit, but she said it was a rite of passage into motherhood. She figured it out. I'll give her that.

"Got it, baby." Baby. In the next few hours, I'm going to be someone's dad. We're going to be a family. The thought is still both terrifying and thrilling at the same time. "Okay, one more second. Let me warm the car up." Our little miracle isn't due for another two weeks, but evidently she's decided that the day after Christmas would be a good time to arrive. I couldn't agree with her more. I can't wait to meet her.

I run out the front door, nearly slipping on the freshly fallen snow before reaching the car door. I duck inside the car and turn the ignition on to blast the heat. Come on. Warm up. This little girl is not waiting for anything tonight.

When I get back in the house, Ellie is standing in the same spot, still holding onto the couch for support. Her eyes are squeezed shut, her teeth clenched together. Drops of sweat are forming on her forehead, and her breaths are quick and loud. I gently wipe her brow with my fingertips and smooth her hair back away from her face, trying my best to soothe her as I wait for the contraction to subside. When it lets up, I take her by the arm as she grabs her purse from the side table. Slowly helping her outside, I hold her up as best I can so she doesn't slip on the snow. "We're doing this, Ell. We're really doing this!" I tell her. She smiles and nods at me, focused on trying to catch her breath and slide into her seat before the next contraction begins.

I settle Ellie in the car and skid across the driveway until I climb into the driver's seat. As I close the door, I pull in a sharp breath and look over at her briefly—the smile on her face and the tears in her eyes. "I love you," she says, placing her hand over mine. "This is going to be the best day of our lives."

"Just the first best day. There are so many best days ahead of us now," I reply with a smile.

Although it feels like forever, it takes us less than twenty minutes to pull up to the emergency room's sliding glass doors. "You're not leaving me, are you?" Ellie asks. It's the first time I've seen any fear in her eyes during this entire pregnancy. She's kept her calm through everything while I've been doing my best to hide my nerves.

"I don't want to make you walk across the parking lot, Ell."

"I'll be okay. I just—don't leave me." Without another thought, I press on the gas and pull into the parking garage, thankfully finding an empty spot on the first floor and fairly close to the front entrance. Another contraction is moving through her, and she's beginning to groan from the pain. "Four minutes apart now," I say, looking at my watch.

When the contraction ends, I take the opportunity to jump out of the car and help her out. I place my arm under hers and walk with her as fast as she can move. Once inside the door, I spot a wheelchair and help her into it. I'm trying to remain calm for Ellie's sake, but inside...Oh God. I'm freaking out.

I push her along to the main desk, one hand on the wheelchair, my other hand firmly gripped around her shoulder. "My wife is in labor," I tell the receptionist.

"Third floor. They'll take it from there," the woman says, smiling brightly. "Congratulations, Mom and Dad." Mom and Dad. We're going to be parents. We're going to be parents! This is amazing. This is incredible! I can't wait to see her little face. I wonder if she'll look like Ellie. God, I hope so. I want her to have Ellie's blonde curls and her big hazel eyes, and her smile that lights up an entire room. I hope she has my humor and Ellie's brains. I just know she's going to be perfect.

"Can you believe this?" Ellie asks, rolling into the elevator. "Three years doesn't seem like such a big deal now. I'd wait forever for this little girl."

"But we don't have to. We're so damn lucky, baby." I wheel her out of the elevator onto the third floor where a nurse immediately greets us. She takes one look at Ellie and ushers us over to a small office.

"I just have a few questions for you, Eleanor. Then we'll get you checked in."

I try to remain calm, or at least make it look like I'm staying calm, but I'm still losing it. What kind of questions could they possibly have right now? We pre-registered. Did everything the way we were supposed to, and I called Ellie's doctor's office to let them know we were headed over her. The nurse asks Ellie to confirm her basic information and creates her a hospital wristband. Then she leans over her desk and places it around Ellie's wrist. Although she's breathing through another contraction right now, Ellie grunts out the words "thank you". That's my girl—always polite, no matter what the situation.

"I will page your doctor to let him know you're here. In the meantime, you two can follow me." The woman leads us out the door and through a set of double doors into a large room separated by what must be a dozen curtains. "One of our triage doctors will examine you and determine if you're in active labor." She places Ellie's chart on the door. "There's a gown for you to change into, and we'll need a urine sample as well," she says as she points to the cup.

How could she not be in active labor? Of course she is. I mean, look at her. I'm trying to keep my cool, but I just want someone to take her pain away. I can't watch her suffering like this.

As if reading my mind, Ellie says, "Don't worry, Hunt, everything is going to be okay." I wish I could say her laughter comforts me, but I know she's forcing it for my sake. What am I saying? I should be comforting her right now. I'm already failing as a husband and father.

I've pretty much been acting like this since the day she got the blood work back, confirming the pregnancy. There was so much to do to prepare for our baby, and I couldn't let either of my girls down. I can't let them down now either.

Ellie is trying to get her clothes off, and I'm just standing here staring at her. I force myself to snap out of my daze and take her by the arm, helping her step out of her pants. I grab the gown from the bed and slip it over her head. "You look so beautiful right now," I tell her, and I mean it. She's glowing. She's happy, despite the pain. She was placed on earth for this purpose and I can see that right now. I'm the luckiest man on earth.

"Sit down," Ellie whispers. "I'm going to use the bathroom. Don't worry. Just relax." She leaves with a smile. She's smiling. I should be smiling, too. So why does the room feel like it's spinning around me? I shouldn't be practicing the breathing exercises without her, but I have to, or I'm going to pass out. She's in labor and I'm the one having trouble breathing. I have to breathe harder because it feels like I can't get enough air right now.

Ellie returns within a few minutes and hoists herself up on the bed before pulling the sheet up around her chest to get comfortable. "The contractions are getting closer together," she says. "I didn't think it would happen so fast."

The class we took said that first-time moms usually have a long labor, so it's okay to take our time when coming to the hospital. They gave us this five-one-one rule. Five minutes apart, lasting for one minute, and for more than an hour. At least, I think that's what it was, but right now my mind is drawing a blank. God, I hope we didn't wait too long. They'll think I'm a horrible husband and father-to-be.

"What is going on in that mind of yours?" Ellie asks, seeing the look of distress on my face.

I bring my focus over to her pale face. "Nothing, baby. I'm just excited. Anxious."

She reaches her hand out to me. "Me too."

A doctor comes in to check her, and he causes her more pain by doing so. Part of me would like to hurt him for hurting her, but again, I refrain from saying anything, since I know I'm overreacting. "Well then, you are almost nine centimeters. I can feel the baby's head, and we need to get you into a room immediately."

"Um, I need to speak with my doctor first. It's important," she says, panic suddenly filling her voice.

"Ell, he'll be here. Don't worry, okay?" I say, trying to reassure her. She's looking at me with a blank expression, like she doesn't want to respond, or maybe it's another contraction coming. I'm not sure.

"Okay," she says, uncertainty filling her eyes.

"Can you get her an epidural? Anything for the pain?" I ask the doctor.

"Mr. Cole, there's not enough time for pain management," he replies. That only means more pain for Ellie. I did this to her. I should have brought her here earlier. I've caused her pain.

"I'm sorry, baby. I'm so sorry," I tell her solemnly, as someone lifts the brakes on the bed she's lying on.

"It's okay. I'll be okay but I need my doctor," she moans out. I keep her hand in mine as we run down the hall into another room where two nurses help her onto a larger bed. They're hooking her up to a bunch of wires and an IV. Is this how it always is? Everyone looks so serious.

"Her blood pressure is low," one of the nurses says. "We need to turn her onto her side." Ellie's eyes are set on mine, ignoring all of the fuss around her. Our fingers are still interwoven and she's squeezing tightly. "I can't get a heartbeat on the baby," the nurse goes on to say.

What? "What do you mean you can't get a heartbeat on the baby? Is she okay? What's happening?" I spit out all of these questions at once as I feel the blood drain from my face...from my entire body.

"Mr. Cole, please relax," the nurse says calmly. "Eleanor, when is the last time you felt the baby kick?"

"Um, uh, a couple of hours ago I guess. I haven't been feeling much through the contractions."

The nurses all share a look, and one runs out the door. God, help us. What is happening right now? I drop down to my knees and take Ellie's hand, bringing it up to my lips. She gives me a small smile and says, "Remember, the class said this stuff happens sometimes, Hunter. I need you to find Dr. Moore, though. It's really important. He has my birth plan and I need him." I'm worried. I'm so unbelievably worried right now, and although I hate to ignore her wishes, I'm not leaving her side to go find her doctor, wherever the hell he is right now. There are fine doctors on call who can deliver our baby, and if Dr. Moore doesn't get here in time, they'll have to be okay.

"Hunter, I am worried, and I'm scared," she whimpers. "Something's wrong."

"Our baby is okay. She is," I say, squeezing Ellie's hand. She has to be. Where is that fucking doctor? And why is nobody talking to us, telling us what is going on?

An on-call doctor finally jogs into the room with a portable ultrasound machine. "We're just going to make sure the baby is in the right position to come out," the doctor explains calmly. That's all they're checking for? It doesn't seem like that's the case. Is he just trying to keep us calm? If so, it isn't working. "Okay, we have a heartbeat, but it's not as strong as I'd like it to be. I hate to do this with you being so close to full dilation, Mrs. Cole, but just to be on the safe side, I think we need to get the baby out right away."

"A C-section?" Ellie asks, through tears. "I didn't want to have one."

A nurse hands Ellie a pen and has her sign a few papers, which takes less than ten seconds. They're already pushing her out of the room, back into the hall. Someone throws me a set of scrubs and tells me to put them on and follow them down to the operating room. Is this safe? Is Ellie going to be okay? She seems so afraid...but I know they do this all the time. They said that in our class, too.

I struggle to get the scrub shirt over my t-shirt as I run down the hall toward where I see doctors piling into a room. Shaking and weak, I walk into the OR in a daze and a nurse guides me over to a stool next to Ellie's head. "Just relax, the nurse says," smiling and patting my hand. "She needs you right now." I wish everyone would stop telling me to relax. How the hell am I supposed to relax? My wife is on an operating table, and my unborn daughter is in trouble. Who would relax in this situation?

I try to breathe through my nerves, but it isn't working. I comb my fingers through Ellie's soft hair and push it out of her face. "You okay?" I ask. Stupid question. Of course she's not okay, but right now, I don't know what else to say.

"As okay as I can be," she says quietly. I know she's terrified.

"There isn't enough time for a spinal," a doctor shouts. It's Ellie's doctor, thank God. I don't know when he got here but he's here. "Mr. Cole, we need you to leave right now."

"What? Why?" I ask, feeling totally helpless. A nurse inserts another tube into Ellie's IV. "What's that?" I ask.

"We need to put your wife under general anesthesia to perform the C-section. There isn't enough time to give her a spinal or an epidural without putting the baby at risk, so I need you to say your goodbyes and wait in the room next door. As soon as the baby is born, we'll let you know what is going on." I can't be here for my daughter's birth? I can't be here for Ellie? "Mr. Cole, we need to do this right now," her doctor shouts over, snapping me out of my panic-stricken haze.

Ellie already looks dazed as I lean down and press my lips against hers, feeling the tears fill my eyes. "I love you, Ell. When you wake up, we're going to be a family." We are. Right? Her hand lifts weakly and she places it over my face. "Let's name her Olive," she mumbles.

"You said you didn't want to name her until you saw her," I remind her. But her eyes are already closed, and I'm being pulled out of the room. "I love you, Ellie," I cry out. I shouldn't be crying. I'm supposed to be the strong one. I don't cry. I haven't since I was a kid. Why does this all seem so wrong? I shouldn't be leaving her right now. It's my job to be by her side.

Now I'm alone in a small room with a water bubbler and a TV. I only sit down because I feel like my knees might give out. I might pass out, and I didn't even see a drop of blood. Holding my head in my hands, I count the seconds as they pass, wondering how long I'll have to wait before I hear something.

The dryness in my throat is making me feel strangled so I lean over to the water bubbler, grabbing a paper cone and filling it with water. This wasn't our plan.

After what feels like an hour, a doctor walks through the door but it's not Ellie's doctor. "Mr. Cole," he says. I stand up, pushing through my bodily weakness. "Your daughter is perfect. She had the umbilical cord wrapped around her neck two times, but she's receiving oxygen right now and will be just fine. A nurse will be in to take you to the neonatal care unit so you can be with your daughter." With a proud smile, the doctor reaches for my hand. "Congratulations, son. She's a beauty."

"How's Ellie?" I ask, breathing a little easier. "Will she be in recovery soon?"

"Eleanor is just fi—" The doctor stops talking as he looks down at his pager. After a long second, he looks back up at me with wide eyes. "I'll have someone come speak with you in a moment." He runs out of the room, and I'm left staring at the door he just ran through. The look in his eyes—was that about Ellie? Is she okay? I push out of the door and find myself in an empty hallway, spinning around, looking for a nurse...or anyone who can help me understand what is going on. Not finding anyone, I head back into the waiting room.

A nurse finally walks into the waiting room and sits down beside me, placing her hand on my back. "Do you want to meet your daughter?" she asks with a gentle smile.

"Is Ellie okay?" I ask.

"The doctors are taking good care of her," she says with a hint of unease.

"What does that mean? Did something happen?" I ask, more firmly this time, while trying not to panic.

"When they know more, they'll let you know," she says, seemingly trying to sound reassuring. "For now, you should focus on your daughter."

"Olive. Her name is Olive." I feel like we've walked a mile down this hall before we turn in to a room surrounded by windows. The nurse takes me over to a little bassinet with plastic sides. And I see her…Olive. She's perfect. I look at her fingers—counting them—and her toes. Ten and ten. Her nose—she has Ellie's perfect little nose. She's absolutely beautiful.

"Do you want to hold her?" A nurse asks. Ellie should be able to hold her first.

"I don't feel right—" I begin.

"She would want you to hold your daughter," the nurse says with a small smile, "especially since the delivery required general anesthesia. She wouldn't want Olive to wait until she wakes up before being held by her Daddy." She reaches into the bassinette and carefully pulls my little girl out, keeping her wrapped tightly in a pink blanket. "We need to keep the tubes in her nose for a little while longer until her oxygen levels are where we'd like to see them. So just be careful not to move them."

The nurse pulls over a wooden rocking chair and takes me by the arm, guiding me down into the seat. Stiff as a board, scared of hurting this tiny little person, I hold Olive against my chest, feeling her warmth. It soothes me. Olive opens her eyes, looking up at me with a lost look—a curious look. I melt instantly. I'm in love. This little girl is mine. She belongs to me—forever. How did we create something so perfect? "I'm your daddy," I cry through a weak voice. "And I don't usually cry this much, but you're just so beautiful."

The nurse returns with a bottle and holds it out in front of me. "Do you want to feed her?" she asks.

"Oh, no. Ellie is planning to nurse." That was one thing she was dead set on. She knew her birth plan could change, but she made it clear she wanted to try breastfeeding, totally avoiding bottles if at all possible.

The nurse pulls up a stool and sits down beside me. "We'll give it a little while then," she says.

"Do you know something?" I ask her, looking at the expression painted across her aging face. Because her expression tells me she does know something or she's seen this before. Something. There's sympathy in her eyes, not the happiness she should have for a dad meeting his daughter for the first time.

"I—I can't. I think a doctor will be in to speak with you shortly."

My heart is aching. There is something they aren't telling me, and with absolutely no information, I feel like the wind has been knocked out of me. "Could you take her for a moment?" I ask the nurse. I don't want anyone to touch my daughter. I want to keep her to myself, but right now I can't breathe. The nurse takes Olive. My Olive. She takes her from me and rocks her gently as I lean forward, trying my hardest to inhale a little deeper.

"Is she going to make it? Will you at least tell me that?" I ask with a touch of hostility. I'm trying to control my anger. I'm in a nursery, so I know I can't lose it. But I'm about to. If someone doesn't tell me what's going on, I'm going to fucking lose it.

The nurse looks back up at me again and doesn't even answer me this time. Oh shit. Shit! Ellie! No! I stand up and lean over, placing a quick kiss on Olive's head. "I'll be right back, baby-girl."

I run out the door and back toward the OR before anyone can stop me. When I approach the OR door, I press on it, knowing very well I should not be going through these doors, and by now I'm somewhat surprised no one has stopped me.

When the door opens, the sight of a whole lot of blood—my wife's blood, immediately assaults me. Why isn't anyone working on her? Why isn't anyone stopping the blood? I scan my focus around the room, looking at everyone's faces until I see her doctor. He's looking at the clock. What is he doing? No...no...Ellie! I run to her, grabbing her hand and pulling it up to my chest. I fall to my knees. "No. Ellie, baby. Ellie!" I scream out. Continuing to shout, I call her name over and over. Why isn't anyone stopping me? I wonder, but deep inside I know the answer to that question. I know why no one is stopping me. It doesn't matter, does it?

"Time of death—"

"Don't say it. Don't you fucking say it!" I yell.

"Eleven, twelve," the doctor says quietly.

"No, she's not gone! You can't just take her from me like that. She's not gone. Bring her back. Do something. Anything!" How could this happen? She's healthy. She had a picture perfect pregnancy. No morning sickness, no blood pressure issues, nothing. So what is this?

Silence consumes the room after my outbursts. A blur of activity happens around me, and I'm being pulled up to my feet by several hands.

All of the hands release me as another hand settles on my shoulder, but I can't look away from Ellie. Her eyes are closed. Her cheeks are pale. Her lips—they're blue. "Please, Ellie. You can't leave me. We have our family now. Ellie—" I sob.

"We did all that we could," the doctor's words float into my ear and twist tightly around my brain, shutting off all logical thoughts. "She suffered from a ruptured aneurysm."

"Isn't that in the brain, though?" I ask, confused, looking at the blood-soaked blue sheet covering the lower half of her body.

"Unfortunately, the strain from her contractions caused an aneurysm to rupture. It happened very fast. She didn't suffer, but yet, her brain is no longer functioning."

"How did we not know she—"

"Some people don't know until it's too late, I'm afraid," a doctor, not Ellie's doctor, says.

And just like that, my family has been broken apart before it was even united. The love of my life—the other half of my heart—has died. "Son, this is not an opportune time to discuss this with you, but time is of the essence. When her oxygen levels depleted, we placed Eleanor temporarily on a ventilator because she elected to donate her working organs if she were to pass. I wanted to inform you of this before we begin the procedure. The surgeon is on his way over as it needs to be handled right away." There's too much going through my mind to tell myself this is what Ellie would have wanted. This isn't what I want. What about me? What about Olive? We were supposed to have all parts of her, and selfishly, I don't want to give her parts to anyone else. I want her whole. I want her with me. Alive. I can't do this without her. "I'll give you a moment."

"So she's still alive? I mean, her heart is still beating?" I ask, baffled. "Can she hear me? Are you sure she's really gone? Didn't you put her under general anesthesia? Maybe she just hasn't woken up."

"This happened as we were preparing to put her under, son. I'm sure. We did several tests to confirm what we immediately assumed. Her heart is still beating but I'm afraid the rest of her is gone."

The room empties out around me, leaving me alone with my Ellie. My girl—the woman I knew I was placed on this earth for. I kneel back down by her bedside, unable to comprehend how we've gotten to this moment in time.

Five hours ago, we were laughing at our favorite TV show. She was making a long list of baby names and spitting out the most ridiculous ones she could find in the baby-name dictionary. Five hours ago, our life was perfect.

I always tried not to think that God didn't want us to have a baby. We tried everything, including infertility treatments. Nothing worked, but we kept trying. Maybe we should have taken the hint. But we didn't. We needed Olive. We needed her like we needed air to breathe, and now I know Olive really was Ellie's air to breathe.

"Ellie, baby, I never considered the thought of having to say goodbye to you today. How can I say goodbye? I don't want to. I want to beg you to stay, but it won't matter, will it? God. Life is cruel...so damn cruel. It shouldn't have been like this." I place my lips over her cool cheek. She's gone. I can feel it. Her soul is gone. My beautiful Ellie is gone. I watch her for a moment, stupidly thinking...hoping...she's just going to open her eyes. "Open your eyes," I cry into her ear. "Please. I can't do this without you." My heart feels like someone just ripped it out through my throat and is now choking me with it. Everything hurts so damn much, and this isn't a pain that will ever go away. "Ellie, I'm going to raise our little girl the way you wanted to raise her. She's going to know everything about you—every single detail—right down to the heart-shaped freckle under your right eye. I won't let you down. I won't. Please, Ell, just know how much you are loved. I've loved you since the day we met, and I will love you until the day I die. You are my wife, my best friend. My forever. Just like I was your forever."

I really was her forever. We met on the first day of Kindergarten when we were five. We were best friends until high school, then boyfriend and girlfriend until our senior year of college when we got married. There was never anyone else...for either of us. We had our lives planned out, and this was supposed to be the beginning…not the end. I stand back up and place one more kiss on her forehead. Am I really saying good-bye to her right now? This isn't real. This isn't happening. Someone wake me up.

But no one does. This is real. What was supposed to be the best day of my life just became a living hell.

I touch Ellie's hair one last time because it's something I'll never be able to do again. I don't think I'll ever be able to comprehend the loss standing in front of me. How can this lovely creature, who was such an integral part of my past, not be part of my future? I touch her lips, her eyelids, her ears, her cheeks, and her neck. The heaviness of her hand isn't something I recognize, though. This isn't my Ellie, the warm, beautiful woman who I haven't spent a day without.

This isn't happening. This can't be real. Someone please tell me this isn't real. Everything inside of me is screaming with an alarm of panic. My mind doesn't understand what I'm about to do. My mind doesn't know how to say goodbye to the love of my life. I shouldn't have to say goodbye. I can't.

"Ellie," I say sweetly as if my calm, soothing voice will pull her back to me. "You don't understand, baby. I can't do this. Life. I can't do this without you." My words in the form of a plea go unheard, unanswered, ignored by God, Ellie, and anyone and anything that was ever supposed to support me. This isn't fair. This isn't fair. "Ellie, I need you. We need you. Please, come back."

CHAPTER TWO

I'M PACING IN circles around the living room, desperately searching for a neon blue backpack. How can something that bright just disappear? God, she's going to be late for her first day of kindergarten and I will have already failed before the school year begins. "Olive?" I call out. "Have you seen your backpack?"

I yank up the cushions on the couch, knowing the bag can't exactly fit under here but I'm running out of places to look. I'm freaking out right now. That's what this is. I'm definitely freaking out because I'm not ready to send her to school. She's too young. She's not ready. She won't want to let go of me. I should just homeschool her—maybe that would be best, but then I'd have to quit working with AJ, and he'd kill me if I did that. Not to mention that Olive and I would both starve.

"Daddy, what are you doing?" Olive asks, in her squeaky little voice. I turn around, dropping the cushion down. "Did you lose something?" She walks toward me with her backpack firmly perched on her shoulders, lunch bag in hand and wearing a smile that tells me she's not nervous to leave me. It's me who doesn't want to let go of her, not the other way around. Having her with me for these last five years has been my lifeline...my way to keep a piece of Ellie near me. My heart aches for a brief minute as I stare through her, imagining what this moment would be like if Ellie were here. Would Ellie be crying? Probably, but she'd also be excited for Olive, and she would help me be brave as we send our little girl off to her first day of kindergarten. At least I know she would approve of the eye-blinding blue backpack. It was her favorite color, too.

"Nope, I didn't lose anything. I was just straightening up."

"No," she croons with a toothy smile. "You were looking for my backpack." I swear there is a twenty-year-old living inside of my five-year-old. "Don't worry, Daddy. I'm going to be okay today. And so will you. I made you lunch and breakfast. And I plugged your phone into the charger because the battery bar turned red."

I kneel down and open my arms up, waiting for her to run to me like she always does. "You made me lunch and breakfast?" I ask as I tighten my arms around her tiny body.

"Yup. I made you cereal for breakfast and bread and mayonnaise for lunch. Now you won't have to make lunch by yourself today." A tiny breath escapes her lips and her eyes look at me with as much seriousness as a five-year-old could muster up. "You told me yesterday that you would be sad not having anyone to help you make lunch while I'm at school, and I didn't want you to be sad."

My chest tightens a little more. "You are the most thoughtful little girl in the world, Olive. Thank you for making me meals." Her wet lips press against my cheek and her hands squeeze against my back.

"We're going to miss the bus," she says. I look up at the clock, seeing we have five minutes to get to the bus stop down the street, so I scoop her up and head out the door. I don't want to let her go. I've kept her by my side for five years. And to show for that, she's probably the only five-year-old who could install a carpet with her eyes closed. Every day has been a "bring-your-child-to-work day" and I've loved it. Today will be the first job without her next to me in five years.

By the time we reach the end of the driveway, AJ is pulling in. His window is down and his head is craned out of the window. "Is my big girl finally going to school today?" he shouts over.

"Uncle AJ!" she shouts, wriggling herself free from my arms so she can run to his truck. "I'm going to school!"

AJ throws the truck into park, hops out and swings his arms around Olive. It's seconds before she's sitting on his shoulders. "You are going to have the best day, little girl." He tickles her senselessly until she's hanging upside down and completely out of breath.

"We're going to miss the bus," I tell him.

"Well, Mr. Serious Pants said I have to put you down," AJ says in a mockingly deep voice. "Can't miss the bus on your first day, Ollie-Lolly." With one last giggle, Olive runs back to my side, slipping her hand into mine.

"Come'on, Daddy," she drawls.

"I'll be back in twenty," I tell AJ.

"I'm heading right over to the job site. Just meet me over there when you're ready," AJ says. I give him a quick nod and continue toward the bus stop. "Hey, Hunt."

I look back at AJ as we continue to walk. "Yeah?"

"She's going to be great, bro. Don't worry." AJ is a man of many words, but most of them are filled with humor, sarcasm, or things I don't need to hear. It makes up for my serious disposition, but when he says something from the heart, it means a lot.

"Thank you," I say, waving over my head.

"I'm excited," Olive says as we approach the bus stop.

"I'm going to miss you today," I tell her, taking in the scene of a half dozen moms and what must be ten kids. What if the bus driver doesn't see her get on?

"It's just kindergarten," she whispers into my ear.

I chuckle against her cheek and place her down. She's quick to take off, throwing her backpack to the ground so she can join the other kids running across the grassy area. She doesn't know any of them but she doesn't care. Olive makes friends with everyone she meets, just like Ellie did. I could learn a thing or two from my intelligent daughter.

"Hi there," one of the moms says as she approaches me with her hand outstretched. "Are you new to the neighborhood?"

I clear my throat from what feels like a gummy substance lodged between my tongue and tonsils. Keep your shit together, Hunter. "Yeah, ah, Olive and I just moved in a few weeks ago," I manage to get out while shaking her hand—her warm, inviting, and surprisingly strong hand.

"Oh, you're the new neighbors in the yellow house?" she says, pointing down in the direction we walked from. I don't look to where she's pointing, though, since the wind blowing through her long, auburn hair seems to have caught my attention.

"Yes, Ma'am, we are." Ma'am? Really? Smooth.

She chuckles quietly. "I'm Charlotte Drake. Welcome!" With an awkward pause because I can't figure out how to say my name, she continues, "Well, I'm sure you and your wife will be happy here. This is a wonderful neighborhood to raise a family as you can clearly see." She emphasizes her statement by looking back at all the children playing.

My wife…my wife who should be here with us today, but isn't. And just like that, I'm reminded how nothing about this day is as it should be. A pain forms in my stomach at yet another thought of what can never be. I don't know how many important events in Olive's life will be stolen from Ellie…from us as a family, but with as many as I can count so far, it is still as heartbreaking every time we experience another first. Ellie would have been so proud of Olive today…to see what an amazing little girl she is already becoming.

Charlotte's words are innocent, but they pack a punch harder than I've felt in a while. It's not like I haven't gotten the single dad questions before, but today I didn't need a reminder that our family is broken. I was also hoping a new neighborhood would mean a fresh start, a life without sympathetic looks and the outpouring offers of help. Although appreciated, I wish everyone would give me the benefit of the doubt and realize I can handle things. At least, I say I can handle things, although some things I'm still not great at.

"It's just Olive and me, actually," I say, offering her this peephole of information—information I'm only giving because I know it won't remain hidden for long here anyway. My response causes her to loosen her grip and slide her hand out from mine.

"Oh," she groans, her captivating lake-blue eyes squinting tightly as if she wants to punish herself for accusing me of having a normal life. "A divorce. They're horrible. I just went through one myself. At least the asshole left me the house." She lets out a loud sigh and covers her face with her hands. "Sorry. TMI." Her eyes for a brief moment and she drops her hands down by her sides. "Anyway, it's been a long summer, and I was starting to feel like the only one in this neighborhood among the fifty other happily married couples. You know, we should start a divorcee club here. Right? We should. That should be a thing."

Her rambling is humorous and so are her assumptions of me being divorced. I have, in fact, tried to convince myself over the past five years that I've been going through a horrible divorce. I have even tried to make myself believe I hate Ellie and this was my only option. But in no world could I ever hate her. "I'm actually not divorced," I say. "My wife and I had a great marriage." Charlotte looks dazed for only a second before her pretty eyes grow wide. The meaning of "had a great marriage" and not being divorced must have clicked in her head.

"Oh my God," she breathes. Placing her hand over my shoulder, she pulls in a sharp breath and asks, "Did your wife—did she—?" There's no beating around the bush with this one.

Again, I have to do the nod and force my lips into a straight line across my face, hoping she doesn't force out any further details. I'm not sure if it's normal or not, but even though an entire five years has passed, it doesn't matter how many times this question has been asked, everything inside of me still aches the same way it did that night I had to say goodbye. After this long, I think it's safe to say this pain will never go away but I don't think it should, and I'm not sure I want it to. Ellie's missing out on the life we were supposed to live together. I get to live it and she doesn't. I should feel the pain for her. "She's no longer with us," I say, looking past her, watching Olive's unbreakable smile as she holds an invisible microphone up to her lips and belts out the new Taylor Swift song she's had me playing for her on repeat.

When I refocus my attention on Charlotte, leaving the moment of despair behind me, I find her with her hands clasped over her heart. "That little girl is lucky to have you," she says. "You're a good man. I hope you know that."

I'm a good man for taking care of my daughter? She turns around and calls her daughter over, then Olive, too. Her daughter looks like she might be a bit older than Olive, but probably no more than a year. Both girls come running and Charlotte kneels down in front of them. "Lana, today is Olive's first day of school. Will you sit with her on the bus?"

"Mom," Lana says, exasperated. "We're already new best friends." Lana giggles and snatches up Olive's hand. "Olive is so funny."

"Yeah, we're already friends, and you know what?" Olive says with delight. "We live right across the street from each other. Isn't that great, Daddy?" I look up at Charlotte, wondering why she failed to mention living across from the "new neighbors." I guess maybe it is because we've been hermits since we moved in, and with the car in the garage, we haven't been out front much.

"That's great, girls. I'm so glad," Charlotte says.

The yellow monster coming to steal my daughter catches my eye and I know now that I have to come to terms with letting her go. "The bus is coming," I tell them. The sinking pit hits the bottom of my stomach as the bus comes to a screeching halt. I'm supposed to let Olive climb onto this contraption that some random person is driving and let her go off, alone, to God knows where. I can't do this. I grab Olive and hold her against me, running my fingers through her blond curls. It takes all the courage I can conjure to say, "You're going to have so much fun today, and I'll be right here waiting for you when you come back. Okay?" I place a kiss on her cheek and squeeze her a little harder.

She kisses me back and pulls her bag over her shoulders. "Don't forget to eat your breakfast," is the last thing she says before making the hike up the three mountainous steps of the bus. My throat is tight and my heart is pounding, but I have to control myself—if not for Olive's sake, then for the fact that I'm surrounded by six smiling women. Why are they all looking at me the way they are? And why do I feel like a little girl whose balloon just popped?

I watch through the windows of the bus as Olive plops down in the second seat. She's so tiny, I can only see the top of her head above the windowsill. I can't see her face. I can't tell if she's scared or happy. She has to be happy. She has to be. As the bus door closes, her hand slowly pokes up above her head and she waves—this slow, unsure wave. Shit...that does it. I'm done. I turn around, avoiding goodbyes, as well as the staring faces of all the moms looking at me like I'm crazy, and I jog down the hill toward the house.

When I get home, I lock myself inside and lean against the door. I need to destroy something. I take all of the mail on the coffee table and throw it against the wall. That didn't suffice. Next is the damn coasters Mom gave me as a housewarming gift—I chuck each one of them against the wall individually, still feeling only the slightest bit of relief. It's just school—she's just going to school but letting her go hurts like fucking hell and I shouldn't have to do this alone—that's why I'm mad. A logical reason, as far as I'm concerned; regardless of the fact that if I were watching someone behave the way I am right now, I'd tell them to man the hell up. I'm not interested in taking my own advice, though, not today anyway.

A knock on the door pulls me out of my moment. A moment similar to others I allow myself to have far too often. I jump up; worried it could be Olive...or something—even though that wouldn't make any sense. She's on a bus. To school. A normal part of life.

Whipping the door open, I find Charlotte on my doorstep. Her hands are tucked into the pockets of her jeans and the expression on her face tells me she's as unsure about standing on my front step as I feel about everything right now. "You okay?" she asks sincerely—the "I get it" type of sincerity, not the type of sincerity where she's talking to me like a child. Without giving me a second to respond, she continues with, "We've all been there. You're just the only one with a kindergartener this year. The rest of us went through the pain last year. There were six of us standing on the curb in tears as the bus took off for the first time." She pauses to catch her breath and then lets out a soft laugh. "At least Olive went willingly. You wouldn't believe what I had to do with Lana last year. I had to drag her onto the bus kicking and screaming. It was like this horror movie. You would have thought I was dropping her off on the side of a deserted road."

"Yikes," I offer as a condolence.

"Yeah, I know, right? Once she was on the bus, she stood up on the seat and pressed her hands up against the window, crying for me. I felt like the worst mother in the whole world for the entire six hours she was gone. As you may have noticed, this year seemed a little easier."

I look at her for a long minute, unsure of what to say since I already used up my "Yikes" remark. What else is there to say? "I'm glad things went better for her today." Could I sound less interested, or humored by her approach to making me feel better? I tell myself every day to snap out of it and act like a decent person, but it's like everything inside of me is black and cold. I only have enough warmth inside for Olive. The bitterness just pours out of me and chases everyone away.

"Well, if you want to talk—I..." she points across the street to what I now know to be her house. "I'm just across the street." Charlotte turns on her heels and releases what sounds like a lungful of air.

"Did I do her hair right?" The words slip off my tongue before I realize I'm calling out for help. What the hell am I doing? I don't ask for help, encouragement or sympathy. I close doors in people's faces and hang up on phone calls filled with questions I don't want to answer. I am closed off and not concerned with what anyone else thinks about my life or me.

Charlotte releases a hearty laugh as she turns back around. "She has great hair and the headband is adorable. You really are doing just fine."

"I grew up with a brother. Having a daughter sometimes feels like I'm living in a foreign country where no one speaks English." This is exactly how I've felt since the day Olive turned two and grabbed her first Disney Princess doll off of a shelf.

A mischievous look spreads across Charlotte's face and she retraces her steps up to my front door—where I'm standing. "Do you have coffee?" she asks.

What kind of question is that? Is there a parent awake at this hour that doesn't drink coffee? "How could I survive without it?" I laugh.

"Do you have more than one coffee cup?" Is she inviting herself over? Is this what parents do when their kids go to school for the day? Hang out and drink coffee while they share secrets on how not to screw up their kids' lives?

"I have four, believe it or not. They all came in one box—so I didn't really have a choice," I answer, smirking a bit. The wittiness pouring out of me is something that has felt unnatural for so long, it feels foreign leaving my lips, but standing in front of someone who understands my current pain, the camaraderie isn't unfortunate. In fact, I'm surprised to realize it feels kind of nice.

"Do you have enough coffee to fill more than one cup?" Charlotte continues, squinting through one eye as if is she's waiting for me to say no.

"Would you like to come in for a cup of coffee?" I finally ask, not that I wasn't cornered into asking, but I can do coffee. I can be a normal human being for just a few minutes today. Plus, it doesn't hurt that she's incredibly gorgeous. A distraction that looks like her would be okay, I suppose.

"Oh my gosh, thank you so much!" she says, as if it's an unexpected invitation. "I ran out of coffee this morning—mommy brain. If you didn't invite me in, I was just going to beg you for some coffee beans. I don't even have a grinder, but I'm so desperate that I would have pounded the hell out of the beans just to get my fix."

Her joke makes me my laugh—a real laugh—not like the laughs I offer AJ when I'm trying to make him stop a bad joke before it completely rots.

I lead Charlotte into my house, through the living room, and into the kitchen. I wonder what she's thinking about the couch cushions, coasters, and mail lying on the ground from my recent Tasmanian Devil fit. "A Keurig," she says, eyeing the coffee maker. "I like the way you think." I pull a chair out from the table and offer her a seat. "You're settled in pretty well for moving in so recently."

"I don't like feeling displaced," I say while pulling down a couple of mugs from the cabinet.

"I hear ya," she mutters in return, looking at her nails, inspecting each one as if using that as a distraction. Her sudden shift in mood has me questioning if I said something wrong.

I retrieve the sugar and cream and place them both down in front of her. "You okay?" I ask.

"I'm sorry for being rude," she responds without skipping a beat. "I shouldn't have so slickly invited myself in after only knowing you for twenty minutes. I really did just want to ask for coffee, but...that's weird. So is asking you if you had more than one cup. Considering the circumstances, that wasn't funny. I'm sorry. I don't exactly know anyone else on our street since we're the only two with kids, so knocking on their doors would have been even weirder. And the bus stop moms all live two streets away." She lets out a loud groan. "Hi, I'm Charlotte and I like to ramble and make a fool out of myself immediately after I meet a nice person." Her nervous laugh actually puts me at ease.

"I did the inviting; you're fine," I grin. I'm smiling. I almost forgot about sending my child off to war.

With the mugs both filled, Charlotte pulls a napkin from the pile in the middle of the table and wipes away a sprinkle of fallen sugar. I find myself watching her hands, remembering the way Ellie's hands looked as she was wiping down our counters. Our counters were always very clean. Everything was always very clean. Ellie was what she'd refer to as a clean freak. I think it was a little OCD, but she preferred the term "clean freak."

The clattering of the two mugs clinking against each other pulls me from my thoughts of Ellie, forcing me to refocus my attention on the stranger sitting before me. If we were in the old house, I probably would have clawed Charlotte's eyes out at the thought of another woman placing her hands anywhere Ellie's hands had been, but that is one of the many reasons I needed to sell our house. I was basically living in Ellie's coffin with her. Except I'm still alive.

Charlotte hands me one of the mugs as I sit down across from her. This is suddenly weird. I don't know her at all and she's sitting at my kitchen table. "I can't even begin to imagine what you've been through," she says.

I hate sympathy. I really do. When there is too much of one thing, it becomes the least desired part of life, my life anyway. "It's been a rough road," I say, running my fingers through my hair.

"One of my closest friends lost her husband," she says, placing her mug down. "I saw how it took her years to pick up the pieces of her life. Nothing anyone did made the process easier for her, so all any of us could do was just be there for when she needed us."

I know I haven't made it easy on AJ or my parents. Actually, I know I've been a complete pain in the ass. They've all tried to pick up the pieces for me and put them back together in a way they thought I should now be, but Charlotte's right, there is nothing anyone can do for a person who lost half of their heart. "It's a horrible thing to go through," is all I can respond with.

Her focus shifts from me to the empty space beside me, to the picture frame I keep at the third place setting on the table. Ellie's seat. With a smile, Charlotte traces her finger down the side of the frame. "She's beautiful. Olive looks just like her." She pulls her hand away from the frame and rests it over mine. The sensation of her touch causes everything within me to stiffen—everything. With a thick breath lodged in my throat, my eyes lock on our hands—the connection and the disconnection. "Did she pass recently?"

I nod my head, feeling some anger stir within me. Why is she making me answer all of these questions? Most people I don't know will tiptoe around the subject and just offer the sympathetic stare, but not Charlotte. She's prying open this closed door that I have tried hard to keep shut. "She died five years, eight months, and twenty-seven days ago while giving birth to Olive."

I was wondering when Charlotte would crack, but I'm guessing that's right about now. Her eyes are still wide, staring at me, but now they're filling with tears. I don't want someone crying for me or over me. I don't want anyone talking to me, looking at me, or being near me. I want to feel like I've died, too, because it just makes this all so much easier. With no more tolerance, I stand up, pulling my hand away from her grip. Debating on fleeing this scene altogether, I remind myself I can't exactly run out of my own house, so I put the cream and sugar away, doing my best to stall and hint that I'm ready for this coffee date to end before I say something regretful.

Delaying and all, there is still silence and there are still tears in her eyes, so I walk out of the room. I leave her there crying because—because I don't think I know how to avoid being an asshole to anyone who dares to step foot into my life.

I circle the living room a few times, trying to even out my breaths, waiting for my heart to give up on the boxing match with my ribcage. But it never relents. The heart always wins over everything else. Whatever it needs to feel, it feels, and it will bring everything down with it.

I fall onto the couch and release all of the air from my lungs. The pain is as prominent today as it was five years ago. It's like shrapnel in a wound. If the wound closes around what is causing the pain, the pain will forever be embedded. I've come to accept this. "I don't even know your name," Charlotte says, stepping out of the kitchen, wringing her hands around her wrists.

"Hunter," I mutter softly.

"I'm sorry for being pushy or nosy but you look like—it seems like you might need a friend. We're neighbors, so I figured..." I could be a great charity case or pity project to make her feel better about herself.

"Thank you," I say gruffly. "I'm usually fine. It's just days like today—firsts in Olive's life—when everything comes to a head, it feels as fresh as it once did. I'm not usually this much of a mess."

"I went to therapy with my friend after her husband died—it was the only way I could get her to go. The doctor always told her the pain would never go away but that eventually the good days would outweigh the bad. They also told her that the hard days would be harder than they ever had been before, no matter how much time has passed. Grief is like a scar—you can cover it up all you want, but it will always be there." She's saying what I have always thought. Everyone who is someone in my life has told me the pain will lessen, things will eventually get easier, and I'll move on and forget about her. But in truth, the pain reminds me of her, and I don't want to forget her so I endure the pain, and I carry it around like a heavy bag on my back. Sometimes I carry it with pride and other times I let it weigh me down until I'm at the point I'm at right now.

Charlotte exhales loudly and looks around the room, focusing on the mess my couch cushions are in. "What do you do for work, Hunter?" she asks hesitantly, sitting down in the recliner across from me.

And I'm done. Time is up. Did she just become my therapist? Because, yeah, I'm all set with that.

"I'm a carpenter. I run a company with my brother." How the hell do I get this chick to leave? I need time to deal with Olive going off to school before I head to the job site, and instead, I have Charlotte, dredging up every detail of my life. More than I care to share in one day.

"You aren't with Harold and Sons, are you?" she asks, straightening the pillow behind her, becoming more comfortable. I don't want you to get comfortable on the chair that Ellie and I spent two whole wasteful weeks fighting over. I hated it, and I won. Then I bought it after she died. Now it's my favorite chair.

"I am with Harold and Sons." There are only three carpentry companies here in Sage. And only one of them is family run.

"Shut up!" she squeals. "My parents used you guys a few months ago to refinish their hardwoods."

I think for a minute, recalling the few hardwood jobs we had. Only one of those couples were on the older side. "The Olsans?" I ask.

"Yup," she grins. "That's them. Such a small world."

"Great folks you have. They were very kind." Does my voice sound as monotone as I hear it? Why would anyone want to sit here and continue a conversation with me? I did technically invite her in, but that was before I knew she was a female praying mantis, or in this case, "preying" mantis. "What do you do?" Why did I ask that? I don't care what you do. But I should. So I ask. I should make an effort to talk to a beautiful woman, especially a forward one who almost but not quite, invited herself into my house. I should be thinking inappropriate thoughts right now, and hoping she's sharing in those inappropriate thoughts. Instead, I'm staring at Ellie's photo hanging on the wall behind Charlotte.

"I'm a software engineer," she says. Her response draws my attention back to her face, but I'm guessing it would be incredibly rude to look shocked, so I do my best to restrain my reaction. She doesn't have the look of a software engineer, but that's sexist. I'm just not sure I've seen a woman of her type, involved in such an intense profession. Wow, I am a total sexist.

"Very cool. Do you work from home?" She's dressed well for eight in the morning, but not exactly in corporate attire. Jeans, chucks, and a long sleeve white t-shirt wouldn't be acceptable in any white-collar company I've ever seen. But times have changed, I suppose. That dress code was one of the very reasons I made the decision to take up carpentry instead of finance like I had gone to school for. Stuck in a suit, working ten hours a day, and coming home with a headache has never appealed to me. Although, now that I'm about to hit thirty, some days the body aches from carpentry make a job requiring a suit seem more appealing.

"I do. I run my own company," she says with a bit of pride. "Ever heard of the 'TheLWord.com'?" The dating site. Oh boy. Internally, I sneer at the mention. Those things are the epitome of love. Matching up strangers based on a couple of common interests doesn't seem like the most natural form of a connection, but hey, it works for some people. Just, definitely not my thing. Of course, AJ would completely disagree since "TheLWord.com" is where he met Alexa, the female dictator of his dreams.

"I definitely have. It's your company?"

"I have a passion for helping people fall in love. What can I say?" She looks shy or reserved while saying this, which is a bit shocking considering her previous assertiveness. "Kind of ironic that I ended up divorced, huh?" Right. That's like being a doctor with an incurable disease, I would assume.

"We live and learn. I bet your divorce will help you grow your company in a way that helps others avoid the path you went down." That may not have come out right. Actually, I'm hoping it didn't so we can end this—whatever this is. It's not unreasonable to want to be left alone right now. I mean, I just let Olive out of my sight for the first time in five years, and I'm here with a woman I met an hour ago. I don't do this. I've actually avoided people and the thought of making new friends for this exact reason. Charlotte looks down at her watch and her eyes widen in suit.

"Oh wow, that hour went by quickly." She looks back up at me. "You going to be okay until three?" Am I that pathetic? Yes. Yes I am.

"I'll be fine. I have to be at a job site in an hour, and Olive was kind enough to leave me a bowl of cereal for breakfast that I must tend to." Air is beginning to percolate in my lungs again as I feel this meet and greet coming to an end.

"I was wondering about the overfilled bowl of lucky charms, but I went on the assumption that you were either starving or still looking for that pot of gold." With a cunning grin, she flashes a quick wink at me and stands up. "Well, Hunter, it was a pleasure finally meeting my new neighbor. If you need someone to talk to today, my doorbell is only a hundred feet away."

"Same for you. Single parents unite, right?" Did I just say that? I did. And she's looking at me with the same look I would be looking at me with if someone said that to me.

"We do. We'll get through this," she says quietly. "Thanks for the coffee." We. There is no such thing as a "we" outside of Olive and me. I stand up and meet Charlotte at the front door, opening it and standing to the side as she passes by. "I'm glad we met," she says.

I don't respond. Nothing good would come out of my mouth if I did. It was never my intention to shut the world out after Ellie died, but it was sort of an unofficial commitment I made to myself. If Ellie couldn't move on with her life, then why should I? I know it's irrational, as are most of the common decisions I make, but it makes sense in my head. I think.

I watch Charlotte walk down my driveway and cross the street, but now I'm closing my eyes so I don't stare at her ass because...why do I want to stare at her ass? It is a nice ass, that's probably why. I'm trying so hard to keep my eyes closed, but with as much restraint as I thought I had, I come to the conclusion that I obviously have none. So I surrender to my weakness and take in the last couple of ass-watching seconds before she disappears inside of her house. I'm a prick—a prick whose day just got a little better, despite my effort of avoiding what could be a lucky charm in my life—one that isn't overflowing from a cereal bowl.

CHAPTER THREE

FIVE MINUTES. FIVE. Five more long minutes, and then I'll take off. This day is going on forever. I look back down at the nails I'm supposed to be hammering but I'm unable to concentrate as I look back up at the clock again. Four minutes and thirty seconds. What if the bus driver gets there early for some reason? Olive wouldn't know what to do. She'd be standing there alone, crying, wondering if I forgot about her after she had been gone for so long. Oh God. I can't take this. I have to go.
"Dude, what are you doing? It's only two!" AJ shouts in from the adjacent room.

"The bus could get there early."

"An hour early? Doesn't school get out at three? Because if that's that case, I'm pretty sure it's virtually impossible for the bus to get to the bus stop before Olive is actually dismissed from school. I have a point, don't I? Yes, I have a point."

"There could be traffic," I try to reason; although reasoning with AJ is like reasoning with a stubborn five-year-old. Olive and AJ go head-to-head quite often and there is never a winner. Ever.

"We're two blocks away, so..." AJ needs to add in. Then he looks up at me and stops mid-sentence. I'm pacing the uncarpeted living room, pressing my fingers through my hair, trying to make sense of my ridiculous apprehensions but there is no clarity coming along with my irrational worries. I'm just so uneasy being away from Olive. "I'm sorry, Hunt. You're right," AJ says, placing his hammer down and flipping the light off. "Let's go get our little martini garnish."

"Really?" I punch him in the shoulder. "I told you to quit calling her that now that she's old enough to repeat shit. She's going to tell someone at school."

He snorts and rubs the spot on his arm that I punched. "I said it to you, not her."

"Just knock it off, will you?" I snap, causing him to roll his eyes at me. If I ever had to describe him to someone, I could pretty much sum him up as the kid that was always in the principal's office for doing something stupid, like pantsing a teacher or shooting a spitball into someone's hair. Years later, AJ hasn't changed. His brain hasn't matured along with his twenty-eight-year-old body.

"Why were you so late this morning?" AJ asks. "Knocking boots with the old lady who brought you a pie last week? Oh, did she bring you her pie this week?"

Drowning in a fit of laughter, he regains his composure when I say, "Actually, my neighbor dropped in. She came over for coffee."

AJ stops in front of me, preventing me from walking any further. "There was a chick in your house?"

I push him to the side and continue forward. "My neighbor. Not a chick," although that was what I mentally referred to her as just a few hours ago.

"You said she, which makes her a chick. Is she married?" Why is that always his first question? Why did I bring this up to him at all?

"No, she's not."

"And she wanted to have coffee?"

"Yes, and it was just coffee. She didn't pin me up against a wall and have her way with me." Those were the thoughts I was avoiding the entire time, though, but AJ doesn't have to know that.

"But I bet you're thinking that would have been pretty fucking sweet, huh? What does she look like? Is she hot? Big tits? Nice ass? I need details, bro." God, shut up. I close my eyes and pull in a struggling breath while ignoring each of his questions. "You would have said no, if she didn't meet some, if not all, of those criteria," he continues, despite my lack of encouragement. I can see his shit-eating grin in my peripheral vision, and I'm now absolutely sure that telling him about having coffee with Charlotte was a horrible mistake. Though, it was not as big of a mistake as bringing him to the bus stop where Charlotte is currently standing. "Bro." AJ grips his hand around my shoulder and forces me to stop walking. "What's gotten into you today? You've been doing well lately and it's the first time I've seen you with that 'rock-bottom' look in on your face in a good while."

"Today's just hard. It's been hard," I say, keeping my eyes set on Charlotte.

"You know she didn't just go off to college, right?" he asks.

"Yes, I know, AJ." But it's all a downward slope from here. First kindergarten...then the next thing I know she'll be driving. She'll be dating. She'll be sneaking into gardens at night with some dude who wants to carve her damn name into a tree.

I try to continue walking, but his hand tightens around my shoulder. "Hunt, what is this chick's name? Give me that at least."

"Hey!" Charlotte yells over. It is forty-five minutes before the bus is supposed to arrive, so I guess I'm not the only crazy parent here. I turn to tell AJ that, but he is too busy taking quicker steps ahead of me toward Charlotte.

"I don't believe we've met," AJ says. "I'm AJ, Hunt's brother." He points over to me and I place my head in my hand. How were the two of us cut from the same cloth? "Are you by any chance Hunter's neighbor? The one who joined him for coffee this morning?" Peeking through my fingers, I watch as Charlotte slips a bookmark in between the pages of the book she was reading and stands up, facing AJ.

"Nope," she grins. "We definitely haven't met. I am your brother's neighbor, and yes, I did have coffee with him this morning. Is that a problem?" Charlotte lifts her hand to shake his, but AJ finds it necessary to first turn around and cup his hand around his mouth, shouting through a whisper, "You don't have to answer my questions. I answered them myself." I love how he's pretending to whisper, like any type of volume matters right now. If I look at AJ for another second, I might go after him with a swinging fist, so instead I look up at Charlotte, noticing she is not the slightest bit embarrassed by this horrible encounter.

"I've been around his type, plenty," she says, leaning to the side so she can see me around AJ. "This isn't new to me." Her smile is sarcastic and adorable. Adorable? I didn't know that word was even part of my vocabulary, aside from referring to Olive.

"We're here early because Hunter was hoping you would be here early, too." You have to be fucking kidding me. I'm going to knock him out.

"AJ, maybe you could sit down and stop talking. Or better yet, go back to the site and keep working," I suggest.

"But I'd like to get to know your new neighbor."

She gives me a quick wink and sits down beside AJ on the bench. "What would you like to know?" Charlotte complies.

"Well, I already know you're single. But now I know you're a single mom—I never would have guessed that, honestly. You live across the street from Hunter, so now I'm wondering when the two of you will cut to the chase and go out for dinner now that you've had coffee? I can watch the kids." Still wanting to crawl out of my skin, I keep my eyes locked on this scene, waiting to hear what comes out of Charlotte's mouth.

Thankfully, I don't have to wait long because she stands up and walks over to me with a blank expression. "Your brother..." she begins. I like wherever this is going. I think. "Is a nutcase, and kind of funny. Why are you here so early?"

"Hey now!" AJ yells over. "We were in the middle of a very serious conversation."

Charlotte turns around and gives him a look I can't see, but then immediately turns back to face me. "Are you okay? Did you survive the brutal six hour wait?"

"I'm good. I just wanted to make sure I was here when the bus gets here. I know I probably sound crazy, but maybe not since you're sitting here, too."

The corners of her lips perks up. "Yeah, for the past year, I have come down to the bus stop an hour early and read, using this time as my daily late lunch break. At least I know I'll never be late."

"That's fantastic. Hunter, you won't have to stand here alone every day," AJ interrupts again, with a cunning smirk I still want to punch.

"Really, you should get back to work so we're not there until six, finishing up." AJ doesn't like to work past five, so I'm using the only weapon I can think of right now. He looks down at his watch and squints one eye, debating what choice is better— torturing me or getting out of work on time. "Alexa will kill you if you're late tonight." That should do it. It's their anniversary. And when I say, "Kill" I mean she will make his life a living hell for an indefinite period of time.

"Shit," he says. "Fine. You win this time, bro." Win. What exactly am I winning? "It was a pleasure to meet you, Charlotte." AJ tips his invisible hat and heads back down toward the job site.

Charlotte doesn't respond. Instead, she immediately turns her attention back to me. "You have to go back to work after you get Olive?" Charlotte asks.

"Yeah, Olive is no stranger to carpentry. She's been with me at every single job for the past five years."

"What a lucky little girl," she says, slipping her hands into her pockets and rolling back onto her heels. Charlotte looks up at the sun and squints from the brightness as she exhales a soft sigh. "Boy, you seem to have this single parent thing down pat."

"What choice do I have?" It's not the option I would have chosen. Ever. Watching Olive grow up without a mother, or any female influence for that matter, has made this single parent task even harder. What do I know about raising a little girl, or a teenage girl? Nothing.

"Let me take Olive home with me while you finish up at work. She and Lana can play for a bit. It'll be a great way to finish the first day of school for both of them."

I think about it for a brief second, but then I realize I haven't seen my little girl in six hours and there's no way in hell I'm not keeping her by my side for the rest of the day and night. "I appreciate the offer, but—"

"What am I saying?" she says, placing her hand up against the side of her cheek. "You haven't seen that precious little face in hours."

"Yes, that," I chuckle awkwardly. Was I always this awkward around women? I can hardly remember, considering Ellie and I grew up together. We promised to marry each other when we were children.

The minutes with Charlotte pass with a series of short conversations about weather and the horrible grass seed our lawns were sodded with. The awkwardness between us begins to lessen, but with each second, as my comfort level increases, guilt seeps into to my veins—guilt for enjoying the company of another woman, and guilt for talking to a beautiful woman—which is now causing me to feel like I am somehow cheating on my dead wife. It's okay to move on. It's okay to do all of this. I've told myself this for years and through dozens of horrible first dates, but each time, I still question if it's wrong.

Relief sets in when the bus creeps down the road. The thought of seeing Olive fills me with relief—the only little thing in this world who makes me feel like I'm alive and not walking among the dead. My daughter is the blanket I couldn't give up as a child, and the bed I used to hide under during a thunderstorm. She's the calm voice always telling me everything is going to be okay. Mostly, she is the voice I've longed to hear for five years—the voice I know I'll never hear again. She is Ellie. Everything about her is Ellie. It's as if Ellie created her entirely on her own without my help. And I wouldn't want it any other way. She, alone, makes my life worth living.

As the wheels of the bus come to a screeching halt, my heart freezes. The doors crank open and I watch each child hop off the bus one by one until I see the blonde, springy ponytail I've been waiting for all day. "Daddy!" she yells, running toward me at warp speed. The pride highlighting her face melts everything inside of me. Her arms wrap around my legs, squeezing me as tightly as I want to squeeze her. Her embrace tells me she missed me as much as I have missed her today and I lift her up, holding her tighter, relishing in the warmth of her cheek against mine. I feel her tiny heart beating through her back as a small shudder escapes her mouth. "I missed you so much today. I was so worried about you being all alone."

My world stops. My mind stops spinning, and my heart...my heart hurts. What have I done to her? "Why were you worried? You should never have to worry about me." The words come out, but they feel stuck in my throat, like I'm trying to convince her of something different than what she has obviously grown accustomed to.

Pulling away, she takes my face in her hands and stares me straight in the eyes, just like Ellie always did when she wanted to get her point across. "Because you don't like to be alone. You need me." Her words are spoken through a wisdom no five-year-old should have. Those words define a parent who has no right taking care of a small child when he can clearly not always take care of himself.

"Olive," I breathe out. "You need to listen to me." Her lips purse together with a hint of the attitude I know is looming. "You do not ever need to worry about me. I have never liked being alone because I love being with you. And yes, you are a million percent correct: I will always, always need you, and I hope you will always need me too. Plus, I wasn't alone today—I had Uncle AJ with me all day at work."

"Oh, Daddy. You're so good at avoiding the truth," Olive responds. She is not five. I'm convinced of this. Rather than fight with the warrior of all fights, I pull her back in and her arms loop around my neck as she rests her head on my shoulder. "Whether you like to believe it or not, I was sent to you for a reason." While there are many times when I feel like the use of her words surpasses her age, I'm beginning to question where she is getting these insightful statements from—or rather, who read them to her.

"Olive," I sigh. "Who read your baby book to you?"

"Auntie Alexa," she giggles. It has been a couple of years since I have opened Olive's baby book. I used to read it to her every night, the parts that Ellie insisted on filling out before Olive was even born. A writer never has a shortage of words, and as an English teacher, it should never have surprised me how many letters she wrote to Olive in preparation for her life. There were nights when I would sit in Olive's room after she had fallen asleep and read Ellie's words under the glow of the moonlight, imagining the sound of her voice as if she were speaking the words into my ear. Some of the pages had stains from tears…tears of happiness she felt when dreaming of a life she was creating. I used to trace my finger over the soft, puckered spots on the paper, wishing I could wipe away another one of Ellie's happy tears from her face rather than from a page in a baby book.

It got to the point where I couldn't read it anymore. The pain it was causing me to imagine the words that had gone unspoken after Ellie's death began to haunt me. I wanted to write the words for her—explain in great detail what Olive looked like, how the sound of her cry was nothing less than a soothing lullaby from heaven. I wanted to describe the incredible color of Olive's eyes— how they are blue, but with greens, yellows and purples mixed in like a splash of watercolor. I should have been able to write about the time Olive looked up into the sky and said "Ma". I know it was nothing more than baby babble, but to me it was a sign connecting our family.

It never fails, the second I place a pen down to the glossy paper in Olive's baby book, the words seem to float above my head like a breeze, drifting just out of reach and causing me to forget how to put a sentence together. I'm not a writer. I'm a reader of a writer's words and the only writer I have ever wanted to read words from can no longer breathe the air needed to form a syllable.

Olive slips herself out of my arms as we approach our driveway. "I'll get the mail!" she shouts, running ahead. She whips open the door to the mailbox and pulls herself up on her tiptoes to reach whatever is inside. As she retrieves the mail, she looks at it quickly, flipping through it like she does every day. I'm not sure I understand the excitement of looking through mail, considering the amount of bills I receive, but for some reason she enjoys thumbing through it all. I can assume that might change some day when she has financial responsibilities. "Daddy, there's a letter from that lady."

Ellie. Her heart. I jog over to Olive and take the letter from her hand. Turning it over, I'm hopeful for a return address, but once again, disappointment sets in when I see that this continues to be a one-way message.

Olive stands in front of me, looking up, waiting to hear what the note says. Before I open it, I look back down at her pleading eyes. Does she feel what I feel? Does she yearn for a connection to the heart surviving my wife—her mother?

"Inside," I tell her, pointing to the front door. "We only have a few minutes because I have to get back to work with Uncle AJ."

"Not until you read it, Daddy," she says, walking ahead toward the door.

We sit down on the couch as Olive peels her backpack and sweater off. She pulls her leg up and twists toward me, waiting with eagerness. We haven't received a letter in a couple of months and I was beginning to wonder if things had gone wrong in this woman's life. But as long as her heart is beating and she's well enough to write this letter to me, it all has to be okay. I slide my finger under the flap of the envelope and tear it open slowly, keeping the envelope intact.

Whenever I pull one of these letters out, my stomach turns heavy and my chest tightens. I find it hard to swallow or conjure up an intelligent thought. This isn't just a letter from a stranger. This is a letter from the person caring for the last of what is left of Ellie.

When I was a child, I remember Mom telling me that when a person dies, it is only their body that passes on because their soul remains intact forever. If a soul stays behind, wouldn't it make sense for it to remain attached to the heart that created this soul? I know it's a foolish way of thinking, but it makes sense to me. I know the body I fell in love with is gone, buried deep under the soil of this world, but the heart I watched grow with age, the heart that adapted to a greater love as life evolved, perhaps it is sheltering at least a part of her soul that remains. At least that's how it seems from these letters I continue to receive.

My hands shake as I unfold the typewritten letter. "Daddy!" Olive snaps me out of my haze. "What does it say?"

I wish the letter were created with handwritten words, offering just one minuscule hint of who she is.

Dear Mr. Cole,

I stood on the cliff of a mountain today and took a breath of sweet summer air. I closed my eyes and felt warmth embrace her heart—it felt full, as if it were taking up all free space in the cavity of my chest. When I squatted down and stretched my arms over the ledge, the strength of her heart pounded harder and sped up as if it were knocking on my ribcage, reminding me of her presence. This heart is so alive. I am alive.

When I laid down along the stony rippled edge of the cliff, I placed my hands over her heart and stared up into the sky, feeling the brightness overwhelm me as if heaven were covering me with a blanket, and her heart calmed under my touch. I felt her. I felt her life living within me, and I am grateful. I am alive because of her, just as her heart is alive because of me. The connection was strong today and I knew I needed to send you this letter. I hope it offers you a bit of comfort through the pain that must follow you around like a dark shadow.

Take care,
Her Heart

Rather than soak up the beautiful words from this stranger who might be the most familiar person in my lonely world, I can only focus on the mountain, and the question of where this mountain is. I need to find it, in hopes of finally meeting this woman. Although, I shouldn't be dumb enough to think she's just sitting around some mountain waiting for me to show up.

"Maybe she was at that mountain Grampy took us to last year," Olive says. Mountain. What mountain? I don't know if this woman even lives in this state, or on this side of the country. I don't know how she knows who I am, and I certainly don't know who she is. I always thought the donation and recipient process was anonymous. I've contacted the hospital several times, pleading for information, but each time I have been led to another roadblock. I did find out that this particular donation wasn't completely anonymous, but the recipient requested to keep her identity private. I've looked up the laws and it doesn't add up. Any time I've tried to get somewhere by arguing this, I get nowhere. "We should go to that mountain." There is no mountain in this town or the surrounding area. Olive snags the letter from my hand and turns it over. "Look, Daddy." During the short second it takes for me to take the letter back and flip it over, I pray that there is contact information.

But there isn't.

Instead, I find a drawing.

"That was mommy's favorite," Olive whispers. "She likes them, too." The letter falls from my limp hand, and I watch it float like a feather to the ground.

CHAPTER FOUR

NOVEMBER
-TWO MONTHS LATER -

"YOUR SANDWICH IS in the fridge and your cereal is on the counter," Olive says, pulling on her backpack.

I kneel down and wave her over. "You don't need to make me food anymore, Ollie."

"You can make me food," AJ says from the couch. "You know Uncle AJ is always hungry." He rubs his hand over his growing gut.

"Uncle, you eat all of our food! You're going to turn into a piggy," Olive says through laughter.

"Well, if your darn aunt wouldn't keep me on this clean-eating, inhumane diet, I wouldn't be so hungry every time I come here." Olive just looks at him with question. She may sound older than five, but she's five and has no clue what a diet, let alone a "clean-eating" one is.

"Well," Olive says, turning back toward me. "If you don't want me to make you food, maybe Miss Charlotte can make you lunch again, I guess." A tiny smile pinches at her lips. "I think that would be okay. Don't you, Daddy?"

"Olive, I've already told you—" She places her fingers in her ears and hums loudly, avoiding the words I'm trying to speak.

"That-a-girl, Ollie-Lolly," AJ says, pointing at Olive with a wink.

"Come on, we're going to be late," I tell her, giving AJ the look he was desperately trying to get out of me.

As we step outside, Charlotte and Lana are coming out of their house, as well. Olive's hand slips out of mine, and she books it down the driveway, stopping momentarily to look both ways before crossing the street. Within seconds, Olive and Lana's hands are interlocked and they're running down the street ahead of us.

"I take it she's feeling better today," Charlotte says. "Did the soup help?"

"I guess it did," I laugh. "Thanks for bringing it over."

"It was the least I could do after Lana was nice enough to share her germs with Olive." Charlotte folds her arms over her chest and shivers against the brisk wind. "I guess autumn is here, huh?"

I look over at her. Her cheeks are rosy against the rest of her pale skin and her eyes are a bit puffy. For a second, I wonder if she has been crying, but then she sneezes. "Oh no. You're sick?"

"I'm fine," she shoos me off, sniffling a bit. "Moms don't get sick."

"You should be wearing a coat," I tell her. She's wearing a flimsy, long-sleeved t-shirt and I'm guessing the chill in the air is seeping right through the fibers of the shirt. I might be a frigid person, but I'm still a gentleman. I unzip my hooded sweatshirt and hand it over to her. "Put this on."

"I'm good, but thank you," she says, pushing my hand away.

"Put it on," I say firmly. "I don't make the best chicken soup, so—"

She looks at me with an arch in her brow and her lips press together. "Thank you," she groans begrudgingly, giving in. Slipping on my sweatshirt, she scrunches up the sleeves and pulls her hands through. The fabric drops down to her knees, making the size difference between us quite apparent.

Her sniffles continue for the duration of the walk, and I notice an increased flush across her cheeks when we reach the bench at the bus stop.

"Do you have a fever?" I ask, taking a closer look at her face.

She shakes her head. "I'm sure I'm fine."

"She's not fine," Lana says from the grassy area. "She was up all night coughing and sneezing. I gave her my cold." Without thinking, I place my hand over Charlotte's forehead, instantly realizing how cold my skin must feel against the scorching sensation of hers. I may be cold, but she's burning up. She recoils at my touch, pulling back with a wide-eyed look as if it were a shock that I touched her. Actually, it's a shock to me that I touched her. I've done a good job at keeping things very vanilla.

"Oh," she says, finally coming to terms with having a fever. "Good thing I work from home, then." With a garbled coughing laugh, she pulls her hands inside the sleeves of my sweatshirt and curls her arms up over her chest. I like the way she looks, all cuddled up in my sweatshirt.

"I have to run a couple of errands this morning, and the store is one of them. What can I get you?" I ask. "Do you have anything you can take to get your fever down?"

"I'm sure I can find something, but if you don't mind picking me up some ibuprofen, that'd be great," she says.

Lana runs over to us and wrenches her hand around my shirt, pulling me down to her level. She cups her hands around my ear and whispers, "Mom was tearing the medicine cabinet apart this morning, saying she couldn't find anything that wasn't meant for a—a damn kid." I pull away, trying to maintain a straight face, but she pulls me back again, resuming her secret-telling position. "Then she said…'Goddammit, why isn't there ever anyone around to take care of me?' She said a bad word. Two, actually." I want to laugh at what Lana took out of that statement, but I know exactly how Charlotte feels. We spend every second of our lives caring for someone else and there is never anyone to take care of us when we need it.

I twist around to the side of her face and cup my hand around Lana's ear, "I'll have a talk with your mom about saying bad words." Lana pulls away and slaps her hands over her mouth, giggling loudly, before running back over to where Olive is playing.

"What was that all about?" Charlotte asks.

I clear my throat and slip my hands into my back pockets. "Evidently, someone needs to wash their mouth out with soap," I say, in my best mock-scolding tone.

Charlotte scrunches her nose and forehead with curiosity. "What did she say?"

"Don't worry about it," I laugh. The other moms arrive in their group and the roaring chatter that grew from halfway down the street stops almost immediately as they come within earshot. They are all very friendly, but I can't help feeling as though they get quiet because they don't know what to say to me. I assume meeting a single, widowed father isn't the norm around here.

"How's Olive feeling today?" one of them asks.

"She's much better, thank you," I respond.

"Chicken soup is always the cure-all," another one sings with a cynical grin painted across her tinted lips. I know Charlotte doesn't converse with any of these women, which means someone likely saw her walking across the street with the pot of soup yesterday.

Fortunately, the bus interrupts whatever conversation could have ensued and Olive runs over to take her backpack out of my hand. "Don't forget to eat your mayonnaise sandwich today, Daddy. You're going to get sick if you don't eat." Rather than argue with my little Ellie, I lift her up and place a kiss on her nose.

"Have a good day at school. I'll see you when you get home."

"Bring me home a jasmine today," Olive whispers in my ear. "My last one died." She drops out of my arms and runs for the open door of the bus. "Bye, Daddy!"

Once the bus pulls away, the other mothers begin to crowd but I break away just in time to hopefully make the obvious a little less obvious—that being said, I don't want to answer any soup questions. Charlotte isn't as lucky, though. She's in the center of the conversation, and I decide not to look back and catch the look in her eye that would most likely tell me she hates me right this second.

She feels awkward around the other mothers, too, since we're the outsiders—the single parents who aren't lucky enough to have a normal family.

I jump right into my truck the second I get home, heading out to the gardens early enough to beat the daily crowd of elderly visitors. I've learned if I arrive within five minutes of their opening, I can have thirty minutes alone without the gawking eyes and whispers.

The fifteen miles between Sage and the gardens in Glenn blur by as I catch myself thinking about Charlotte. For the first time since Ellie's death, my mind feels torn between mourning and healing. Mourning and memories are all I have left of Ellie, so if I let go of the mourning, Ellie is really gone. Moving on feels like betraying her, so healing has never been an option for me before, but lately, I find myself wondering if it's possible to mourn and heal at the same time. Maybe I finally have room in my life for both.

In another life, a life where Ellie didn't leave her permanent footprint, Charlotte would be a woman I could see myself wanting to spend more time with, maybe even pursuing something more than a friendship. Not that there is anything wrong with the friendship that has budded nicely between Charlotte and me over the past couple of months, but I've made it clear...maybe a little too clear...that whatever we are—will continue as is. She hasn't exactly asked for more or even insinuated anything, but the reason I keep thinking about it may be because recently, the consideration of something more has crossed my mind more times than I'd like to admit. There is something about her that has me looking forward to the moment she walks out of her house in the morning, and waiting for the first laugh that escapes her lips each day. Being around her has brought me a sense of peace I've been missing in my life.

I pull into the gardens, seeing only two vehicles. One belongs to the groundskeeper, which means a visitor is already here.

I step out of my truck and head down the narrow, gravel-covered path. The scent of lilies and jasmines permeates the air, pulling me down the earth-made, moss covered steps toward the tree. Our tree. My tree.

We had these plans. Horrible plans that no twenty something year olds should ever be discussing. But we did for a reason I can't even recall. "Let's be buried together by the tree in the gardens. That way we can always be together in the one place we love." I laughed at her that day and told her never to bring up the thought of dying again. It was the one and only time we ever spoke of it, but at least that terrible conversation made things easier when planning my twenty-five-year-old wife's funeral. Her parents hated the idea. They were angry that it was my right to make the arrangements and decisions. I understood their desire to bury her in the cemetery that contained the rotting bodies of their relatives, but I had to carry out Ellie's wish, regardless of how much her parents would hate me.

The one thing I didn't plan for was the owner of the garden telling me it was against regulations to bury a body on their grounds. They would only grant me permission to bury an urn. I had to burn Ellie's body into dust. Dust had always been an annoying particle I was used to sweeping into the trash can, but now, my wife's remains are nothing more than dust and it's the most beautiful, precious dust in the world.

When the cremation procedure was complete, I was called into the office to pick up the urn. My wife was handed to me in a fucking vase. I placed it in a small box down in the passenger seat and then secured Olive into her car seat. It was the one and only time our entire family was together. Pretty screwed up.

I kneel down by the tree, along with the cliché carving of our names surrounded by a heart with the word "forever" below it. Who knew forever ended at twenty-five? With my hand placed up against the heart, I close my eyes and allow the words to flow. "I miss you, baby. So much." I pull in the thick air that never seems to find a way through my lungs easily while I'm here. Even if I could breathe freely, the knot in my throat makes it hard to speak the words I save for these moments. But with a slight breeze blowing against my skin, comfort blankets me like a warm hand touching my back. "Olive is learning to read. Can you believe it? She wants to be a writer like her mom. She wants to be just like you, Ell. I've done my best to keep you alive in her mind. I want her to know you like I know you. I wish she had years with you like I did, but I'm doing the best I can. I know I say this every time I'm here, but I just need you to know how hard I'm trying." I open my eyes and remove my hand from our engraved heart. "I hope you don't mind, but I need to steal a blue jasmine for Olive. She requested it." I lean down and pull the clippers from my coat pocket. If it weren't for Ellie's strict rules on how to remove a flower from the soil, I would yank the thing out, but that would be a sin to her. I clip the flower and replace the clippers in my pocket. "I love you, baby. I'll see you next Friday."

I stand up and turn toward the jasmine-lined pond. This was the place that sparked Ellie's passion for flowers, jasmines in particular. They aren't naturally grown here, but I guess the groundskeepers maintain them; though the temperature is dropping quickly now, so I'm guessing this will be it for a few months. As I pick a couple more, my focus catches something pink across the pond.

A woman is kneeling down, collecting flowers and placing them in a box. I realize I have no right to say anything, especially since I've just picked some flowers, too, but I'm not stripping the area of all the flowers. What is she doing with all of them? I've never seen her here before, so I'm guessing she isn't a new groundskeeper. Not dressed like that, anyway.

I stand up and make my way around to the other side of the pond. "This is a privately owned garden," I tell her. I know I'm no more an owner than she likely is, but I have an arrangement with the owner, who allows me to pick a couple of blue jasmines when I'm here.

Her head pops up, startled by my presence. I didn't mean to sneak up on her, and normally I wouldn't approach someone like this...but these flowers—they should wilt on their own. I'm a hypocrite. Why am I over here?

Her jade eyes meet mine and she looks completely distraught like I have accused her of a heinous crime. "Are these your flowers?" she asks in a honeyed voice.

I look down at my hand gripped around a single Jasmine. "No," I reply, despondently. "I—I got permission from the owner of the garden."

"I did, too," she says. "I help the groundskeepers out sometimes since I manage a flower shop downtown. The shop I work for supplies the seeds in the spring and takes what's left at the end of the season. Since we're getting an early freeze, I'm making my rounds sooner than normal this year."

"I had no idea," I tell her, feeling like my tail is between my legs. She is the reason these flowers continue to grow here.

"It's okay. I'm sure it looks a little odd to be cutting down flowers in the middle of a beautiful garden," she says, closing the box up. Tucking it under her arm, she stands and flips her coffee brown hair behind her shoulders. With a couple steps in my direction, she tilts her head subtly to the side with an inquisitive look in her eyes. "Do you come here a lot?"

"Every Friday." I point over my shoulder toward my tree. "I come to visit my wife."

The woman places her hand over her chest and clenches the loose pink material of her shirt. Her eyes break contact with mine as she looks down toward her feet. "I'm incredibly sorry for your loss."

"Thank—" before I can offer her my complete gratitude, she takes off past me. I turn and watch her jog up the moss steps, leaving me staring with wonder. While I'm questioning what I said to make her run, the box she is carrying abruptly flies out of her hands as she trips up one of the steps. The flowers spring out from between the flaps and the woman falls down to the step, looking defeated. Defeated from running away from me? I take my steps toward her slowly, with caution, since I don't want to scare her again if I already have somehow.

I scoop up the flowers and take the box, laying it flat on one of the steps. I place them in one at a time, careful not to rest any of the leaves up against each other. "Are you okay?" I ask. She looks up at me with a tear streaking down her red cheek. "Did you lose someone, too?" I don't know why I would assume that, but she's crying and I feel like I was a dick to yet another poor person.

She nods her head subtly, staring me straight in the eyes again. "I'm sorry," she says, her voice shaky.

"I think we covered the unnecessary apologies," I say, feeling a ghost of a smile find my mouth. I don't think I have smiled in these gardens since the last time Ellie was here with me.

"Yes, I lost someone," she says.

"Life sucks sometimes," is all I can think to tell her. "It's what I've told myself every day for the last five years."

"Sometimes, but it can be really sweet some days, too," she argues. "Sorry for this dramatic scene." Quiet laughter escapes her lips as she runs the back of her hand against her cheek, drying the one lonely tear. "I don't know what to say to myself to make my pain better, and I definitely don't know what to say to someone else to ease their pain. So, the only logical thing I can think to do is run away." She stands up and takes the box from my hand.

"Words aren't always needed," I tell her.

"Words are almost always needed," she retorts.

"Is that what they say?"

"Who?" she asks, appearing puzzled.

"Whoever they are. You know, those who make up all of the crazy sayings that make no sense."

"Those sayings are like art. You have to let the words sink in, and you have to forfeit your mind to the greater meaning of what is on the surface. It will all make sense then."

"You must be a philosopher," I tell her.

"Just a florist," she reminds me.

"This has been the most confusing conversation about words I will probably ever have." All because I wanted to accuse a poor woman of stealing flowers from a garden. I really know how to keep topping myself with every stupid decision I make.

"I hope not," she says, a grin transforming from her grimace. "But I do need to get going. I need to get the shop opened."

"Where is the shop?" I ask, wanting to know where I can buy these jasmines.

"It was nice to meet you," she says, avoiding my question.

"Likewise," I say in return.

I give her a head start before I follow her up the steps and out to the dirt lot, where I look toward my tree once more, sending my last "I love you" to Ellie for the week. When I make it out to my truck, I see the backside of a navy blue hybrid pulling out onto the main road. And that's that, I guess.

My thoughts feel scattered as I make my way through the grocery store, picking up food for the week, as well as a get-well kit for Charlotte. I may not have been married for a long time, but I think I know what makes women feel better. Or I'd like to think that.

She has made a much larger effort to help me than I have made to help her, so this is an opportunity for me to thank her and maybe prove I'm not as big of an asshole as I sometimes appear to be.

After putting my own groceries away, I jog across the street and knock on Charlotte's door. I believe I hear what sounds like a crow squawking at me to come in so I open the door slowly, finding her curled up on the couch under a blanket. "Guess working from home isn't going so well for you today," I say, closing the door behind me.

"Not at all," she croaks.

I sit down at the edge of the couch and pull the grocery bag up to my lap. "I got you some stuff." I pull the tissue box out and place it on the coffee table beside us. Next is the Advil and Nyquil, then a box of chocolates, and finally every single chicky magazine I could find on the racks. As her eyes settle on the magazines, she props herself up on the couch.

"Wow," she says. "You are quite the desirable bachelor."

I don't know why, but her words cause me to back up and switch from sitting on the edge of the couch to the edge of the coffee table. The irony of just rehashing the fact that she doesn't "go there" only a couple of hours ago, tells me I might have jinxed myself.

Charlotte places her hand on my knee. "Hey." Her eyebrows knit together with an accompanying look of frustration. "Are you okay?"

"I don't know," I tell her honestly.

"Was it weird that I said that?" She squints one eye closed as if she were preparing to take a blow to her head.

"I—I am so fucked up, Charlotte." Truth. Nothing but truths here right now…no point in being anything but honest, as she's beginning to learn just how fucked up I am.

"I'm well aware," she laughs through another fit of coughs. One thing I've liked about Charlotte is that she doesn't tiptoe around off-limits subjects. "I have no filter, but I'm not sorry I said it. It's the truth."

I look down at my hands, searching my mind for a non-asshole-like response, but nothing comes to me because I know I shouldn't say anything rude since I've been thinking the same thing about her being a desirable bachelorette.

"How was the garden?" she asks, kindly changing the subject. For my sake, not hers.

"It was fine," I sigh. "Want me to make you some tea or something?"

"No, thank—," she says through a sneeze.

I stand up and take the empty bag into the kitchen, dropping it into the trash bin. "If you want me to get Lana off the bus today, I can."

"Okay." Awesome. I just ruined the only friendship I've managed to maintain for longer than two weeks. "Oh, your sweatshirt is hanging on the closet door," she adds in.

"Thanks." I grab it and at the same time feel my phone vibrating in my back pocket. Pulling it out, I see that it's Olive's school calling.

"Hello?" I answer, immediately hearing the school nurse explain something to me in a way that I can't understand. Or maybe I don't want to understand. "What do you mean? Is she okay?"

Panic drives me out of Charlotte's house without a goodbye or explanation. Panic drives me down to Olive's school going twice the speed limit, and panic has me racing through the school doors, passing by the preparing EMT's, praying that God spares me any more heartache.

CHAPTER FIVE

THERE WAS A time in my life when I questioned why I was so lucky. I had two parents who beat the age-old odds of divorce, good grades were just something that happened for me, money was never an issue thanks to Dad and his successful business, and then in the girlfriend department—getting the girl was never an issue because I always had one. I sometimes sat down at the edge of my bed and asked God, "Why me?" It wasn't that I ever expected things to come easily, or for the luck to ever continue, but I was always grateful enough to fear the day when my luck might change. Maybe part of me always knew it would.

Until the moment I saw Ellie lying on the hospital bed, dead, I didn't realize that she was my luck—all of my good fortune clumped together into one being. Those other things in my life:

happy parents, money, intelligence—that wasn't luck. I thought I was good at appreciating what I had, but I came to find out that I never truly appreciated it the way I should have. I appreciated the wrong parts of life. Now I appreciate time—the time I had with Ellie, the time I take to be a dad and raise Olive, and the time Olive is awake and home from school. Time is what I'm grateful for, because without time, nothing else matters.

I bust through the front office doors and into the nurse's office, searching around the room until I see the school nurse, principal, and receptionist hovering over Olive. "What happened?" I snap. They already told me over the phone, but I need to hear it again. I need every single detail.

The EMTs are on my tail and I'm forced to back away so they can take care of her. One of them is pulling up her eyelids checking her pupils with a flashlight while another checks her limbs. I hold my gaze on the EMTs as the nurse describes in detail about this "misfortunate accident" on the playground.

"She climbed up to the top of the play gym and stood on the monkey bars while reaching for the sky. By the time her teacher saw, it was too late…Olive's foot had slipped through one of the openings and she fell off the side. The drop was about seven or eight feet, and she fell directly onto her head."

This was one of my biggest concerns during open house. I asked them how carefully they watch the children on the playground. They explained how great their teacher/student ratio was, and that each child would be carefully supervised. Don't they know it only takes one second?

"Looks like a grade three concussion," one of the EMTs says, matter-of-factly, without a hint of emotion in his voice. As another EMT rushes past me with a stretcher, they place a brace around Olive's neck, and it nearly covers her face. I can't even touch her because they have closed in around her, keeping me away. I can only see through the cracks of their bodies, allowing me a view of the dirt staining her pink leggings.

Again, for the second time in my life, my heart physically aches. It's beating the shit out of me from the inside out, and I'm having trouble catching my breath. Whoever the hell said, "What doesn't kill you, makes you stronger…" can kiss my ass.

"Olive!" I shout, worthlessly. "Olive, sweetie, wake up!" A warm hand clenches around my shoulder, and a chest presses against my back, but I don't turn around. I don't care who is behind me—who is trying to show me sympathy or comfort. My little girl is lying in front of me unconscious, from a goddamn seven-foot tall fall. "Is she going to be okay? I need to know. Is she?" No one responds, so I grab one of the EMTs by the shoulder, the one who doesn't have his hands on Olive. I yank at him until he turns around. "Is she going to be okay?"

"I'm not a doctor," he says. "I'm not able to give you any definite answers."

The hand that was on my shoulder is lowered to my bicep and another hand rests over my other bicep. The hands squeeze harder, but I still don't turn around. I will not take my eyes off of Olive. As the EMT I was just speaking to moves to the side, I see that Olive is missing her shoe. She looks uncared for; she doesn't look like my daughter.

The two minutes it takes to have her strapped down on the gurney feel like an hour—an hour of impatiently waiting for her to blink or say the word, "Daddy".

"Sir, you can ride along with us."

The hands around my arms release and a voice echoes in my ears. "I'll meet you there," she says.

As the EMTs rush by me, the wind of their speed knocks into me. I run, unable to feel the soles of my shoes hitting the ground, or hear the panic in everyone's voices, or focus on the dozens of children lining the hall with fear in their eyes. I know it's all there, but I feel locked inside of a tunnel with only darkness at the other end.

I climb into the back of the ambulance, still forced to sit far enough away from Olive that I can't touch her. Maybe if she knew I was here, she'd wake up. "Olive," I call softly. "Can you hear me?"

The EMT I'm sitting beside looks over at me and shakes his head slightly as if to tell me not to bother. Why wouldn't I bother? "She's alive, isn't she?" I spew angrily.

"Yes, she is," he says. "I'm just afraid she can't hear you."

"You don't know that," I grit. "You're not a doctor, remember?"

"Take it easy, sir," he says, remaining calm. Unlike me.

"Take it easy? Take it easy?" I shout. "My wife died giving birth to this little girl. She is my entire fucking world. I wanted to homeschool her just so I knew she'd be safe. So don't you tell me to take it easy—you understand?"

"That's irrational," he says, looking away from me. Cocky, arrogant, doctor wannabe.

I want to hit him. I want to punch him square in the goddamn jaw right now, but I know they'd kick me out of this claustrophobic vehicle, so I shut my mouth and clench my jaw.

We arrive at the hospital. This hospital—this horrible place of death that I promised myself I would never to walk into again, and yet here I am. It already stole Ellie and now it's threatening to take my sweet, little Olive.

As I walk down the endless hall of white, an image flashes through my blurry mind—Olive at two days old in the car seat I spent hours learning how to take apart and put back together, just to make sure I knew exactly how to operate it when it came time. She was buckled in snuggly, looking up at me as I held the seat firmly within my embrace. I remember thinking it's just you and me now as I wondered how I was going to do this—be this little girl's sole provider for every single thing she needs. Then I wondered how I got to that point, and why? How could I ever imagine leaving this hospital without Ellie? That wasn't the plan.

The sight of the EMTs rushing Olive into one of the triage areas pulls me from my thoughts. A nurse greets us just as Olive is transferred from the gurney to a bed. "Sir, you're quite pale," she says as she pulls up a chair and taps the armrest. "Have a seat." I do as she asks because I don't think my legs are strong enough to support the weight of my heart any longer. "A doctor will be here momentarily." She places her hand on my shoulder and I look up at her.

A familiar face stares back at me, but I don't say much to confirm the similar question swimming through her eyes. Yes, I do look familiar. Yes, you were the one who handed Olive to me just as she was born and just as my wife died. I'm guessing I only look familiar to her. This hospital sees hundreds of people a day, I'm sure. "Thank you," I say.

"Mr. Cole," she sighs. "It has been a while." Her bottom lip quivers and her eyes fill with tears. "We'll give your little girl the best care possible. I promise."

"You remember me?" I ask, shock lacing my hoarse voice.

"I have never forgotten you. I could never forget you. You and Olive have weighed heavily on my mind for years. I think of you often, wondering how you are doing." She breaks her stare from my eyes and focuses on Olive. "She looks just like her. She's beautiful." The nurse squeezes her hand around my shoulder and croaks, "I'll be right back."

As promised, a doctor comes jogging around the corner and up to Olive's bedside. He introduces himself and then checks Olive over from head to toe, inspecting her pupils and neck first. He turns to me, saying, "We need to send her for a CT scan right away." He lifts the phone and puts in the order to whoever is on the other end of the line. In less than two minutes Olive's bed is being rolled out of the room and down the hall. When we enter the new area, I'm asked to remain in the waiting room because I can't go in with her for the CT scan. Once again, I'm forced to sit in a waiting room, waiting to hear the destiny of the one living person I love.

"Can I get you some tea or coffee?" the nurse asks—the same nurse who remembers me. The same nurse who was able to communicate that Ellie wasn't going to make it with only a look in her eyes. She doesn't have that look now, but maybe she's gotten more experienced at hiding her emotions.

I shake my head and drop my face into my hands. "My name is Caroline," the nurse says quietly as she takes the seat next to me. "You're doing a wonderful job with Olive."

I lift my face from my hands and look at her with nothing but question. How in the world could anyone sit here and tell me I'm doing a wonderful job? My daughter is lying unconscious in a hospital bed. I'm thinking that's qualification to have someone second guess my ability to care for a child, never mind doing anything less than an okay job. "I beg to differ," I reply, sounding less cynical than I truly feel.

"Oh, honey, her clothes match, her hair had two barrettes evenly placed on both sides of a straight part down the center of her head. Her socks match. Her teeth are clean. Her belly is full.

These are only the few things I noticed within the minute she arrived here. I know it isn't much, but I could immediately tell she is a cared-for child." Caroline takes my left hand from my lap and points to my ring finger. "And you're caring for her yourself, aren't you?" She knows about Ellie, which means she's questioning if I moved on.

"Yes," I respond, looking at my empty finger along with her. I struggled with the decision to take my ring off. I finally did last year and placed it in a box with Ellie's ring.

"Olive is going to be okay," Caroline tells me.

I remember asking Caroline if Ellie was going to be okay, and she wouldn't answer me. But here she is, offering this information unprompted by me. "She is?" I need hope. Please give me an ounce of hope to hold on to.

"Hunter!" a voice cries from the door. "Hunter." Charlotte runs in and throws her arms around my neck as if we do this sort of thing—hug when in need of a hug.

I'm still looking at Caroline, though, as well as the small smile unraveling across her lips. As the wrinkles on her cheeks smooth out, a happy gleam encompasses her face. She places her hand on my back and stands up. "I'll give you two a moment, and I'll check on Olive."

"Thank you," I tell her, then turning to Charlotte with what I'm sure is a puzzled look, I ask, "How did you know I was here?"

"When you left my house so quickly after you got that phone call, without even saying goodbye, I suspected it might have been the school calling about Olive, so I called them. I was with you at the school but… Anyway, I heard what happened and I followed you here because I thought you might need me. And I didn't want you to be alone. I would have gotten here sooner but I was looking all over for you," Charlotte says, breathlessly. It was her hands trying to embrace me at the school. It's Charlotte who is always here for me lately. And yet, I get scared when she tells me I'm a desirable man. What the hell is wrong with me? "The administration desk wasn't entirely sure where you might be and I called your phone a dozen times. As I was running through the halls, I thought security was going to escort me out, but instead, they helped me find you. How is she? Is she okay? Are you okay? Do you need something? I was so worried about her." Charlotte sounds wild and out of control. The worry in her voice is pure and full of honest compassion for Olive—for me. It's something I haven't heard in a while since I've pushed everyone away—everyone including my own parents. I wouldn't allow the presence of compassion in my life because it made everything worse. AJ is the only one who I haven't burned, because he isn't compassionate. He's an asshole like me, just in a different way—a way I can tolerate most of the time.

"Thank you for coming," I tell her, honestly. "She's getting a CT scan, but she is still unconscious." Charlotte's arms remain around my neck as she whimpers into my ear. The sympathy-coated knife I usually feel stabbing into my chest when someone is trying to "make me feel better" is more like a senseless dull puncture this time and I have no energy to put up my protective wall. Instead, I close my eyes and try to ignore everything around me but the sensation of Charlotte's arms encircling my neck, and for the first time, I don't force myself to imagine Ellie on the other side of this embrace. For the first time, I feel a comfort I haven't imagined ever feeling again. But it's uncontrollable, and leaning into Charlotte, I allow it. I allow it because I am in such desperate need of consolation that I suddenly feel dehydrated from the drought of affection that I now realize I desire. I think I need Charlotte to quench my thirst for closeness.

Surrendering all restraint, my arms find their way around Charlotte's slim waist and I pull her down to my lap, burying my head into her shoulder. "Why?" I groan.

"She won't let anything happen to her," Charlotte whispers into my ear.

"Who?" I reply, knowing what I want to hear, but also understanding that no one thinks the way I do.

"What is your wife's name? You haven't told me."

You haven't asked. "Eleanor. Ellie."

"Eleanor Cole," she repeats her name in only a breath of a whisper, one that makes Ellie's name sound as if it, too, were nothing more than a ghost. Following a sharp breath and a shaky exhale, Charlotte softly utters, "Ellie is yours and Olive's angel. She won't let anything happen to either of you. I believe that."

My arms tighten around her as her scent infiltrates my senses. The scent I have refused to inhale in fear of loving it—seeps through the sealed cracks of my cold heart. The fight I have fought to keep an emotional distance from Charlotte has been lost. Flowers. She smells like the vanilla from a Clematis. I inhale as much as my lungs will allow, surprised at how much I'm able to breathe in at once. For years, my lungs have felt deflated, as if I were unable to fill myself with enough oxygen, but right now, I can breath freely.

The momentary relief in my chest is quickly clouded over as the doctor comes through the door. He doesn't draw out his words or thoughts, or even look at me with any type of concerned grimace as he likely conjures up the appropriate words needed to reach down into a person's throat and rip a heart out of its chest cavity. Again. Charlotte moves from my lap over to the chair, as if she senses the space I desperately need.

"Charlotte Drake," the doctor says, interrupting the information he needs to give me right this second. "How unusual to see you around here again. It's been a couple of years, has it not?"

"How is Olive?" Charlotte yields the focus back to where it should be.

The doctor breaks his momentary shift of attention from Charlotte back to me. "It's a moderate concussion, but she woke up right in the middle of the CT scan," he says with a soft chuckle. "She's quite a spitfire, huh?" The release of agony, fear, and all other emotions pulls me from my seat and over to the doctor where I restrain myself from lunging at him with open arms.

"Is—is she going to be okay?" I stammer.

"She's going to be just fine, Mr. Cole." He looks down at his chart and back up at me. "I want to keep her overnight for more observation, however. We're still waiting for a couple more test results, but I'm sure everything will come back as I expect."

"I'm staying with her," I tell him, demandingly.

"And that's completely fine." The doctor turns back for the door. "We'll have her settled in a room within the next few minutes and you can go be with her. It was nice to see you again, Charlotte." He waves from over his head, disappearing into the haze I'm staring toward.

When the door closes, I turn back to Charlotte, who appears to be sending someone a message on her phone. "Just asking Rosy—" one of the bus stop moms, "—to grab Lana from the bus."

"You don't have to stay," I tell her. I'm used to being alone and internalizing my fears and pains, relying on no one but myself to move forward from one moment to the next.

"I know I don't." She holds her phone up, watching the screen for a few seconds before placing it back down onto her lap. "Lana will be picked up, so I'm all yours if you want, but I can go, too. Whichever you need right now."

I don't get it. I don't understand what this is. "Why? Why do you continuously want to be around me? I hardly know how to form a smile, let alone release a joke worthy of laughing over. I push you away. I'm not a very good friend, and quite frankly, I'm an asshole to you more often than not. So why, Charlotte?" There has to be a logical reason for this outpouring of undeserved kindness.

She lifts her chin and narrows her eyes as a faint smile takes form over her lips. "This may sound a little cocky, but I'm an excellent judge of character. I like to think I have an ability to look into a person's eyes and know exactly who they are inside. Everything you portray on the outside is a mask so no one knows who you truly are or what you're feeling."

I feel like laughing, not because it's funny, but because I want to tell her what she sees is what she gets. There is no difference from the coldness I show on my face to the chill that has permanently frozen my heart into stone. "Inside, there is a hopeless, lost soul with no direction. That's what is inside. So if that is what you're seeing, it still doesn't answer my question as to why you would want to be friends with someone like me." I'm not sure I want to hear her answer. I'm not sure I know how to pry open the lid of my lonely world to make room for someone who cares about me.

"I'm aware," she says. "I don't want to fix you, and I don't want you to change," she says, looking away from me and down to her candy-red chucks. "So don't go thinking that either." She only breaks eye contact when something is stirring inside of her or when she's uncomfortable saying what she's trying to say. "You are this incredibly strong person who takes weeds and turns them into beautiful flowers—literally." She laughs and looks back up at me, her cheeks now a little pink. "Look, Hunter, I don't have an honest answer, but there's a pull I feel toward you and I've followed my gut. Like I said, I don't wish for you to change every time I see you. I only wish for you to gain the ability to heal. I know I won't be any help in that department, but that doesn't mean I don't want to be around you as it happens. Because, whether you want to or not, you are going to heal." With a smirk, she goes on to say, "We're also neighbors so we're sort of stuck with each other. We might as well make the best of it."

Normally, I'd feel anger when someone tells me this pain won't last forever. I think I might actually be a glutton for the pain I won't let fade. I hold onto it like a lifeline, but as Olive grows older and more aware of who I am, I think I might have to allow some of my pain to ease, even if only for her sake.

"Okay," I tell her. "Fair enough." I guess. I'm not sure what I just agreed to, though.

Nurse Caroline comes back out and nods her head for me to follow. I walk past Charlotte, who is looking at me and waiting for a decision I'm supposed to make on whether or not I want her to stay. The person who I've been—who I might still be—would tell her goodbye and thank you. However, I might be sick of being that person. I reach my hand out to her, close my eyes, and take another deep breath. This is the right thing to do. For me.

Charlotte swallows hard and loud enough for me to hear then takes my hand and stands up to join me. Her hand is warm, soft, small—perfect, compelling me to interlace my fingers with hers and squeeze a little tighter, all while fighting the stabbing pain running through my nerves. On second thought, maybe it's not pain; maybe it's that comfort thing again. How could a person be so lost that a feeling of pain and comfort could be confused with one other?

As we walk down the hall, Charlotte's free hand wraps around my arm, her body pressed against the side of mine, and the closer we get to Olive's room, the less my chest aches. I consider releasing Charlotte's hand before walking into Olive's room, but I don't.

"Daddy! Charlotte!" Olive squeaks. She immediately does what I knew she would do and peers down to our interlocked fingers and smiles—that smile, the one that takes over her entire face. Just like Ellie's.

Our hands separate as I run to Olive's side, kneeling so I can bring myself as close to her little face as possible. "You scared me so much, Olive. I was so worried about you." I wrap my arm around her and hold her tightly until she groans and squirms from my grip.

"I'm okay," she says, as assuring as ever. She's always "okay."

"What were you doing up on top of the play set?" I ask, looking into her apologetic eyes.

She doesn't blink as she stalls on a response, and her look has me questioning whether she doesn't remember or just doesn't want to tell me. After a long minute, a soft sigh expels from her lips as she says, "Someone asked me where mom was and the top of the playset was the closest I could get to her." Just as I think I'm going to be okay, her explanation devastates me.

When Olive asks me where heaven is, I have always told her heaven is in the clouds because for now at five, it's easy to understand. When I first told her this, she responded with confusion, telling me she can't touch the clouds; therefore, she couldn't touch Ellie. I told her if she reached high enough and closed her eyes, she could feel the clouds, as well as Ellie. This is my fault. "You told me if I reached high enough—"

"I know what I told you, sweetie, but I was wrong. I—"

Charlotte steps beside me and kneels down too. "Olive," she says, her voice soothing and warm. "If you close your eyes, no matter where you are standing, you can feel your mom—in heaven. You don't need to climb up high in order to reach her—" Charlotte pauses as the sound of breath hiccups in her throat, proving a difficulty in offering Olive this sound advice. Her breaths even out and a smile returns to her lips as she continues, "because your mom is right here." Charlotte presses on Olive's chest, over her heart. "Close your eyes, honey."

Olive closes her eyes but opens one slightly to look at us both, skeptically. "Now what?" she giggles.

"You have to keep your eyes closed and imagine what your mom looks like, what her skin might feel like, and what her voice sounds like." Charlotte's words morph from sweet to soothing, serious, and believable, a combination that makes Olive relax into the bed and close both eyes.

I watch as Charlotte continues to talk about Ellie as if she knew her, and I watch as a smile tugs at Olive's lips in response. The connection between the two of them right now is almost too overwhelming to take in. I haven't seen Olive this calm and peaceful, no matter what the occasion.

"I think I can feel her," Olive says in a whisper. "Mom's voice sounds like a pretty song, and her skin feels like a flower's petal. She looks like me, but bigger I guess." Olive's smile grows wider and her cheeks turn a little rosier. "She really loves me, doesn't she?"

"More than you could ever imagine," I tell her, feeling my throat swell into its familiar knot.

"She loves you too, Daddy."

CHAPTER SIX

DECEMBER
-ONE MONTH LATER-

"CAN I PLEASE go out and play with Lana?" Olive begs. I've kept her inside for the past couple of weeks, not wanting to take my eyes off of her for even a second after the scare she gave me.

"Hunter," AJ shouts from the TV room. "Let the kid go out and play." Sometimes, living with AJ is like living with an annoying wife—he's constantly whining and he badgers me like the best of them. The funny part is, he doesn't live with me, he just spends more time here than he does at his own house with Alexa, which I'm not sure I can blame him for. Although, Alexa is here with him today—she's here with AJ every Sunday morning for "Family Breakfast".

"Breakfast is going to be ready in just a few minutes," I holler out to both of them.

"Grammy and Grampy just pulled in!" Olive yells from outside the front door. What is she doing out there? I poke my head around the corner as raw eggs drip from the whisk in my hand.

"Olive, get in the house! Why are you wearing snow pants and boots?"

"I want to go play in the leaves with Lana," she whines.

"Okay, first, we don't need snow pants and boots to play in the leaves, and second, you're wearing a summer dress over it. Third, your grandparents just got here."

"You're a stick in the mud," Alexa says to me as she finds Olive in the living room. "Olive, you look fabulous in that outfit. Come here and let me do your hair." I return to the eggs and waffles, my Sunday morning ritual. The coffee maker is in full swing and I have everything under control.

"Come on over for breakfast, there's plenty!" I hear mom's voice shouting from the driveway. I don't know who's she's inviting, but I'm going to assume it's Charlotte. "No, don't be silly! Come on over. I brought coffee cake and muffins!" Silence commences but only for a few seconds. "Okay. Sure, dear, I'll ask him."

The door swings open and Dad's crowing at Olive in his Cookie Monster voice, "Where's my little princess?"

The squeals coming from Olive make me laugh. She lives for Sunday mornings with the entire family. There's something about a full house that makes Olive feel on top of the world, and that is the reason I continue to do this every week, regardless of how much work it is. I can't give Olive a normal family, but I can give her a family full of love.

"Sweetie, what are you wearing?" Mom asks Olive. I knew that was coming.

"I saw it in Vogue," she answers. I close my eyes and shake my head. Alexa is such an amazing influence on her...

"Very funny," Mom says. "Hunter, dear." Mom's voice grows louder the closer she comes to the kitchen. Finding me at the stove, her hands cup around my shoulders as she presses up on her toes to place a kiss on my cheek. "Hi, sweetheart. I brought a few things this morning."

"Hey, Mom."

"Hunter, I invited Charlotte over. She was bringing in groceries from her car so I figured I would extend the invitation, but she didn't want to impose. Would you mind if she joins us?" I smile, only for the fact that I asked Charlotte a few days ago and she declined due to awkwardness. I haven't officially introduced her to the rest of my family yet since AJ was enough of an explanation, but thanks to AJ, Mom knows all about her.

"That would be nice," I tell her.

"Are you two," she clears her throat. I look over at her, feeling a rush of heat run through my cheeks. Mom and I have never talked about relationships or women at all for that matter. Ellie grew up in our life and everything fell into place at the appropriate times so "the talk" was never necessary. Looking at her now with her raised brows, I feel the need to tell her not to ask.

Instead, I say, "Are we what?"

She slaps her hand on my back. "Oh, Hunter, you know what I mean."

"We're friends," I remind her for the fifteenth time in the past month. We are friends—friends who look at each other the way friends don't look at each other. Friends who hug much longer than friends should hug when saying goodbye at the end of a late night chat session on one of our couches. Friends who haven't dared to take things one step further in fear of losing the only friend each of us has. I have fallen for my friend...and I don't know what to do about that.

"Hunter, I know how you feel about my prying into your personal life, and I have truly tried my hardest over the past couple of years not to push you," This is true; instead, she has planted little tiny bugs in AJ's ear, knowing he can't keep a damn thing to himself. She's even tried her hand with Olive. They've both ratted Mom out, but she doesn't know this. "I just think that woman is darling and she has a little girl Olive's age."

"You have never met her," I remind Mom.

"But I would love to."

"Then go invite her in," I laugh. "It'll certainly make Olive's morning."

"Did you say my name?" Olive says, turning in to the kitchen with four ponytails lining the center of her head from front to back, shaping a perfect mohawk.

"Really, Alexa?" I yell.

"You're welcome," she says. Mom rolls her eyes, feeling the same way about Alexa as I do.

"I'll be right back. I'm going to go extend your invitation to Charlotte." Normally, I would be too concerned to send Mom across the street to talk to anyone I'm associated with, but I have warned Charlotte about Mom. Nothing could come as a surprise, I would hope.

I finish up the waffles and bring out the paper plates and napkins just as I hear Mom and Charlotte laughing as they walk in to the house. "Lana, I hear that you and Olive are best friends. Is that right?" Mom asks.

"Bestest friends in the whole wide world," Lana says.

"Well, she saved you a spot at the table in the dining room. Why don't you go on in and see her so your Mom and I can keep talking?" Without so much as an agreement, I hear Lana flying through the living room, followed by a shriek from Olive. The amount of noise two little girls can make is incredible.

One by one, I shuffle the filled plates into the dining room, and Charlotte is quick to meet me in the kitchen to help with the distribution. "I'm glad you came," I tell her.

"How could I say no to your mom?" she says quietly with a crooked grin.

"I don't know. I figured the same way you said no to me." I nudge her playfully in the shoulder as she sweeps past me with a jug of OJ and two coffee mugs.

I'm in the process of rinsing off the frying pan when Charlotte returns for more. She wraps her arm around my back and presses her cheek into the side of my shoulder. It feels nice. "Your family is really great. With my parents always traveling, I haven't felt this welcome anywhere in a long time," she says. Learning about Charlotte over the past couple of months has been a process of slowly breaking down a barrier she has tried very hard to keep in place. While she is usually one without a filter, her past is a different story—one that seems like it's buried in a place only she knows. I guess we sort of have that in common.

"I hope I'm not interrupting anything," Mom says, walking in with a now empty jug of OJ. The look on Mom's face is almost menacing like she's plotting out my future with Charlotte right this very second. I know she means well but I don't know how to break it to her that a future is an unlikely definition of what comes after today—it's something I refuse to consider or think about. If I don't think about a tomorrow, I won't end up heartbroken when I find myself in another empty world full of only yesterdays.

"Nope, we were just coming out to join everyone," I tell her, pulling away from Charlotte and taking the jug from her hands. "Go on out, I'll refill this and be right there." Mom kindly places her arm around Charlotte and guides her back toward the dining room.

When I hear the growing chatter, a moment of contentment fills me from within, bringing along a feeling of something right, something unfamiliar, and something I think I kind of like. Warmth soothes the inside of my chest and I'm nervous to feel the way I do. From the second Charlotte walked into the house today, I haven't thought about Ellie or the fact that Sunday morning brunch was a thing our families did together for years until she passed.

The only meals I share with Ellie's parents now are the forced ones that they plan so they can see Olive once a month. They look at me like I killed their daughter, like I planted a destructive seed in her uterus and took away everything they loved. Sometimes they look at Olive the same way and I want to hurt them and make them feel an ounce of what they make me feel. Though, as much as I hate living with the loss of my wife, I don't know what it's like to lose a daughter and I will not judge them for their behavior toward me, but I don't understand how they can do the same to Olive, their granddaughter, and the only piece of Ellie they have left.

"Hunter," Mom calls. "The food is getting cold." I put down the dishrag and dry my hands on the sides of my pants. The sight I'm greeted with when I walk in to the dining room can only be described as happiness. However, I'm quickly faced with a reality I've been too closed off to realize. As everyone's focus moves to my face, the smiles disappear, and my heart sinks a little. I'm making everyone around me feel the way I feel—my misery, my self-loathing pity. The silence accompanies the straight faces as I take my seat between Charlotte and Olive.

"Did I say something wrong?" I ask, knowing I haven't said anything at all. "You were all smiling until the second I walked in." I need to hear the truth. Am I that bad? Does Charlotte feel this way too? Olive?

"You aren't the happiest person," Alexa chimes in first. "It's hard to be happy around you sometimes because I think we all feel guilty that you can't be happy along with us." Mom and Dad both nod their heads in agreement, probably grateful, for once, that Alexa had the courage to say something…something they were also feeling but didn't know how to say out loud. Olive is stifling a laugh with her hand cupped over her mouth, proving she doesn't understand what Alexa is talking about, thankfully. And Charlotte, she's looking at me the way I don't want her to look at me, like she just came to a conclusion I might have been trying to hide from her.

I draw in a deep breath, hoping to clear out some of the pain in my chest, but strangely, the extra air only makes me feel more suffocated. I can bail right now and make a scene, I can ignore everything Alexa just said, or I can tell her the truth. Making a decision that surprises even me, I blurt out, "You're right." She is right. "I'm sorry for what I have put you all through over the past five years." How many times can I say this to all of them before it loses its meaning?

In the support groups I used to attend, I witnessed some people healing quicker than others. Some widows began to date only months after their spouse's death, while some swore off the thought of a new partner entirely. I was part of the latter group for a long time, but the fog has cleared enough for me to see a little further ahead and I see a long road, a long life, one in which I'm not sure I want to remain alone, in a constant state of misery. Then again, I'm not sure I ever made the decision to be miserable; I just haven't been able to figure out how not to be. Sometimes I feel like I'm banging on a glass window, trying to get the attention of everyone I love, but they don't hear me. I feel like we have this conversation way too often and I really wish they could have let it go today with Charlotte here.

"Do you know how many times you have said this?" Dad says. "The number of times you have apologized makes this one a little less meaningful, Son." This. This is not something I wanted Charlotte to be a part of, and by the looks of it, I can sense she feels the same way.

"My best friend lost her husband," Charlotte states like a peace offering. "Believe it or not, Hunter is doing far better than she was doing five years after his death."

"Oh dear, I am so sorry," Mom pipes in. "I can't imagine what she must have gone through, the poor thing." Yes you can! Hello? You've watched me go through it.

"Well, sure you can, Mrs. Cole." Charlotte lets out a long sigh before placing her napkin down over her lap. "It's pretty similar to what Hunter has experienced; however, my friend doesn't have any children, which made it easier for her to slide down a slippery slope—one that included drugs, alcohol, and other things that are not appropriate to discuss at the table." Charlotte wraps her hand around her coffee mug, squeezing it as if it were a stress relief. "I know I only met Hunter a couple of months ago, but I think he's doing great, considering." I feel odd being talked about as if I weren't sitting here, but I feel flattered that Charlotte stuck up for me to my family. What she just did takes balls.

Mom looks a bit taken aback. Her eyes are wide and her eyebrows are pinned about an inch higher than they should be. Dad, though, his lips are sewn tightly together into a small, twisted smirk. He likes Charlotte's confidence. He has told me many times during my life that he finds confidence in a woman beautiful and sexy.

We all wait in silence for someone to respond, but I'm not sure a response is necessary. "Look," I finally break through the silence. "Yes, I have been an unhappy person, miserable to be around, I'm sure. I realize it has been five years and maybe I should have gotten over my pain four years ago, but she was part of my life for twenty years. Time hasn't healed me yet, so what am I supposed to do? Do you want me to pretend I'm all better?" I force a stupid grin. "How's this? Does it look real enough?"

"Hunter," Mom says, disappointedly.

"Better yet," I continue. "Maybe I should have just called it quits. Maybe I should have done what I thought about doing so many goddamn times after she died."

Charlotte's hand sweeps across my lap until her fingers touch mine. She squeezes tightly, silently telling me to stop going in the direction I'm heading in.

"You're right," Mom says. "Charlotte, you are right, as well. We have all tried so hard to help you become happy again that we have failed to realize how far you have come and what you have overcome. I think I speak for all of us when I say we can have a little more understanding for the time it is taking—will take—for you to find something that will make you smile the way you once did."

I see them once a week, and Charlotte isn't normally here, so what they don't see is that I do smile like I once did. And it isn't because I'm head over heels in love with this woman sitting next to me, it's because someone has had enough patience to listen and truly understand what I've gone through, what I'm still going through, the grief and sadness I'm living with. Her patience has been something no one else has offered me, and yet, despite my emotional baggage, she enjoys my company as much as I enjoy hers. "I do smile," I correct Mom. I look at Charlotte, then take her hand and pull it up above the table for everyone to see, eliciting a surprised look from her. "This woman makes me smile, and no, we aren't a 'thing' since I know you love labels, but she is my best friend...and more, I guess." More, I guess. What would more entail? More as in what I think about doing, more as in, what I've carefully avoided doing? More as in, when I finally cross that line, will Ellie's memories slowly disappear? Charlotte's look of surprise has changed into a glimmer of delight, and I see an accompanying sparkle in her eyes.

"I knew it," AJ shouts across the table. "Lucky dog, you. That's a big win right there...trust me."

Well, that was an easy way to divert the attention away from me. Mom is gawking at AJ, and Alexa is winding up to slap him. "AJ," mom scolds.

"Whoa, I meant, a big win for him." AJ's words of explanation don't work as well as he probably thought they would, and I'm starting to wonder why the blood just drained from his face and why he looks like he might puke.

"Maybe I should say, I knew it," Alexa says, excusing herself from the table. "Charlotte. I should have known."

"Am I missing something?" I ask.

Alexa has one foot out the door when she says, "Oh, you don't know, do you?"

Charlotte's hand slips from mine and I am instantly drawing conclusions that won't do me any good.

"Girls, are you all done?" Mom asks Lana and Olive.

"Yup," Olive answers, confusion filling her eyes, probably matching the look in my eyes.

"Why don't you two go on upstairs to play, then? I'll come check on you in a few minutes." Both girls flee from their seats and head up the stairs, leaving this room feeling somehow even more constricting.

"Is someone going to tell me what's going on or—?" I don't know how to finish that question, and the words coming from my mouth sound breathless, like someone just punched me in the gut.

"Can we talk for a minute?" Charlotte asks, standing up from her seat. I hear her talking, and I can feel her staring, but I'm eyeing AJ and the look on his face, which tells me there's something I'm going to lose my shit over.

"I haven't gotten to have one bite of the food I spent an hour cooking. I think our talk can wait." I keep my focus on AJ's face, watching as the hue of pink on his cheeks continues dropping shade by shade, ever so slowly, morphing into a paleness resembling a ghost.

I shovel bites of food into my mouth, one by one, as I try to think. Maybe it's not as bad as I'm assuming it is, but what I'm assuming is that AJ's lips have touched the lips I have restrained myself from touching for a reason I shouldn't have. I'm assuming AJ has seen what lies beneath the clothes of this beautiful woman standing beside me. I'm assuming he knows whether or not her breasts are real or fake...a question I ponder every time I see her coming toward me. Whatever it is he's done, I don't know whether it has been recently or before I met Charlotte, and that is the only question I have right now, because depending on the answer, it might cause a conflict with one of the ten commandments of respecting thy neighbor.

Charlotte doesn't leave the room or sit back down, but I can feel her eyes boring into the top of my head. Mom has her face buried in her hands...words have finally managed to escape her, and Dad is sitting at the edge of his seat, waiting for the show to continue. What does Alexa know? How did she figure out so much from such a simple remark? AJ didn't tell her to stop and come back, or ask her what she was talking about, which confirms the right Alexa had to accuse AJ.

Several minutes pass and all of us are still in the same position we were in when Alexa took off. Mom finally makes the first move and stands up from her chair, clearing as many dishes as she can grab within reach. "Harold, come help me in the kitchen," she says to Dad.

Dad follows, picking up some more of the dishes along the way. Now, it's just AJ, Charlotte, and me.

"I'm sorry," AJ says.

CHAPTER SEVEN

"SORRY" WAS ALL I needed to hear. That one measly word packs such a goddamn punch sometimes. Sorry for your loss. Sorry your life sucks. Sorry you live like you're a zombie. Sorry I slept with the one woman who has seemed to understand you since the day Ellie died. Screw all the sorrys. Screw everyone.

I didn't give him a chance to explain because as much as I'd love to hear every detail surrounding how he cheated on Alexa with Charlotte, at the same time I don't want to hear a word about it. How did he even know her? The fucking Olsans' job, her parents' house—that must be how—Charlotte must have been there supervising one of the mornings I wasn't there. Motherfucker. Why didn't Charlotte tell me? Their stupid encounter at the bus stop that first day—it was a cover up. Why the fuck didn't either of them tell me?

I'm through the front door before anyone has a chance to stop me. I know Olive is in good hands with Mom and Dad here so I'm leaving. I'm running away like I always do because, really, what other option do I have? I tried dabbling with facing reality this morning at breakfast, and that ended up blowing up in my face. If I keep running, maybe life will trip over its own feet and stop chasing me deeper into the gloom that closes in on me a little more each day I survive through this hell.

By the time I peel out of the driveway, Charlotte has one foot out the door and Dad has Olive in his hands, watching me from the window. Jesus. He couldn't just distract her for a few minutes?

I have to put it all out of my mind. I need to breathe. I need to catch my breath away from all of them—away from everyone. With no direction in mind, I find myself at the one place I always instinctively end up when I run away.

I shove the gear into park and kick my door open as if I'm being suffocated. I am suffocating. With tunnel vision, I jog down the steps, but I slow my pace when I come closer to the tree. "Tell me I shouldn't be thinking about other women, Ellie." My heart is in my throat as I try to suck back in some of the wind that has pinned my lungs against my ribcage. "If you had a chance to tell me what you wanted to tell me before you died, would you have told me to move on or would you have wanted me to live out my life, waiting until it was my turn to join you up there? I need to know. I need to know that what I'm doing isn't wrong, Ell. I need your blessing on what I do with the rest of my life."

"You know that's a tree you're speaking to, right?" A soft voice pulls me from the darkness of my outspoken thoughts. I turn to face her, failing to recognize the woman at first glance. After a moment, though, I remember her—the woman plucking every last jasmine out of the pre-frozen soil.

"Uh," I fall short of finding more words to fill the awkwardness between us. I was, in fact, speaking to a tree, very personal words not meant for anyone but Ellie to hear. I look past her and over to the pond, confirming that there is no trace of a flower left to be picked. "There aren't any flowers here anymore."

What else is there to say to a complete stranger I shared less than a minute worth of conversation with?

She looks over her shoulder to where I was looking. "Nope, there are no more flowers," she confirms.

"Yeah," this is becoming more uncomfortable by the second. "Well, I was just venting away over here. Family drama, you know?"

She smiles gently, unveiling a perfect, glowing white smile. Every one of her teeth are perfectly even, and the tip of her nose is aligned with the split of her two front teeth. Her eyes, though, while incredibly symmetrical, are larger than her other features—sort of like an anime character—jade green disks floating in a sea of snowy white. Brushing away a strand of her wavy hair, she breaks her gaze from mine. "I know a lot about family drama. Trust me."

"Who doesn't, I guess." I run my fingers down the side of my face, trying to inhale as much as possible in hopes of stretching out the aching muscles in my chest.

"Tell me about her," she says, pointing to the root of the tree. "Your wife."

I forgot I had spewed off this piece of information to her the last time we met. I must have gotten a lot off my tongue in a matter of sixty-seconds. Maybe the conversation was longer than that.

I take a few steps to the side, over to the bench along the stone-covered wall. Sitting down, I wonder if she'll follow. She hasn't moved from her spot, but she's looking between the tree and me as if she's contemplating a decision. "I don't bite."

With hesitation she makes her way over, taking up the spot beside me. "I'm Ari," she says. "Ariella."

"Hunter," I respond, offering her my hand as a gesture, making this awkward meeting more official.

"So?" she urges me on, leaning forward, pressing the tips of her elbows into her knees.

"We were friends since five years old, never left each other's side. We were inseparable until the day she gave birth to our little girl. That pretty much sums up the story." My explanation of Ellie's death gets shorter and shorter each time I repeat it. They're like preprogrammed words that just roll off my tongue. It makes it easier to have an automatic response, saving me from digging into my rotting brain to retrieve bits and pieces of the why, what, when, and where of Ellie.

Ari doesn't blink or react when she takes in my words. Her focus remains solid on the small patch of grass in front of us.

"Do you know that poem by Robert Frost? 'The Road Not Taken'?" she asks, finally looking over at me. The look in her eyes makes my gut hurt, but not in a bad way. It hurts in a way that tells me my nerves are still alive, functioning at a normal capacity when I see an attractive woman; although she isn't the definition of attractive, she's more ethereal, dream-like. Her skin is smooth and flawless and I imagine it would feel like satin or silk if I touched it. I'm staring at her now and I should look away. I am sitting in front of my wife's grave, for God's sake. How much more disrespectful could I be?

With that last thought, I break our eye contact, moving my focus to the patch of grass she was hogging with her stare just seconds earlier. "Yeah, I know that poem," I say, my voice coming out more stern and short than I intended.

"Well, he says that there are two paths to choose from and he took the one less traveled by. It really is a beautiful thought..." she trails off.

"Yup, it is. It's a really great poem," that I cannot remember the words to. Eighth grade English class was quite a while ago and I suddenly remember asking myself what I would ever need poetry for in life. My question has been answered—it's so I don't look like a complete loser when a woman asks me about a poem.

"It's total bull," she says, shocking the hell out of me. My focus swings back to her face, forgetting what Ellie may or may not be thinking of me right now.

"Oh yeah?" I ask, feeling intrigued.

"No one has a choice in life. No one really gets to choose what path they go down. Every single second of every minute of every hour, day, month, and year we are alive was predetermined for us the moment we were born." Her voice is growing in volume as if she's angry with Robert Frost himself. "I mean, how can one person say, 'whatever is meant to be will be' offer so much truth, only to be completely called out by Robert Frost, who's talking about us having choices in life. No one has a choice. Everything that happens was meant to happen and we're just passengers on this ride. Right?" Holy hell, this woman is fired up. She must have really been screwed over by fate, but this may be the most intelligent conversation I've ever had, or potentially the most therapeutic, at least.

"Who said 'whatever is meant to be will be' anyway?" I ask.

"Them, that person, whoever 'they' are—you know, the person with all the sayings," she says. Her smile returns, accompanying a soft breath of laughter.

The longer I look at her, the more at ease I feel. I'm not sure why, considering the despise I normally have for being around other people, but something about her takes that distaste away, kind of like what Charlotte has done for me over the past few months. Except Charlotte was fucking AJ. "You may be the smartest person I have ever met," I offer as a compliment in lieu of a response to her criticism of Robert Frost. In truth, nothing that comes out of my mouth could hold a flame to the intellectual thoughts she just shared.

"Why are you here?" I ask her, not only for the reason of moving away from the poetry discussion I will eventually stumble on but also because I truly want to know why a florist is here in a place where there are no more flowers. I have never seen anyone visit these flowerlesss gardens at the end of fall, besides a straggling elderly person looking to get his or her number of steps for the day accounted for.

"I..." she stammers on a response. "I just like it here. I feel connected to this place for a reason I can't explain. It just makes me feel whole when I'm feeling a little broken, you know? So I come here almost every day." How have I only run into her twice?

"And why are you broken?" I continue.

"I'm literally broken from the inside out. Trust me, it's not something I'd want to waste your time explaining."

"There he is!" Olive's voice shouts from the top of the hill. I turn to find Dad holding her tightly in his arms as he stares down at me with sympathy. Always sympathy. "I told you we'd find him here." As Olive is lecturing Dad, he takes the stone steps one by one. I want to tell him to turn back and let me have just a few more minutes here but he wouldn't listen.

"Dad, I'll—uh—I'll meet you up at the car in just a minute," I tell him, hoping he'll stop coming toward me.

"Who is she?" Olive asks in a sing-song voice. "She's pretty, like a Disney princess. You look like..." Olive pauses for a moment, tapping her little finger against her chin. "Oh, I know! You look like Rapunzel, but with brown hair." Yes, Olive's right. That's exactly who she looks like.

Ari giggles in response and stands from the bench, making her way over to Dad and Olive. "Well, I'm not Rapunzel, but thank you for saying that. You are absolutely adorable," Ari says.

A smile sprouts over Olive's lips, stretching from ear to ear. "Thank you," she says through a fit of quiet laughter.

"If you don't mind me saying, Miss, you look familiar, but I can't quite place my finger on where I know you from. Are you and Hunt friends? Did you go to high school together, maybe?"

Ari takes a couple of steps back, fussing nervously with her hair. "Uh—oh, no, she—we just see each other here sometimes—a common interest, you know?" I chime in.

Dad stares at me for a minute, looking between the two of us with a look I can't decipher. "Huh, well then, maybe you just have a familiar looking face," he follows up.

Ari's cheeks have deepened into a dark shade of pink as she stammers over her next words. "Yeah, I—um—I—I get that all of the time," she says. She does not get that all of the time. She's exquisite, honestly—like no one I've ever seen before. A lot of it has to do with her eyes though, not just the way they look, but the way she looks at things like she's exploring everything for the first time, seeing things with amazement. Or at least that is what I have noticed in the thirty minutes we've now known each other.

"You know, I really do think I know you from somewhere," Dad says again.

Ari turns around, reaching for her bag below the bench. "I don't think that's possible," she says, looking as if she's about to run, yet again. "I just moved here from San Diego a few months ago."

San Diego? Who would leave San Diego to come all the way across the United States to Connecticut of all places...to work in a flower shop?

"Ari, what is the name of your flower shop?" I say, reaching for her arm before she's out of reach.

She shakes her head subtly and slips out of my loose grip.

"Dad, Charlotte is real-l-l-l-l-l-l-l-ly upset that you left her," Olive says, loud enough that Ari turns to look at me once more as she jogs up the stone stairs. "She said it's all a big misunderstanding. And a big, big, big, big mistake."

"Olive, hush," Dad says to her. And now her bottom lip is in place and Olive is officially pouting. "Oh stop it with the lip. I need to talk to your dad for a minute."

"I'm sorry," Dad begins. "I didn't mean to scare your friend away."

"She's not my friend," I reply coldly. But I would have liked her to be my friend, I think. What am I thinking? Saying? I haven't dated anyone in the time Ellie has been gone because it didn't feel right. Now I'm sitting here confused as all hell about how I got my emotions wound so tightly around Charlotte that I actually feel pain for what she did with AJ, and now this...a complete stranger has captured my attention in less than thirty minutes. This isn't me.

"What's going on with you, Hunt?" Dad asks. Placing Olive down on her feet, he then turns to her, saying, "Go find me ten little rocks by the bench over there. Ten." Dad holds his fingers up one at a time for Olive to count.

"I know how much ten is, silly Grampy." Olive skips over to the bench where she begins her search, counting out each rock slowly, one at a time.

"Hunter," he begins again. "Talk to me, Son."

"I don't know, Dad." I don't. I don't know what to think or feel. I don't know what's appropriate or what's wrong.

"You're scared of getting hurt again," Dad says. His accusation is partially correct, but I've been more concerned with what Ellie would think if she could see everything I'm doing.

There were times in our life together when she would get this unsettled look in her eyes, a look worth a million thoughts. It would sometimes take me an entire day to crack the code. She didn't like to vocalize her worries; instead, she would write them down. A lot of times I wondered if I had done something to make her upset or if I just completely messed up or forgot something, and I would have to pull it out of her if I had any hopes of figuring out what I did wrong. That was the only part of her that truly made me nuts sometimes. I'm a fixer. I like to fix problems, especially ones that I cause. The only thing I don't seem to know how to fix is myself.

"Yes and no," I tell him. "Do you think she can see me? Do you think she knows what my life is like, the decisions I make, and the feelings I have? Do you think she can sense all of it?"

"You know I don't believe in that stuff," Dad says, shifting his weight around to lean back against a tree. "I think once a person is gone, they move on to the next part of their life, and I don't think that's here on earth. She's gone, Son, and it is okay to move on with your life. It's okay to be happy." Dad leans over to pick up a dirt-covered penny from beside his foot, bringing it back up to inspect it under the bit of sunlight poking through the trees. "Huh, will you look at that?" His attention is quickly diverted to the penny as he brings it up closer, flipping it from side to side. "This isn't just a lucky penny, it's a 1955 double-die penny. This thing is worth money."

Dad has a thing with coins. Nope, not just a thing, an obsession. I spent most of my youth with a metal detector in my hand, combing beaches for pennies. The world could freeze around us, but if he's looking at copper, nothing else matters. "Dad," I say, trying to pull his attention back.

He slips the penny into his front pocket and refocuses. "I'm sorry. What was I saying?" he pauses for a second. "Oh right. If God forbid, you were the one who died and you had the chance to tell Ellie one last thing other than 'I love you', what would it be?" I would want her to be happy and to live a life that we could both be proud of. "You'd want her to be happy, wouldn't you?"

Then it hits me. I promised her I would live for both of us. I have broken that promise in every single way possible. I have taken care of Olive and I have been a good dad to her, but when that little girl isn't looking at me, I feel sorry for myself and I know it has taken over who I am. "Yes, I'd want her to be happy," I reply simply.

"That is what she would want for you, too. I know for a fact that she would want you to be happy," Dad says.

"You know for a fact? What—what are you talking about?"

"Remember the car accident you two were in?" Dad asks.

"I found ten, Grampy! Ten!" Olive shouts, running toward us with two handfuls of rocks.

"Good, now go find ten little sticks that are green inside." Olive looks at him, puzzled at first but then runs to the grassy area, falling to her hands and knees.

"Yeah, I remember the accident." Obviously. We both almost lost our lives that day. Some drunk asshole in an eighteen-wheeler sideswiped us on the highway, pushing our car down into a ditch. I was told the car had rolled four times before a tree stopped us. We were both airlifted from the scene and taken to Mass General.

"She woke up before you did, you know that right?" Dad continues.

"Yeah, I know," I tell him. It may have been twelve years ago, but I remember it like it was yesterday.

"I remember sitting with her right when she woke up. Her parents were in Scottsdale or something, I don't know. Anyway, your mother was with you and I sat with Ellie so she wasn't alone." Dad pulls in a deep breath and sinks back against the tree a little harder. "One of the nurses came in to tell us you had woken up and everything looked like it was going to be okay." He reaches over and places his hand over my shoulder, squeezing it during a pause in his story. "I cried like a goddamn baby, Son. You know that?" He laughs an uneasy laugh. "Anyway, within minutes, a doctor came in to tell Ellie that one of her ribs had slightly punctured her lungs and she needed emergency surgery. She was so scared when they were taking her away." Dad closes his eyes briefly, smiling through silent laughter. "They told her she was going to be just fine, but she didn't want to believe them, so right before she was rolled out, she grabbed my hand, looked me in the eyes and said, 'If anything happens to me, I want you to tell Hunter to live a happy life. Tell him not to worry about me. Tell him I want him to live his life without regrets and to always keep that smile I love on his face.' Naturally I told her not to worry about a thing, but her words hit me hard." Dad takes another couple of short breaths before continuing. "Anyway, her parents finally arrived some time while she was in surgery and asked me to leave, so I wasn't there to tell her 'I told you so' when she got out. Otherwise, I would have."

"Why didn't you tell me any of this before?"

"Because she woke up from the surgery, survived just like you, and went on to live a happy life." He pushes himself away from the tree, peeking around me to see what Olive is doing. She's peeling sticks apart, looking for a green center, and appears to have now killed an entire tree with the pile she is creating. "Honestly, I hadn't thought of it again until just now when you asked me what she would be thinking. I just remembered her saying all of that."

"Do you think that accident had anything to do with Ellie's aneurysm?" I don't know why I never considered this before, but I have to wonder if that could have been the reason?

"I'm guessing it's possible," Dad says. "You both had head damage from that accident. Although I don't remember hearing anything about her CT scans. She got all of those tests back after her parents came in so I don't really know what those results were."

"She would have told me though, right?" Surely she wouldn't keep something like that from me. She wouldn't. We told each other everything, unless she was mad at me, of course.

"I would assume so," Dad says. "You ever ask her parents?"

"No, it never occurred to me that the accident could have affected her seven years later."

"And it may not have. I don't think it's something you need to figure out at this point. It won't bring her back," Dad continues.

There's no sense in arguing this with him, and it's just another question that will nag at me until I come to the conclusion that there is no answer available. "Olive, how are you doing over there?" Dad calls out to her.

"Almost done!" she shouts.

"Look, my point here is that Ellie would want you to be happy. You got a great girl back there at home. Charlotte cares about you a lot. You shouldn't be so quick to push her away."

And just like that I remember exactly what brought me here. "Dad, she was sleeping with AJ."

"Hunter, what have I always told you since you were a young boy?" I roll my eyes and throw my head back, focusing on the branch above us while waiting for what I know he is about to say. "Don't you know what the word assume means?"

"Yeah, Dad. I know," I tell him.

"Then don't be an ass," he says, thumping his hand against my back. "Go get Olive and let's get back to the house before we miss lunch, too."

Dad and Olive head up the stairs, leaving me to Ellie for just one more minute.

I dig my toe into the dirt, staring straight into the center of the etched heart on the tree. "Ell, is it true you want me to be happy?"

Now's the time when the wind is supposed to blow or the sun is supposed to break through the branches and hit me in the face—any type of sign that she can hear me. But that never happens.

And I think it's because her heart is still holding her soul captive somewhere in someone else's body.

CHAPTER EIGHT

I FOLLOW BEHIND Dad's car on the way back to the house. Breakfast was not supposed to be an all day event, but clearly when my family sees an opportunity to watch some entertainment, they make themselves comfortable and grab their bucket of popcorn.

As I walk back inside, I'm quick to notice the house has been straightened up, cleaned as if breakfast never happened. Charlotte and Lana are gone, Alexa is nowhere in sight and AJ is sitting at the cleared dining room table with his hands folded tightly together.

I want to punch him square in the jaw. And I might if he doesn't have a really great explanation.

"I'm sorry," he begins again.

"Dude, I don't give a shit if you're sorry. How about you tell me what the hell you were thinking."

He looks up at me, and I see grief coating the glassy look in his eyes. "It's not what you think."

"Then what is it? If you think I'm going to sit here and ask you a dozen more times, you're wrong. I'll leave again. I'll cut you out of my life so fucking fast...and I won't hesitate."

"Jesus," he says, likely stunned by my non-Hunter-like response. Continuing with what better be a fucking good explanation, he says, "A year ago, right before Alexa and I got hitched, I was having second thoughts." He leans back in his chair and folds his arms behind his head. "We all know she's a pain in the ass and I wasn't sure if I could really spend the rest of my life with her."

"So you cheated on her?" I ask, trying my hardest to sound unfazed.

"Let me finish," he snaps back. "Look, not that I'm going to place any blame on you or anything, but sometimes I need a friend or a brother to talk to and let's be real, you haven't been much of either to me in the past few years—understandably so, but still."

I suppose I deserve that. It's the truth, but nevertheless I say, "Do not blame your cheating scandal on me. You are a grown man, AJ, and you need to act like one. You can't blame anyone for the mistakes you made or make."

A growl escapes his throat before continuing, "I'm not blaming anything on you. I'm telling you I was going through a hard time." He shifts around in his seat again, this time bringing his elbows to the table. "I needed someone to talk to, so I created an account on 'theLword.com'." He places his hands up, I'll assume to stop me from saying what I want to say. "I know I shouldn't have been on that site looking for someone to talk to." That is not how I figured he met her. What the hell? "Anyway, something weird happened with my account and it got hacked or something, I'm not sure— I'm not real good with computers, you know that. So I had to contact whoever was in charge of the site so I could try to figure out how to fix the problem. Emails were being sent out to my email list and Alexa was one of the recipients. It was a huge fucking mess."

"And that's when it all happened," I chime in. "Charlotte contacted you and you found your person to talk to." My cheeks are burning—all of my skin actually feels like it's on fire. I've needed someone to talk to for years, but I haven't turned to a goddamn dating site, and I certainly wouldn't do that if I were engaged to be married. But that's AJ—he doesn't think things through.

"Well, kind of. We just got to talking while she was going through my page, trying to debug whatever happened. She was going through her divorce and needed someone to talk to, too. Honestly, we only met up a few times because I realized I did want to be with Alexa and we cut off all communication since Charlotte didn't want to be the reason I broke off my engagement." I can tell he's giving me the truth, but I can't tell if he's leaving shit out.

"Did you fuck her, or not?"

"Hunter," Mom shrieks from the kitchen. "Don't use that language while your daughter is in the house." I'm not sure why I would have thought Mom wouldn't be listening in on this whole thing. She is probably standing around the corner with that big bowl of popcorn.

"Did you?" I repeat.

"No," he grunts. "We kissed and maybe a little more, but we didn't sleep together." The 'a little more' fires me up a bit but I tell myself it could be worse. I tell myself that this happened before I knew Charlotte even existed. What I'm pissed about is that both AJ and Charlotte failed to mention any of this before now. What are the odds? I go five years without a female romantic interest in my life, and when I finally find someone whose company I actually enjoy, it turns out that AJ already had his way with her.

"You never came clean to Alexa?" I ask.

"She knew I kissed someone. She knew her name was Charlotte. I think she took a lucky guess when I said, 'That's a big win right there. Trust me.' I should have left off the 'Trust me'."

"You should have never kissed another woman, and 'more', in the first place," I mock him. Then it occurs to me, "Wait a minute, that Olsans' hardwood job wasn't a coincidence, was it? How stupid are you? You were trying to hide this shit from Alexa and then took on a job with Charlotte's parents?"

"Dude, you've told me we're not in a position to turn down work with the way the economy is, so I didn't." Jesus. I drop down into the seat across from AJ, resting my elbows on the table the same way he is. I lower my forehead down against my closed fists

SHARI J. RYAN

and release every bit of air from my lungs. "I am sorry," AJ says. "You know I'd never do that with a girl you were involved with, but you didn't even know her then."

"I know," I say. The words come out muffled against my fist, but he heard me. The sigh of relief he lets out tells me so.

After a few minutes of silence, I look up at AJ, finding regret and discomfort written across his face. "She a good kisser?"

AJ lowers his voice to a whisper. "You haven't kissed her yet? I mean, I thought you guys were fucking like bunnies over here every night." His words send a gnarling pain into my stomach. I haven't kissed or done anything more than that with any woman besides Ellie. Crossing that line is something I've been thinking about, even obsessing over, but I haven't been able to make that move yet.

"No, we're just friends," I remind him.

"If she were just your friend, you wouldn't have stormed out of the house for two hours." He's right. "Where the hell did you go anyway?"

"The gardens."

"Oh," he says, understanding.

"Look, if you want my opinion, get your ass across the street and give that girl the kiss she's been dreaming of—the one I'm pretty sure you've been thinking of, too."

"I'm going to go talk to her, but I'm not going over there to compare spit swap stories," I respond.

"Well, you should," he quips.

I groan as I stand up from my seat. "I love how you boys talk your problems out," Mom says, walking out from around the corner with her hands placed over her heart. "That was just beautiful. It makes me so proud to know I have raised two respectable men." I want to roll my eyes and tell her to knock it off, but the woman is on the brink of tears. "Go ahead, Hunter, go talk to Charlotte. I'll take care of Olive." I take a few steps down toward the TV room and find Olive asleep, tucked under Dad's arm on the couch. Dad's asleep too.

"I think Dad and Olive are taking care of each other," I laugh quietly.

"Well then, I'll just keep cleaning," she says. "And AJ, please go find Alexa. You have some explaining to do."

94

At thirty and twenty-eight years old, AJ and I are still under this woman's power. Never, have we ever been able to say no to her.

I grab my coat from the living room couch and slip it on as I head out the door. I cross the street and hesitate for a brief second before I knock. What am I going to say?

Before I have the chance to knock or figure out what those words are going to be, Lana opens the door. "Hi, Mr. Cole," she says. Her lips are bowed into a slight scowl and I hope I'm not the cause for the look on her face. I don't think my reaction was totally unwarranted but maybe I could have made less of a scene. No. I didn't do this. Everyone should have been honest with me, but they weren't. Charlotte wasn't, and AJ sure as hell wasn't.

"Is your mom home?" I ask her.

"Yes, but she's kind of upset," Lana says, looking away from me and down toward the ground.

"Can I come in and talk to her?" I continue.

"Well—"

"Lana, is someone at the door?" I hear Charlotte shout from the other room.

"Yes, it's Mr. Cole," Lana replies.

A thud in the kitchen tells me Charlotte just dropped something in the sink, probably out of surprise that I'm here. She turns the corner, wiping her hands off on the side of her legs. "Hunter," she says, rushing to the door. "I can explain everything."

"AJ already has," I say, taking a couple of steps inside.

"I should have told you," she continues.

"Yes, you should have," I confirm. While I want to let it all go, I can't just forget about the fact that they were both keeping this from me. "Why didn't you?" I ask.

I take a seat on her couch, falling into the plush cushion. It's one of those couches that has a wide seat, making it so you either fall into it completely to relax or you sit awkwardly on the edge, hoping not to sink so far in that you lose your balance. I've lost my balance and I'm trying to save face by leaning back into it casually. Good thing I've got long legs.

She sits down on her coffee table, only a couple of feet away from the end of my knees. "I," is all she gets out before she sighs. "I don't have a good reason. I realized AJ was your brother the

95

first day we met and I didn't exactly know a good way to tell you that story. Then as our friendship grew, it got harder and harder to bring it up because I figured I should have already brought it up. It has been weighing heavily on my mind since the day…"

"What day?" I cut her off mid-thought.

She breaks her focus away from my face, like she typically does when she's ashamed to tell me something. Except I'm not sure what she would be ashamed of this time. "The day I realized I was falling for you," she says softly, so softly I'm not sure I heard her correctly.

"What was that?" I ask, needing her to repeat it.

"Hunter." She flashes her face upright, locking her sapphire gaze to mine. "I've fallen for you, okay? I know you just want to be friends and I respect that, but I can't control how I feel. I just—"

Everything in my chest aches as if my insides are made of carbonation and someone just shook the hell out of me. There's only one way to release the pressure.

I lean forward, pulling myself out of the plushness of the cushion and lock my hands around her arms, pulling her toward me, allowing her to fall into me as we sink into the bottomless pit of the couch. I cup my hands firmly around her cheeks and shut my brain off—I forget everything—as I close my eyes and crush my lips into hers. I don't think I'm breathing but maybe I just don't realize I am because my brain is not functioning properly. I am only able to think about her lips…the way they taste and feel like a ripe cherry.

Dammit to hell, I'm not coming back from this. Charlotte's body trembles beneath my grip, but her lips interact with mine at the same intensity mine are pursuing hers.

Her fingers slowly comb through my hair, sending shocking sensations down the length of my spine. With her body pressed against me, I realize I have officially lost all control—everything about her is incredible, and the memory of why I was so angry just an hour ago has faded into nothing more than a blur.

My hands explore the length of her back until the tips of my fingers graze the skin between her shirt and pants. The simple touch of her skin is all it takes to make me hard, and I know she's well aware of that as we somehow end up lying flat on the couch with her straddling me.

I almost forgot Lana was home when I hear her shout, "Mom, I'm thirsty!" from the other room. Charlotte jackknifes upward, separating our lips that have been connected for at least five minutes. Lying here, staring up at the flushed look on her cheeks and the heavy movement in her chest, my suppressed thoughts surface one by one. I thought I would feel remorse but I feel free, and while I think it might be a horrible thought, I needed to feel this. I've needed this for so damn long.

"Oh my God. Imagine if she just walked in here," Charlotte says. "We got a little carried away." The mom in her speaks out and I couldn't agree more. I never would have let this happen in my house, not with Olive always peeking around the corner.

"I shouldn't have had that knee-jerk reaction," I tell her.

"Yes, you should have," she corrects me. "That was like the best first kiss I've ever received in my twenty-nine years of life." I wasn't expecting to hear that after nearly forgetting how to use my damn lips.

"Now what?" I ask her. There doesn't have to be an answer to this question but I need to know what she's thinking.

"Now, we're still Hunter and Charlotte. We're still whatever you want us to be, even if that's just friends who kiss and whatever," she says fervently. Whatever. What does she mean by whatever? When would we even be able to arrange "whatever" with the girls running around? Is any of this even possible? "No rules. No expectations. No labels."

"'Whatever' works for me," I tell her. "But right now, I should probably get back home." I point over my shoulder to the window that overlooks my front yard. Why am I pointing at my house like she doesn't know where I live? I'm so out of my mind right now, and it feels nice.

She reaches over and pinches both of my cheeks. "You're looking a little pale. They'll know." She gives me a cute wink before giving each of my cheeks one more slightly painful pinch. "There, now your cheeks are rosy again," she says. The moment makes me feel a bit giddy as I yank myself off the couch. Rearranging my clothes so they fall correctly, she stands up and smoothes her fingers through my hair once more. "Couch head."

"Worth it," I tell her, wrapping my arm around her back as I pull her in to me once more. She's small in my arms and I have to lean down quite a bit to close the space between us, but she presses up on her toes and finds my lips with hers. I grip her tighter, needing to hold on as hard as I can while I inhale everything about her. A quiet moan pulses against my lips and once again, she brings me to another point of losing all control from the waist down.

"I—I might not be able to wait forever for 'whatever', so I just need to put that out there," I whisper into her mouth.

"Well, maybe you both can come over tonight so the girls can watch a movie, and we can just do 'whatever'," she says.

I pull away, gauging the look on her face, taking pride in the flush of her cheeks as well as the lustful look in her eyes as she pinches her lower lip between her teeth. "Okay." My eager agreement comes without much thought. "I'll see you later, Lana," I yell into the other room. "Thank you for letting me talk to your mom."

"You're welcome," she squeaks.

"Tonight then. Six?" I confirm once more.

"Whatever," she says with a quick wink.

CHAPTER NINE

THE PROBLEM WITH brothers is that there is no hiding information from one another. It only takes one look from AJ when I walk in, and I know my face is redder than a Maine lobster. He stands up from the couch with a shit-eating grin from ear to ear as he starts toward me with a slow clap.

"Don't be a douche," I tell him.

"I'm so proud of you, bro." His arms stretch out in front of him, reaching for me. "You're going to make it after all," he continues crooning with obnoxious baby-talk voice. If I were him, I wouldn't take another step closer. His condescending words are quickly eliminating every happy endorphin I walked in here with.

"I should have just stayed there," I say under my breath. Stepping away from AJ in order to hold myself back from punching him, I make my way into the TV room and find Dad still asleep, Mom folding a load of Olive's laundry, and Olive tearing outfits off of each of her Barbie dolls.

"Is everything okay with you and Charlotte now?" Mom asks.

"Yeah, it's fine," I say, kneeling down next to Olive. "Want to have dinner with Lana tonight?"

"Yay!" Olive shrieks. "Thank you, thank you, thank you!" She hops up and jumps on top of me, locking her arms around my neck. "Can I wear a dress?"

"If that's what makes you happy, of course you can," I tell her.

"She has school tomorrow," Mom says, keeping her eyes locked on the pair of pants she's intricately folding into quarters.

"Yeah, I'm aware. I can take care of her, believe it or not."

"What crawled up your pants, Hunter?" she asks.

Besides the obvious, how can she not know what's bugging me? "Am I the only one who sees how much you all consume yourself with my private life?" I stand up with Olive still attached to my neck, giggling like a hyena. She makes it hard to have a serious conversation with Mom, but this needs to be understood.

"It's only because we all worry about you, sweetheart." Mom finishes folding the last of the clothes and lifts the stack up. "And Ellie's death has been difficult for your Dad and me, too. Not only was she precious to us, but seeing our son lose his wife has been heartbreaking. We love you very much and have done our best to help you through the past five years, but it's been a continual learning experience for us too. There's no manual for how to help your son through something like this. Plus, all mothers pry. If I didn't pry, it would mean I didn't care about you. Someday, I won't be here to make sure you're happy and you'll miss this." She brushes by me to head up the stairs, leaving me with her motherly version of a punch to the gut. This is why I normally keep the peace and let her and everyone else take part in my sad little life.

AJ finally meanders in and pulls Olive off my neck. "Sorry, again." He sits down on the couch beside Dad, cradling squirmy Olive in his arms. "You should be smiling."

"You should be looking for your wife," I retort.

"She's at home," he says.

"You should be there, too, then."

"I want a divorce."

And there's the mic drop. Can't say I didn't see this coming the day he spent his life savings on a three-carat diamond only because she wouldn't accept anything less for a proposal, or so AJ said. "Have you thought this through or are you just afraid to fix this problem you caused?"

"Oh!" Olive shrieks. "Did you hear that?"

"Hear what?" AJ turns his attention to her, clearly avoiding my question.

"The mail is here. Mail, mail, mail!" she says, running through the house.

"Where are you going, Olive?" Mom shouts from upstairs.

"Mail!" Olive shouts. She is half way down the driveway before I reach the front door and she is already running back with a stack of mail in her hands. "I knew it!" She runs in past me, dropping the mail on the coffee table, keeping one small envelope against her chest. "It's her, Daddy!"

"Who?" Mom asks, walking down the stairs into the living room. "Who's her?"

"Mommy's heart," Olive says, as if it would make sense to anyone but Olive and me.

"Excuse me?" Mom says. I never exactly told Olive to keep these recurring letters between this woman and myself a secret, but I never intended to let anyone else know about them either. "Why are you getting mail on a Sunday?"

Uh. We don't get mail on Sundays. I didn't grab the mail yesterday, but why would she have thought the mail just arrived. "Olive, did you see the mail carrier?"

"No, I just heard the mailbox." Bionic hearing? Jeez. Wait a second. Running out the door, letting the wind slam it shut behind me, I make it to the end of the driveway just in time to hear a car engine, but whoever it is has already gone over the peak of the hill. Even if I ran down the street, I wouldn't have a chance at seeing the car.

Defeated as always, I walk back into the house and take the envelope from Olive. "Did you see the person who put this in the mailbox?" I ask her. Has she been delivering these letters all along? If so, she's obviously from around here. But, what about the mountains?

Olive shakes her head, her pigtails flopping around. "Nope."

"Did you see a car drive away?"

"Yup," she says. Her one little word makes my heart stop beating for a brief second.

"What color was it?" I ask.

Olive places her finger over her lips as her gaze floats to the ceiling. "Ummmm, hmmm. I think—I think it was green—or maybe it was brown. Gray, yeah it could have been gray, like gray and white maybe."

I kneel down in front of her and take her hands into mine. "Olive, I need you to think real hard. Was it a big car like mine or was it small like Grammy and Grampy's?"

"It was—kind of in the middle I guess. You know what, it could have been a blue car," she says with a large smile. "Yeah...I like blue cars."

This is absolutely not helpful. "Hunter, would you like to explain any of this?" Mom asks me, like I'm a teenager who she just caught hiding weed in his top drawer.

"A lady writes Daddy notes all of the time. She has Mommy's heart," Olive outs me a little more.

"What?" Mom croaks with anger tinting her cheeks. "You know the recipient?"

"No," I correct her. "I don't know who this woman is. I just receive letters from her."

"She obviously knows you and where you live!" Mom says, exasperated. "Well, open it!" I don't want to read this out loud. Not to her. Olive doesn't understand much of what these letters ever say, so I don't mind reading them to her, but this is all I have left of Ellie, and it feels like it should be private.

"Mom, I need this to be for my eyes only," I try to explain, though, I know she won't understand. She loved Ellie as if she were her own daughter. And for that reason, there are tears welling up in Mom's eyes.

She doesn't respond with an argument, just a look like I've hurt her. "Okay," she says. With Olive locked tightly between her arms, she presses her cheek down on Olive's head, her eyes close and a single tear escapes.

I open the envelope, carefully slipping the paper out. I unfold it, finding more text than normal.

"*Dear Mr. Cole,*" I read out loud, succumbing to the guilt trip. Mom's eyes open with surprise, elation, and a plea for more.

Four weeks have passed since my last note to you. In that time, the weather has grown cold and I have spent a great deal of time indoors, reading, cleaning, and writing a bit. I'm afraid her heart feels a bit empty these days and I feel guilty for not doing more to fill it.

I swallow against the tightness in my throat while bearing a sharp pain in my chest. I don't want her heart to feel empty...ever. I spent my entire life warming her heart, filling it with as much love as I could offer. Needing a break from the ice-cold words, I glance up at Mom, assessing her thoughts by the look on her face. Confusion is all I see, though.

I met a man, a man who doesn't know of my weakness, losses or gains. I think he saw me for who I am and wanted to learn more about me, but I fear what he would think or do if he were to learn of my fragile state.

I want to tell her no man is worth the fight if he doesn't love a woman for everything that makes her who she is, but I can't tell her that because I don't know who she is and I probably never will.

Anyway, I hope you and your daughter are doing well. Ellie once told me she dreamed of having a daughter. I know this isn't the way she wanted it to happen, though. I'm sorry I have let Ellie's heart down this past month, I will do what I can to bring back some of the warmth that has slipped away. Maybe this man I met will be different. Maybe he will be the first to love a bird with a broken wing. We can always hope, right? Take care and I hope the holiday season brings you everything you wanted this year.

Sincerely,
Her Heart

I have always thought she might know of Ellie considering she knows who I am and now, where I live, but this is the first time she has mentioned Ellie's name or the fact that she knows Ellie and I have a daughter. That information would have remained private in any donor exchange of information, especially since I have no information about her.

My only thought right now is that she knows Ellie—she knew Ellie, which means I must know her, or I'd like to think I know her. Ellie and I had the same group of friends, aside from some of the faculty she worked with at the school, but she wasn't very close to any of the other teachers.

"Hunter," Mom interrupts my thoughts, tears now spilling out, one after another down her wet cheeks. "This woman knows you and Ellie. This wasn't a random donation, was it?" She's asking me as if I have purposely kept information from her, details I've been dying to find out for myself.

"It seems it, but I have no information about her. I never will unless she reveals herself to me." Mom leans forward and takes the envelope off of the coffee table, flipping it back and forth, looking for the return address I'm always in search of.

"She doesn't want you to find her," Mom says.

"I know." But that won't stop me from trying.

"I'm heading out," AJ says, walking into to the living room. I almost forgot about the atom bomb he dropped on me a few minutes ago.

"Where are you going?" I ask him.

"Home to work things out with Alexa, I hope," Mom interrupts.

"Nah, I'm going to Lion's for a bit," AJ says, brushing her off.

"Oh, AJ, I hope you aren't drinking again. You've come so far."

"Jesus, Mom. I think you and Dad need to hit the road. You're spending way too much energy worrying about Hunter and me today. For your information, I never had a drinking problem. I just like to unwind and enjoy myself sometimes. There is nothing wrong with that. Plus, maybe I'm just going for the bartenders' company." He knows he's crawling under her skin and AJ has always been one to enjoy doing that to her.

"I did not raise you like this, AJ. You should be ashamed of yourself. You need to make things right with your wife, not go down to a—a," she curls her lip in disgust. "Grungy, dirty bar where the girls all have ta-tas bigger than the state of Texas."

AJ lets out a loud belly laugh before placing his hand on Mom's shoulder. "Oh, Mom. Their breasts aren't quite that big, but they sure are something to look at, huh?" With that, he grabs his coat from the couch and leaves without another word.

"Where have I gone so wrong with the two of you?" she asks in a shaky voice. "You want to die alone and he doesn't know how to keep it in his pants." While I know she didn't mean what she said, it still feels like a slap across my face. I never said I wanted to die alone. Yes, the thought has crossed my mind, but I never admitted to it out loud.

"That's not fair," I tell her.

"You're right," she agrees. "But don't look something good in the face and walk away, Hunter. Don't do it. That's all I'm going to say." Except, that's not all she's going to say. "That girl over there, Charlotte, she's a keeper, so don't mess it up. Make yourself happy, even if it's only for Olive's sake." Now, she's done.

"Daddy always makes me happy," Olive chimes in, avoiding eye contact with Mom. "Always."

Mom hands me the envelope she's been holding tightly in her hands and pulls Olive into her. "I know, sweetheart. This is just grownup talk."

Olive looks up at her, gazing straight into Mom's eyes. "He does the best he can," she says, following her last defense.

Mom closes her eyes, hopefully realizing she's gone too far once again. "You're right, Olive," she says. With a loud sigh, Mom stands back up and walks into the kitchen, calling out, "Harold, it's time to go." And this is how most Sundays end. Mom's feelings get hurt and Dad leaves all discombobulated from his food coma.

Dad meanders into the living room, rubbing at his eyes. "What's going on?"

"Just the usual invitation to leave," Mom says to him as if I told them to leave. Her passive aggressive comment isn't worth the argument, though. I learned long ago that I won't win, and she will just end up feeling more hurt.

"Well, I guess we'll see you next Sunday," Dad says lazily. He leans down and squeezes Olive, then thwacks his hand against my back. "Take care of yourself, kiddo."

Mom gives me a cold hug and sighs against my cheek. "I love you even if you hate me." More motherly guilt, but I'm not letting it get to me today.

They walk out together, leaving a gust of silence behind them as the door slams. "It's okay, Daddy," Olive says.

"Am I really doing okay?" I ask her.

She wraps her arms around my leg, leaning her face against my side. "You're doing great," Olive replies. "Oh! I almost forgot! I have to get ready to go Lana's!" I look down at my watch, seeing it's already four. Where the hell did this day go?

After a couple of hours of mindlessly watching the game, I pull out my phone and send Charlotte a text—refocusing on where my thoughts have all been going since I left her house a couple hours ago.

Me: Pizza?
Charlotte: Yeah…'whatever' ;).
Me: Pizza and 'whatever'. Got it.

As I slip my phone back into my pocket, the thought of a decision I've made plays out in my head, where I feel a combination of desire and fear beating the shit out of each other. Growing up, my situation was different than the average guy; I was only with one woman because there was no other woman for me. I don't know what another woman would even be like, whether she would be different, better or worse.

Neither Ellie nor I knew what we were doing when we took that step in our relationship. We were sixteen and her parents had to go out of town for the weekend. She said she was scared to stay home alone all night, so I told her I'd come over, regardless of her parents' strict rules of no boys in the house when they weren't home. When it came to rules for Ellie and me, we broke every single one. Young love isn't something to tamper with since our hormones were raging at a rate I still have trouble comprehending.

We were only friends, best friends, until a few months before that particular weekend.

Everything between us shifted during a birthday party with the good old Spin-the-Bottle game. As fate had it, the combination of momentum and the velocity of the bottle wanted us to kiss.

The moment I had imagined most nights as I was falling asleep was only seconds away from happening. I was going to savor the taste of her lips. She moved toward me first, quickly to start, then much slower as the space between us closed. Her focus was locked on mine. There were no apparent nerves, just a small smile, a smile I would see so many more times throughout our lifetime—her lifetime. She closed her eyes, waiting for me to meet her halfway, which felt like a mile in that moment. My heart pounded, sweat was beading on my forehead, and my breath lodged in my throat. It was a now-or-never moment. I considered it being a never because I thought if I didn't have the balls to do it at that second, I would never be able to do it. My eyes closed and I leaned forward, forgetting about the two-dozen eyes staring at what would be our first kiss. Music was playing in my head, my heart was no longer pounding, but dribbling a slow beat as my fingers swept across her cheek and into her silky blond curls. Our lips were only separated by two inches of air, filled with magnetizing particles of attraction. Adrenaline took over and our lips met. It wasn't one of those passionate kisses like we had when we were older, where I would surprise her from behind and lift her up until she was pinned against a wall beneath my grip. This one was stationary, pretty much devoid of motion, our lips connecting and locking into place as we sat there for what felt like hours. I took the opportunity to inhale her skin and the fragrance of her shampoo. Everything changed and happened in that one second—I fell in love with my best friend. Just before our kiss ended, her lips made one small movement—they curled into a smile I could feel against my mouth.

When she pulled away, and she had to because I never would have, her hazel eyes were wide and I swear to God I saw a twinkle in them. That shit doesn't really happen, but it did in that moment.

What the fuck am I doing? "Olive," I yell up to her.

"Yeah?" she shouts, hopping down the steps in her party dress.

"I'm not feeling so well, sweetie."

"Oh no, do you need me to call the doctor?" she asks. "Do you need soup? I can call Charlotte."

"No, no soup—or Charlotte. I just need to lie down for a bit," I tell her.

"No Lana's?"

I look at her sad eyes for a long minute, trying to think of a way to explain to her why it's not a good idea to go over there but there is no way to make her understand that I'm scared of feeling something even remotely close to what I felt for Ellie. I will tarnish memories. I'll forget sensations, feelings, and what my heart once felt like.

My phone vibrates in my pocket and I pull it out, seeing AJ's mug appear on my screen. I answer, asking, "What's up?"

"I might need you to come get me," he says.

"Where the hell are you?"

"Downtown," he says simply.

"You had too much to drink?"

"No."

"AJ, where the hell are you?"

"County jail," he mutters.

"Jesus, AJ. What the hell did you do?"

"Please," he begs quietly.

"I'll be there as soon as I can." I drop the phone onto the couch and grab Olive's jacket from the coat hook. "I'm taking you over to Lana's. Grab your things," I tell Olive.

"What about you?" she asks. "I want you to come, too."

"I need to go help Uncle first."

I scoop her up, along with the Barbie dolls she planned on taking over to Lana's. We run across the street Charlotte opens the door as we approach. The front step. The poor thing opens the door with a large grin, but I'm about to ruin that.

"AJ got locked up; I have to go get him out," I tell her.

"What?" she asks, shocked. "What the hell did he do?"

"No clue."

Charlotte takes Olive by the arm and pulls her into the house. "Come in, honey, Lana's upstairs. Go on up." Olive turns back around and gives me a quick hug before she runs inside. "Do you need me to do anything?"

"No, if you could just watch Olive, I'll let you know as soon as I find out what happened. I should just leave the moron there, but—"

"That's not who you are," she says, pushing up onto her toes and leaving me with a soft kiss on my cheek. "There's always time for 'whatever' later." Her words float into my ear, crashing into my already confused thoughts, and I respond with a smile.

I should say more to her, like, I can't wait, or something, but words don't come to me, so instead I just wrap my arm around her shoulders and leave her with a kiss on the top of her head. "I'll let you know as soon as I find out what's going on."

CHAPTER TEN

"REALLY?" IS ALL I have to say to AJ as he walks through the alarmed door in the Sheriff's office.

"I can explain," he mutters. His usual happy-go-lucky grin isn't plastered across his face and his eyes are half-lidded. Actually, he's got a black eye. AJ is a lot of things, but he isn't a fighter, so this surprises me a bit and I ease back on some of my anger.

"What the hell happened to you?" I ask him quietly.

He avoids my question as he turns to the security window. An officer hands him a small pile of belongings and AJ turns around, still avoiding me while he heads for the main door.

As we make it out to the car, the silence becomes alarming. He can't find one word to explain how he managed to get himself arrested tonight? "Unlock the door," he says.

"Not until you tell me what happened."

"Alexa happened," he growls, pressing his thumb into his bottom lip, which I now see is split open. My God.

"Alexa did this to you?" I ask, sounding doubtful. That girl is by no means big enough to do the type of damage that has been done to him, so there has to be more to this story.

"No, she had the bouncer do this to me," he says. With the little amount of information I have, I decide to cut him a break and unlock the truck doors. AJ slides in and slams the door behind him. Once I get in, his mouth starts moving. "I wasn't doing anything wrong. I was talking to the bartender when Alexa came in. She said some shit to the bouncer and the next thing I knew, the asshole's fist was in my mouth. Instinctively, I swung back. Once. That was all it took for the bar manager to call the cops. That's why I'm here."

"Look," I say. "This is none of my business, but as your brother, I've been telling you this for years...that girl is no good for you. She never made you happy. You proposed to her because she threatened you. I don't condone your cheating habits, but you need to do what's right."

"I was going to tell her when I got home, you know, that I want a divorce and shit, but I needed a little liquid confidence before I did that."

"You need a place to crash?" AJ has more or less been living at my house or wherever I have lived since Ellie died. He sleeps at home, but the rest of the time, he's with me. I do give him credit for putting up with Alexa for as long as he has, but I'm pretty sure there's no good that will come out of him being under the same roof as her right now.

"Yeah, I do," he confirms, settling his weight against the back of the seat.

It's only a few-minute ride before we pull into the driveway. I hop out and head across the street to grab Olive. There is definitely no 'whatever' happening here tonight, especially with AJ on my heels.

I open the door and let myself in. I guess we've gotten to the point where knocking isn't completely necessary. Actually, I don't remember the last time Charlotte knocked on my door. It's almost like we're in a relationship that doesn't involve the normal parts of a relationship. I've made this weird and she has gladly put up with it. It suddenly occurs to me that she has actually put up with quite a bit from me. I've been so caught up in my guilt over cheating on Ellie that I haven't appreciated Charlotte for accepting me with all my baggage, for being a friend without asking for more than I can give. I need to change that...to let her know how much I appreciate her...how I feel about her.

How do I feel about her? My thoughts are all over the place and change by the minute. It's not fair to do that to her.

"Olive fell asleep about twenty minutes ago," Charlotte informs me as she perks up from the couch. "If you want to leave her, I can bring her home in time for you to get her ready for school in the morning." Charlotte's voice is less charismatic than usual. Although I can't pinpoint the emotion I hear, I actually think she sounds annoyed.

"Can you give us a minute?" I ask AJ.

"Thanks for watching Olive," AJ says to Charlotte. "I'll see you tomorrow." AJ slips back out the door, carefully closing it behind him so it doesn't make a sound.

"Charlotte," I begin.

"It's fine, really. Family comes first," she says coolly as she takes the throw blanket from the couch and slowly folds it in half. "I feel like there's a part of you missing from whatever it is we're doing, anyway." Her focus doesn't leave the blanket. She can't look at me when she says this, which I can't understand. Did I miss something? How'd we go from planning "whatever" to the cold shoulder in a matter of hours?

"Because I went to bail AJ out of jail?"

"No," she sighs. "That's not why."

"What is it then? Am I shitty kisser or what? Because we haven't exactly proven any other way for me to not be 'all in'." I know exactly what she means, but I thought I was hiding it a little better than I am. Guess not.

"Uh, no." She laughs and her cheeks burn with a red tinge. "You're an incredible kisser, probably the best I've ever...like ever...experienced, but I feel like I'm stealing you away from something else, like your heart isn't completely available...if that makes sense."

"What have I done to make you think that?" What haven't I done to make her think that?

"We all have secrets, Hunter. I get that and I would never expect you to open up after only knowing me for a few months, but while I understand, I also can't help wondering what you aren't telling me for other reasons." I wish I knew what she was referring to. What secrets do I have? I feel like I've been more of an open book with her than I've been with anyone else in the last five years.

"I don't know what secrets you're referring to," I say, and I'm being honest.

"Great, well, we're at a place now where I need to know what your plans are. If you need a fuck buddy, just say it. If you want to be friends, that's cool, too. I guess you've just sent me on a whirlwind with your mixed messages today when you kissed me. You already know how I feel about you, Hunter, but despite some sweet words you have nicely offered to me, I don't know what is going through your head and I don't know how long I can pretend to be okay with it." I'm totally baffled by the change in her attitude, and this is the last thing I need right now.

"Well, that makes two of us!" My voice rises louder than I intended but fury is bubbling in my stomach and this is the exact reason why I've avoided getting too close to anyone over the past few years. "I didn't realize you needed to put a label on us or whatever we're doing, especially since we haven't really done anything, but if you want to put a label on us, then go ahead and slap a big fat 'friends' one on."

"I think it's time for you to leave," she says in almost a whisper.

"Daddy?" Olive tiptoes down the steps one by one as she rubs at her eyes. "Are we going home?"

"Let's go, princess," I say, squatting down to lift her up.

"Will you tell Lana I'll see her at school tomorrow?" Olive mutters to Charlotte.

"You got it, kiddo," she says in return. With a smile for Olive, her lips curl into a grimace as she looks over at me. "Now." Her finger is pointed at the door and it's enough of a gesture to make me want to walk out and never walk back inside. It's just unfortunate that our little girls are as close as they are.

What the hell just happened? Did I say something wrong when I dropped Olive off? If she isn't pissed about me bailing AJ out, which would be ridiculous, what is it?

As we walk in through the front door of our house, AJ immediately snatches Olive up. "Boy do I have a story for you, Ollie-Lolly." He starts up the stairs with her and her arms tighten around his neck.

"G-rated, please," I yell up the stairs.

Alone and pissed, I kick my boots off, letting each one thud against the wall. What the fuck am I doing? I drop down into the chair beneath Ellie's picture and let my head fall backwards until I'm looking up at her. "You must be so disgusted with my behavior," I tell her. "Since you're probably already rolling over in your grave, I might as well finish the night off." I get up and walk through the kitchen, whipping the top cabinet above the fridge open to retrieve my bottle of Jack—the bottle I sometimes flirt with after Olive goes to bed.

"Grab a glass for me," AJ says, walking in behind me. I was going to drink straight out of the bottle, but I guess a glass means I have someone to drink with—that at least sounds better than drinking alone. I grab two glasses and fill them halfway, leaving the Jack out in case there is a need for seconds.

"You aren't drinking because of me, are you?" AJ asks.

"Nope," I say, pressing the rim of the glass up against my lips.

"Is it about the letter I found on your coffee table?" Fuck. Fuck. Fuck. I tip the glass a little higher, letting the liquid burn down my throat at a pretty impressive rate. "Or is it about Charlotte? Or maybe, it's about the woman at the gardens." How? Just how? "Dad filled me in. Dude...how many chicks do you have? Here I thought you were impotent and you're banging three of them?"

"Not quite," I say, finishing the whiskey in my glass.

AJ grabs the bottle and walks out into the living room. "Let's hear it."

At some point tonight the hour hand on the clock turned from eight to two and I can already feel the hangover I'm going to sustain tomorrow...or today...in three hours when I have to get Olive up for school. I just hope I'm sober by then. AJ is slurring his words, bitching about Alexa, and I'm staring across the room at Ellie's portrait. "We're both...pathetic fucks," I tell him.

"You're more pathetic than I am," AJ says. "Your wife has been dead for five years and you're still staring at her picture like she's going to start responding to you at some point." His words would normally cause my rage to fire up, but since he's already had the shit beat out of him in the past twenty-four hours, he's been drinking, and there's a little validity to what he's saying, I'll let it go this time. Only this time.

"You need to talk to this chick in the gardens some more," AJ says. "And you need to make up with Charlotte. Wait, didn't you fix things with her earlier today?" He takes another swig.

"I thought so," I groan. "Dude, I'm so fucking confused. I have real feelings for Charlotte...I do. I want to be with her, more than just this stupid friend-shit. I'm always looking forward to the next time I see her and I'm always thinking of reasons to call her at night. That means something, right?" I consider my drunken truths for a minute, realizing I'm running away from what I want because of the amount of unanswered questions in my life. "But then I'm like...what about the chick behind the letters? I want to find Ellie's heart, too. I don't think Charlotte will understand that." Never mind the woman from the gardens. I'll probably never see her again anyway.

"I can see your problem," AJ says. "Oh my God, Hunt, what if—what if the letters are from Ellie's ghost?" AJ says, closing his eyes. "You know what, no—" He wags his finger at me for a long minute. "No, you know what dude? You're my brother, my blood, my blood brother, you know—" His breaths elongate as if he's about to fall asleep. "So, I'm going to help you. Plus, you bailed me out tonight, you're letting me crash here, and you've been a pretty damn good brother. I'll help you, Hunt. I'll help you find this mystery girl of yours."

"Thanks, man," I say, feeling the heaviness in my eyelids begin to take over as well.

"What if?" AJ says, pulling me from my almost tranquil place. "What if you already know this letter-writing woman? Could you imagine?"

"You just told me she could be a ghost," I remind him. "But I don't think that's the case. The way the woman talks in her letters is almost like she isn't from this area. She talks about mountains and shit. We don't have mountains here."

"Maybe she was on vacation?" AJ says, surprisingly insightful for his inebriated state.

"Maybe." My eyelids win the battle, pulling me into a heavy fog, a comfortable heavy fog, a place that is far away from every puzzle piece in my life, leaving me alone with visions of Ellie and the life we were supposed to still be sharing. Is it a problem that I haven't moved on from my dead wife? Is there a rule that says widowers are only allowed a year to grieve before they need to collect themselves and act like normal human beings again? I know it has been five years, but I love her still, as much today as I did then and I don't know what to do with that.

The amount of times I hear Ellie's voice in my head telling me to let her go, makes me wonder if that's her trying to tell me something or if it is my stupid subconscious' attempt to get me to man up and move on. I can't even trust my own brain to tell me what's right.

CHAPTER ELEVEN

"DAD-D-DY," OLIVE'S WHISPER booms into my ear like a bongo drum in an enclosed bathroom stall. "It's nine, zero, zero." Her words ignite my brain and body, forcing me to sit upright in my chair. I slept in a goddamn chair. It's nine, she missed the bus and she's late for school. This is officially the most irresponsible I've been since the day she was born.

"Shiiiiiiit," AJ groans, peeling his eyelids open.

"Uncle said a bad wordddd," Olive sings, dancing around in a little circle. "One quarter please?" She holds her hand out to him, waiting for another coin to put in her piggy bank that is already overflowing from AJ's bad word fees.

"Olive, go play," AJ groans again.

"No, we're late for school!" she squeals theatrically.

"Shit, I'm sorry," AJ apologizes. "This is my fault." As easy as it would be to blame all of this on him, this time, it's my fault.

"This one is on me, bro," I tell him.

"I'm sorry I overslept, Olive. I'm not feeling well. I'm sick," I explain.

"You aren't sick, Daddy," Olive says sternly, crossing her arms over her chest. Add this moment to the number of times over the last couple of years that I've wanted to respond to her with, "Okay, Ellie," but I've refrained.

"I am sick," I tell her. "My head and belly hurt." She doesn't say any more, but just gives me that look, the look that tells me she doesn't know what I'm lying about or why, but she knows I'm lying.

"I'll take her to school," AJ says, walking into the kitchen.

"You smell like Jack, so no," I tell him.

"Who's Jack?" Olive asks. "Was Jack at jail? Like Jack-in-the-Box, but Jack-in-the-Jail?" she giggles ferociously at her own joke—a joke I'd find hysterical, too, if my head didn't feel like it were about to split in half.

"You don't smell any better," AJ tells me.

"Get her ready and I'll take a two-minute shower," I tell him.

I run up the stairs, tearing my clothes off on the way. As I rip the shower curtain across the rod, the squealing from the metal rings zings through my head. Jesus. I need Advil...a lot of it. With the water cranked to full heat, I step inside, letting the shower cascade over me like a warm blanket. The steam fills my head, leaving no room for wandering thoughts or the memories of the thoughts I was trying to drown away with booze last night. Fucking Charlotte.

Come to think of it, I'm a little surprised she didn't come banging on my door when she didn't see us at the bus stop. She must really be pissed off, not that I know why. For someone who runs a dating site and specializes in relationships, she should know better that communication is a key component. So I'm not wrong here, she is.

After soaping up my hair and body, I'm still in need of releasing some of my anger and frustration. I grab my cock, close my eyes and let my imagination run off, hoping to escape for a few minutes, except I don't even know who to fucking fantasize about anymore. My manhood is a limp dud that won't turn on. Maybe it's a good thing I didn't screw Charlotte last night. Maybe my virility died with Ellie.

I grab a towel and step out, snatching the Listerine off the shelf. I fill my mouth with the blue liquid, allowing some of it to seep down the back of my throat. The burn feels good for some sick reason, even if it reminds me of the Jack that's still rotting my gut from last night. At least I won't smell like it now.

It takes me less than five minutes to slip on some clothes and make it back down the stairs where I find Charlotte sitting on my couch.

"Hi," she says. Her voice is shameful, despondent, hurt.

"Hey."

"You okay?" She asks.

"Not really."

She curls a strand of her hair behind her ear, pulling my focus to her glossy eyes. Was she crying? "I figured something was up since you weren't at the bus stop."

"Yeah, I have to take Olive to school. She's late and it's my fault."

"Do you want me to take her?" She offers.

Some of my unreasonable anger from last night simmers in response to her question. "Thanks for the offer. I can take her. But…" I don't know what the hell I did but by the look in her eyes, it's definitely something. "If you want to come along for the ride, you can." Maybe she can shed some light on my unknown mistake.

She takes a minute to answer me, stalling by looking out the window toward her house. I wish I knew what was going through that mind of hers.

"Please," I tell her. I don't want it to be like this. I'd rather go back to her couch and resume what we were doing yesterday, and skip over the whole part where my guilt almost pulled me away from something good.

Olive is ready and waiting at the door with her backpack on and her hair in some funky ponytail that AJ tried to…I don't even know what he tried to do. Charlotte notices Olive's hair at the same time I do and walks over to her, kneeling down beside her. She takes the rubber band out of Olive's hair and slips it between her teeth while she runs her fingers through her curls. Charlotte's face illuminates, like this makes her happy, taking care of my daughter. After a few seconds of studying Charlotte's skill of sweeping up both sides, careful not to miss any loose hairs, she ties it up in a perfect ponytail—something I've yet to master. This is why the poor thing needs a mother. I wasn't bred to do a little girl's hair. "Perfect," Charlotte says, pinching Olive's cheek gently.

Olive wraps her arms around Charlotte's neck and squeezes her tightly. "I love you," she says.

My throat tightens; my heart swells with pain and relief, but mostly pain. Those three little words that have been only mine since the day Olive was born have now been shared with a woman who might hate me, a woman I wasn't sure I could move forward with for reasons maybe I shouldn't even have. The simple act of making her hair perfect brought out those sacred words. Olive doesn't know it, but she needs a woman in her life as much as I do. Am I screwing up that badly?

Charlotte, still holding Olive tightly, looks up at me, this time with distress in her eyes, as if she wants to apologize for what Olive just said. I don't want her to apologize, though.

"Ready to go?" I ask Olive. She walks over to me slowly and wraps her arms around my leg. "I love you too, Daddy." What is going on inside of her little mind today? Sometimes I wonder if Olive feels the same kind of pain I do, but the only pain she really feels is the pain I've instilled in her. In truth, she didn't know Ellie, she doesn't understand what losing someone feels like, and she doesn't understand what it's like to have a mother. These are things only I feel in my head, and when I assume she might feel that pain too, it causes a lot of unnecessary guilt.

"I'll see you at the site," I yell in to AJ, who looks to be working on his third cup of coffee. He gives me a quick wave without separating his mouth from the mug.

While still wondering if Charlotte is going to come along or not, I reach for the door handle of the truck. "The seat is still free," I tell her.

Charlotte looks across the street once more and places the tip of her thumb between her teeth, deeply contemplating this short ride. "Okay," she says, almost inaudibly, before walking around to the other side. The moment we're all settled in the truck, Charlotte spews out, "I'm sorry."

"You have no reason to be sorry," I tell her. I mean, maybe a little for getting angry with no explanation attached but I've never been a fan of people needing to apologize for things. Life's too short for that.

"I shouldn't have expected you to tell me everything," she continues. "I guess—" She pauses for a moment and presses her fingers against the side of her head as if she has a headache. Maybe she has sympathy pains for me. "I guess I just wanted things to work out with us so badly and the thought of you maybe having something else going on with another woman made me feel a little crazy."

Ah, what? Who would I have something going on with? "Why would you think that?" I ask.

"We should talk about this later...when Olive isn't in the car," Charlotte says, looking back at Olive with a smile.

No kidding. Not sure why she even broached the issue with Olive still in the car. What the hell is she thinking? I pull in to the school parking lot and park the truck. "I'll just be a minute," I tell Charlotte.

I grab Olive from her booster seat and jog, hand-in-hand with her, into the school, handing her off to the administrator who is eyeballing me warily. "Good morning, Olive," she says, returning Olive's smile, then glancing at her watch, before peering at me with raised brows. "Good morning, Mr. Cole."

"Good morning," I say, returning her greeting, while also feeling like a five-year-old in trouble as I lean down to give Olive a kiss on the head. "Take the bus home, I'll be waiting for you at the bus stop, okay?" I add, as I sign her in to school.

"Okay," she sings. "Have fun with Charlotte today." She giggles and plops down on the plastic blue chair behind us.

"Yes, Mr. Cole, do have fun with Charlotte today," the administrator says, crossing her arms over her large chest. Her glasses slip down the bridge of her nose and she squints one eye. "These children greatly depend on their education. It's important to make sure Olive's here on time in the morning." Really? I have never made her late before. Cut me some slack, will ya, old lady.

Feeling like I'm doing the parental walk-of-shame down the empty hall, I make my way back to the truck eagerly, with a need for an explanation of Charlotte's accusations.

I hop back into the truck where Charlotte is patiently waiting, scrolling through her messages on her phone. "You're late for work," I tell her, "but I want to talk if you have time."

"Yeah, we need to talk," she says, placing her phone down on her lap. "How about we start with the letters....and the woman in the garden." Oh shit. Olive...my little blabbermouth. Now I'm beginning to understand where Charlotte's anger is coming from.

A groaning noise rumbles in the back of my throat, a habit I have when I can't think of a proper response. I scratch at my head for a minute as I sink back into the driver's seat. "Those letters have been a secret for a very long time, and not just from you, but from my entire family, as well. It's something between Ellie and me, I guess. There really isn't any other explanation for me hiding it, other than it's just something I've chosen to keep private."

"A woman is writing letters to you every week or so. I can't help but wonder if there was something more going on."

"No," I say. "I don't even know her. They're just letters and it's not something I wanted to share with anyone, I guess."

"I should have just asked you last night instead of assuming the worst," she says, fingering a loose thread on the tear in her jeans.

Only a slight tinge of guilt finds me when I think about the way I was looking at Ari in the gardens, but I might not have looked at her that way if I wasn't angry at Charlotte for what I assumed she did with AJ. "Should I remind you of the secret you kept from me about AJ?" I end my question with a cunning grin, trying to call a truce to the argument.

"Fair enough," she says, releasing a relieving sigh.

"I'm not seeing anyone else, or sleeping with anyone else for that matter," I confirm.

"And I probably never would have come to that conclusion if Olive hadn't told me about your rendezvous with a 'Disney Princess,'" she air quotes, "at the gardens."

This one is a little tougher to explain since I don't know much about Ari other than the fact that we share a common interest in a place we both visit. Olive has dug me a nice little hole here.

"There is a woman who I ran into a couple times at the gardens when I was visiting Ellie. She seemed like she was going through something and I chatted with her for a few minutes. I don't know much about her." I feel like I'm on the defense, trying to justify my actions when in reality, I haven't done anything wrong besides notice an attractive woman. It's not a crime—even happily married men do that.

"I understand," Charlotte says. "I do. But I'm sure you can understand my sudden concern, or questions, rather."

"I do. If this all bothers you, I understand, but there are certain things I need to remain constant in my life, for my own sanity—like the letters, and I can't bend on that. I don't want to tell you that you have to be okay with it, but this is just the baggage that comes along with me."

"I get that. And I still want this," she says, placing her hand over mine. "I got angry last night because I really, really want this. You. I just wanted to make sure we were on the same page and I second guessed that."

I look over at her, turning my hand over and squeezing her fingers. "I want this too."

She unhinges her seatbelt and drops her phone into the cup holder. I don't know how she's managing to maneuver herself the way she is, but she's climbing over the middle console, resting one knee on each side of me. Before I have a second to interject, her lips are on mine. Her hands are slipping up the front of my shirt, and shit, we're still sitting in the middle of the school parking lot. I pull away. "Are you out of your mind?" I laugh. "We could probably get put away for like, pedophilia or something, for making out here."

She laughs and removes her hand from the inside of my shirt. Burying her head into my shoulder she mutters, "Crap, you're right. How fast can you get home?"

"Fast enough," I say.

We're halfway home when her hand crawls up my leg. "Charlotte, I'm going to get us killed if you keep going." She doesn't stop, though. Her hand continues up until she reaches my cock. With a gentle squeeze, she slowly starts moving her hand back and forth over my suddenly insane hardness. I'm going to bust through my goddamn pants in a minute. Guess it's not dead.

By the time we peel into her driveway, I feel like my pitched tent is seconds from blowing away. She runs ahead of me, unlocking her door and pushing her way inside. Her shirt is off before I even cross the threshold. Christ, those things cannot be real. Her pants go next and then she's standing before me in a black thong and a black lacy bra that leaves nothing to the imagination. I lift her up and her legs tangle around my body as I carry her up the stairs and into her bedroom—a room I have yet to step foot into since I've known her. I place her down onto the bed and pull my shirt off as she works on my belt, my fly, my button. Pants are gone. Boxers are gone. Her bra is now gone and her panties are hanging off the corner of the bedpost.

I climb onto her bed, hovering over her, leaning down and taking one of her dusty-rose colored nipples between my teeth. It's all it takes for her to start moaning and for my need to grow more intense. My hand travels down the length of her body, reaching between her legs where I'm pleasantly welcomed with wetness. I guess foreplay isn't needed by the feel of her readiness, but I'm not done exploring. I slip two fingers inside of her, feeling her tighten around me, making my poor not-so-dead cock jealous. Her moans grow louder as her movements become greater. Without wanting her to finish before me, I pull my fingers out, giving her the freedom to reach over and pull out a condom from her nightstand.

After unrolling it over my throbbing hardness, she wraps her fingers around me and guides me into her. My thoughts go blurry; becoming lost within the sensations my body is gratefully experiencing. I close my eyes and thrust into her, finding that she likes it hard and rough according to her shouting words. I pin her arms above her head as I ride her like I realize I've wanted to for quite a while. Her legs tighten around me—everything tightens around me as she screams louder than I've ever imagined a chick yelling. Her tremors tell me she's finished, but I think she knows I'm not there yet.

She grips hers hands around my biceps and pulls me down to the bed where she climbs on top of me, giving me the most unbelievable view of her large bouncing tits. I squeeze my hands around her hips, enjoying the way her ass grazes tersely against my palms. With another wave of moans finding her lips, I'm guessing she's about to finish again. This time, I'm with her. The pressure and heat builds within me and as if she knew the exact second to grind down on top of me with all of her weight, I release into her. It's like all of my stress has melted away and liquefied into the bed beneath me. I don't think I can move now. I don't think I want to.

She flops down on top of me, bringing her lips to my neck, leaving them there as a placeholder for whatever else is supposed to happen this second. "You're amazing," she whispers against my skin. "I have never had anything remotely close to what you just gave me."

Her words are a turn on and a compliment. I wasn't sure what I'd measure up to, especially after being nearly dead below the waist for so long, but I'll take this as a nice pat on the back. "You're not so bad yourself," I mutter. "Actually, you're fucking incredible." A grin stretches across my lips as I fold my hands behind my head. I really do feel like a million bucks right now.

"No, I don't think you get it," she says. "No one has ever been able to make me...you know. Never mind once, but twice?" Her words and soft laughter are like a dessert wine—the perfect ending to an amazing meal.

Married for however long and no man has ever made her finish? I don't know whether to be surprised or really proud of my efforts. I'll just assume I'm incredible—easier that way. "Wow, careful not to stroke my ego too much there," I tell her.

"I won't stroke your ego, but—" her words trail off as she climbs down the length of my body, taking my still very stiff cock into her mouth.

I'm never moving again. This is it. I'm done for...whatever.

CHAPTER TWELVE

FEBRUARY
-TWO MONTHS LATER-

VACUUMING UP THE last of the left over carpet shreds, my focus is drawn to AJ leaning up against the far wall, staring down at his phone. An unsettled look is playing across his face and I can't figure out what has gotten into him. "How did last night go? Did you finally tell Alexa?" I ask him.

"It's not important," he mumbles, typing something into his phone. His jaw is grinding back and forth and he's spurting out short breaths, something he tends to do when he's either upset or pissed off.

"Dude, something is obviously going on."

"Shit, Hunter, can you give me a fucking minute?" I walk over to him, ignoring his request because God knows he'd do the same to me. He's done the same to me. Whenever I need space, he smothers me and crowds me into a corner until I break. I guess that's how we show brotherly love. "Don't do this right now," he snaps, as he chucks his phone across the room. I watch as the thing bounces off of the opposite wall.

"This isn't our house," I remind him. "Talk to me. Just take a breath. Something."

"Yeah, I did it last night," he grits out. "I told her I wanted a fucking divorce." It only took him two months to finally say it to her.

"That's good, right?" I ask. "Isn't that what you wanted to do?"

"Yeah," he shouts. "That is what I wanted to do." I'm not sure I'm following right now. What is there to be so pissed off about if this is what he wanted? "Shit. Shit. Shit!" Running across the room, he grabs his phone from the ground—lifting it, inspecting it. I can't tell if it shattered or not but I'm assuming it didn't since he's hitting more buttons.

He lifts the phone to his ear as he runs his fingers through the thick of his hair. His focus meets mine for a brief second but now he's storming off toward the other end of the house. I follow him, though. "What the hell are you talking about?" he asks, his voice is low and soft. He doesn't want me to hear, which is all the more reason for me to listen. "How do you know?" There's silence on his end of the call while I assume he's listening to whoever is on the other end. "Those things aren't always accurate." Another pause follows, likely filled with words I wish I could hear. "Hello? Jesus. Hello?"

AJ turns around, finding me less than a few feet away. Anger is staining the whites of his eyes red. "She's fucking knocked up," he says through gritted teeth.

Oh shit. The words, "Is it yours?" are probably not the best-chosen words at this precise second but it's exactly what comes out of my mouth. Of course it's his. Well, maybe it's his.

"Are you asking me if she's been fucking other guys? Because I wouldn't put it past her! What the hell am I supposed to do? Do you think it's mine? Am I supposed to fix things with her now? Is it even possible to fix things with her? I feel like we were broken from the start. Fuck! What the hell am I going to do, Hunt?" Sweat is beading up on his forehead. He's completely freaking out right now. I'm not sure AJ ever had intentions of becoming a dad. He said something to me once after Ellie died. He was shitfaced, of course, but it was something along the lines of he's never going to risk ending up a single dad because he couldn't do what I do. It was a compliment, sort of, but I can understand why my life might scare the crap out of him. It scares the crap out of me.

"Let's chill for a second," I tell him. "Sit down." He doesn't sit down. Instead, he continues pacing and ripping hairs from his head. "AJ." I try to keep my voice even in hopes of calming him down, even if it's just a little.

"I can't do what you do, Hunt. I can't do it. I can't stay with Alexa and I'm not going to stay in a horrible marriage for God knows how long just because we have a kid together." His anger is simmering a little, but I can tell by the look in his eyes that question after question is festering in his head.

"You need to find out if it's yours," I tell him again. "We can figure things out from there."

"How the hell do I find out if it's mine?" How does he not know crap like this at twenty-eight?

"A paternity test. They can do it before the baby is born." I grab the vacuum so I can finish up the job here. "You just have to convince her to go do it." I adjust the vacuum and lean down to hit the button, but I pause as another thought comes to mind. "When's the last time you two—"

"She hasn't touched me in weeks. She won't go near me. I'm lucky if she sucks my dick once a month." Awesome, I totally needed to know that. Whatever the case, I think he might have lucked out with this one.

"Go find her and get a paternity test. I'll finish up here." AJ doesn't give it a second thought. He grabs his coat from the closet doorknob and jets out the door. It's only a matter of seconds before I hear his truck grumbling against the below zero temps outside. I hope for his sake that the kid isn't his.

I finish up earlier than I thought and head home for a quick minute before it's time to grab Olive from the bus. As I'm pulling into the driveway, I notice the flap on my mailbox is open a crack. The mail doesn't usually come until a little later but maybe I didn't close it all the way yesterday. Or maybe there's something in there. Hopping out of the truck, I jog to the end of the driveway and shove my hand into the box, retrieving an envelope. By feeling the texture of the paper, I already know it's from her. She comes by here to put this in my mailbox and not once have I seen her drive by. For someone who wants to remain anonymous, it's odd that she does this, rather than mailing it. If she knows where I live, it isn't like she can't find my address. How does she know where I live? We just moved here a few months ago.

At first, I consider ripping the thing open right here but on second thought, Charlotte could very well be eyeing me from her window and I'd rather not having another conversation about this anonymous woman.

The moment I step inside, a little out of breath from excitement and jogging up the driveway, I tear the side of the envelope off and pull the note out.

Dear Hunter,

I can't do this any longer. Her heart aches for you every time I send you a letter. Guilt fills my soul and covers me like a heavy blanket I can't seem to find my way out of. I know I'm not responsible for taking her life but I feel like I'm keeping her alive for you and at the same time holding this heart hostage for the sake of yours.

I've debated over the last couple of weeks whether or not this is the right decision, but I think it is.

I asked the doctors to keep my information anonymous because I didn't think I would have it in me to face the family who so unfortunately lost this very heart I protect so dearly. With realization of the unfairness in this situation, given you have not been offered the choice to remain anonymous, I feel I should unveil my identity to offer you proper closure. These letters aren't fair to either one of us, and I have been selfish in pretending they are.

I'd like to request that you meet me at the Borderline Grill for dinner tonight at seven. I realize it is short notice and I know you have to find care for Olive, but if I don't do this now, I may never find the courage to do it again.

I understand if this is too much to ask or if you don't wish to meet with me. In any case, I appreciate your consideration.

Best,
Her Heart

My hands are shaking as I reread the latter part of the letter over and over again. I'm not sure I follow her thought process or what she's feeling. Does she want to meet so she can move on? These letters have been a connection I have needed over the past five years and the thought of not receiving any more makes my stomach hurt. Have I been misleading myself, giving in to a fictional relationship? I have considered the possibility of this being a side effect of completely losing my mind, but I avoid those thoughts, too.

I can't ask Charlotte to watch Olive tonight. I'd have to explain why and I don't want to do the whole lying bit with how well things have been going between us. Even if I tried to explain this to her, she would tell me she understands, but I know better. I've been around women long enough to know this will never make any sense to her. In any other situation, I would never do something as sleazy as hide a secret meeting with a woman, but she is the keeper of Ellie's heart, and that makes her a more than an ordinary woman, and it makes this a less than ordinary situation.

I slip my phone out of my back pocket and thumb in a message.

Me: Could you watch Olive for a couple of hours tonight?
Mom: Of course. Is everything okay?

Without allowing those three little thinking dots to appear for more than a couple of seconds, I respond:

Me: Yes, I have a client meeting tonight. It was a last minute proposal.
Mom: That's wonderful, honey. What time would you like me there? I can make her dinner if you'd like.
Me: That would be great. Six?
Mom: I'll see you then, sweetie.

Lying to her doesn't seem as bad as lying to Charlotte, I guess.

Almost losing track of time completely, I hear the door slam across the street and I see Charlotte making her way down the driveway toward the bus stop. Stepping outside, I catch her attention, as she looks surprised to see me. "I thought you would still be at the site," she says, shivering against the cold.

"We finished early and I ran home for a few." It only takes a few seconds to realize how cold it actually is out. "Should we take a car down there?"

"It's okay, I could use a walk," she says, her words muffled against her gloved fists.

"Everything okay?" Meaning, what's wrong? Something's wrong. There's no smile on her face. There was no hello kiss. Going through the motions of falling back into another relationship, I've come to learn her mannerisms pretty well over the last few weeks. One of the things I like about her is that she won't tell me "nothing" if something is wrong. She'll tell me exactly what's wrong, but not until I ask.

"I saw a woman drop something into your mailbox today. She wasn't a mail carrier. Is it her? The woman who has Ellie's heart?"

"What?" I know what. I'm using the word as a placeholder until I figure out what to say. "Do you know who she was?" I've never wanted and not wanted the answer so badly before.

"Do you know who she is?" Charlotte retorts, firing my own question right back at me. If I knew who she was, we wouldn't be having this conversation.

"No," I tell her.

"Well, did you check your mailbox?" she asks.

"Yes," I refrain from lying, following my earlier intentions.

"So you do know who it is," she kindly informs me.

"The letter was anonymous."

"It was her," she whispers, a cold fog billowing from her mouth.

CHAPTER THIRTEEN

"I'M HERE!" MOM yells from the front door. "Where is my little Olive Oil?"

Olive is watching TV in the family room and I've been staring into my mirror for the last twenty minutes. I'm not sure what I'm looking at but maybe I've been hoping some kind of sense finds my reflection. No such luck, though. Charlotte isn't happy. She's probably pretty rip shit, actually. I can't say I wouldn't be if I were in her shoes, and normally, I would care. I do care, especially after how much I have fallen for Charlotte. But this other relationship— or whatever it is—I've had with this woman who has Ellie's heart has been alive for almost five years. I can't just forego the one opportunity I've wanted more than anything since I received the first letter from her. I owe this to my curiosity, my pain, and heartache...and to Ellie.

What I don't understand is what suddenly made this woman want to change her anonymity. In any case, I will hopefully find out tonight. So many times, I have lain awake at night imagining what she might look like. A faceless woman is the only thing that has come to mind, though—a faceless woman with a heart made of gold, a heart that can outlive the most amazing woman who has ever existed in this world.

"Hunter, sweetie," Mom calls, her voice growing louder the closer she comes. As she turns the corner, stepping into my bedroom, a questioning look lines her face. "Must be a pretty big client?"

"Yeah, it's a huge opportunity—one I've been waiting for." It isn't a lie, just the client part. "Thank you for coming to watch Olive," I offer.

"Why didn't you ask Charlotte to watch Olive tonight like you normally have been lately?" Mom asks.

"I don't want to take advantage of her willingness to help me so often," I respond honestly.

"I see." There's the look, wondering if things are fizzling between me and her dream of a new daughter-in-law. "Anyway..." Mom brushes the hair away from her forehead and releases a soft sigh. "Have you spoken to your brother today?"

Ah shit. I'm going on the probable notion that AJ did not inform Mom of his newfound situation. Problem is, she knows we worked together today. "Yeah, we worked this morning."

"Do you know where he went after work?" Not that she's ever great at giving us our space, but she's definitely fishing for information right now. She must know something.

"Nope, I've been a little preoccupied." Truth.

"Hmm." She sweeps her fingers across the top of my bureau, creating a cloud of dust in the air. "You really need a housekeeper," she says, wiping her finger off on her pants.

"Noted," I sigh. "Okay, I won't be home too late." I don't think. Finally breaking my stare from the mirror, I inhale sharply and swallow against the dryness in my mouth.

"You put cologne on for a client?"

My God.

"Goodbye, Mom." I grip her shoulders and place a kiss on her cheek. "Thank you, again."

After saying goodbye to Olive and shooing off her four million questions, I have slipped out the door and into my car, unnoticeably I hope. Whether or not Charlotte is, in fact, watching me out of her window right now, I don't know, but I feel as though I'm hurting her by doing this, even though I failed to mention this meet-up. I hate that it has to be this way, and I shouldn't have to convince myself that what I'm doing is right or wrong because it's something I know I have to do.

The closer I come to Borderline Grill, the heavier my chest feels and the more painful my gut becomes. How will I even know how to find her? She left me no description or even a name. So now I'm going to have to approach every female in the restaurant and ask if she writes a stranger notes, or "Hey, I'm sorry, this might sound weird, but, do you have my wife's heart in your chest?" What the hell am I doing? Maybe I'll have this unsaid connection to her and I'll just know by looking at her that it's her. Except, that thought is ridiculous.

My racing mind blurred out the last five minutes of this trip and I'm pulling into the half-full parking lot. I glance down the row of cars looking for any type of car that might stand out to me but I'm not sure what would stand out and make a statement. A car is a car.

I find myself short of breath as I step out of the truck. My knees are weak and if I weren't trying my hardest not to fall over, I'd be kissing the pavement.

What should be twenty-five steps to the front door seems as if it's only three, and before I know it, my hand is gripped around the ice-cold handle. The slight gust of wind feels as though it's holding the door in place but it's actually just my muscles not working accordingly. The restaurant isn't large and it's diner style, which means the moment I step in, I will be faced with people looking at me—the reason for the door chiming.

I hold my breath and yank the door open, stepping inside. Looking at several people sitting in booths, I notice none of them are seated alone. Maybe she brought someone with her...her mother, father, sister, or brother? I could be psycho, after all. Though, I don't even know if she has any of those relatives. I know almost nothing about her. Maybe I would have been smart to bring someone, too—Charlotte. Maybe that would have been the right way to handle this. Too late now, though. Whatever, it isn't like this a blind date. I just want to meet her. I just want to be near her heart.

As I continue scanning my gaze up and down the row from left to right, no one is looking at me anymore, which means no one has cared enough to think I could be Hunter. Does she know what I look like? I suppose that wouldn't surprise me since she knows where I live and what my name is. It wouldn't be that hard to figure out.

I pull in another shuddered breath as a waitress with a black skirt and a white blouse approaches me. She's young, maybe a teenager. Her hair is everywhere and there is sadness pooling in her dark lined eyes, telling me she's got a story to tell. I'd like to distract myself with figuring her out but there are no time-outs or pauses in real life, so I won't ask her if she's okay while she's asking me if I would like a table for one. The mere fact that I even notice sadness in others around me makes me realize how different I am today from the grieving Hunter who first met Charlotte at the bus stop just a few months ago.

"Two, please," a voice from behind me answers the question before I have the chance to open my mouth.

"Right this way," the waitress says, pivoting and heading down the narrow path toward the last empty table in the restaurant.

I should turn around. I should face her. She knows who I am from behind and I don't know who she is at all.

Doing what any scared-shitless person would do, I follow the waitress without turning around. By the time we reach the table, the waitress has already placed the two menus down and told us to enjoy our meal. I slide into the nearest bench, which is rude. I've always been big on offering the lady the closest seat first, but I don't have the balls to be a gentleman at this moment. My wife's heart is four inches behind me—close enough to feel the breath being created from Ellie's beating heart.

The coward inside of me would like to run away and never face the outcome to this mystery, but I would have to face her in order to do that, too. I understand now why she has kept her identity secret all of these years. The moment I see her, know her, speak to her…everything will change.

I close my eyes briefly as I feel the booth adjust slightly, telling me she is now seated across from me, staring at me, likely wondering what the hell is wrong with me as I sit here with my eyes pinned shut.

I place my hands down on the table, gripping the plastic coating with the tips of my fingers. My heart is in my throat and I'm not sure I have what it takes to swallow until a hand—a soft, warm hand—falls gently on top of one of mine, and instantly, my eyes flicker open.

My other hand finds my mouth, covering it with shock and awe. "You," is all I manage.

She nods with an unsure, small smile and responds, "Me." With a gentle laugh, she says, "Robert Frost told me to take a different path today."

"You didn't just move here from San Diego, did you?" The tense feeling in my muscles eases at the sound of her voice, "And I thought you didn't believe any of that? As a matter of fact, if I remember correctly, you called it, 'bull'."

She expels a quiet huff and peers down to her lap. After a brief pause, she looks back up at me through her thick, dark lashes. "No, I lied about San Diego," she says, "And I could have been wrong about Frost."

"Why didn't you tell me?" I ask.

"I couldn't figure out how to," she says, breaking her gaze from mine.

I seem to have an abundance of people in my life who don't know how to tell me things...important things. "Hey, I have your wife's heart," I say, offering her the simple words that so easily could have been admitted when we first met. "That would have done the trick."

"Yeah, like that would be the appropriate way to do it and not weird at all," she retorts, rolling her eyes. Her upper body slouches forward, allowing her dark hair to slip off the edges of her shoulders. Creating more silence, she unzips her coat, cautiously pulling each arm from her sleeves, revealing a v-neck black shirt that flirts with her collarbone. My focus is drawn to the very center of her chest where a perfectly straight scar plays peek-a-boo with the covering material. It is her.

"I wanted to tell you but there's something about running up to a total stranger and gutting him," she says.

We aren't strangers.

"Instead, you have written me anonymous letters for five years. Don't you realize that has gutted me, too?" Maybe gutted isn't the correct word but I've felt hollowed out each time I read more of her words. It has kept the pain alive for me. It has also kept Ellie alive for me. "And where was this mountain you wrote about?"

"That was never my intention, Hunter. I promise you." She presses her fingers through her hair, sweeping it away from her cheeks, and I take the moment to acknowledge Olive's description of a Disney princess to be quite accurate. She's flawless. "The mountain is up north. I like to take short road trips to think and be alone sometimes."

Checking off the answers to my questions, I continue, "Did you know I would be at the gardens that day? Those days?" I ask her, wondering how much Ari honestly knows about me.

"No, I had no idea. That happened all on it's own." As if Ellie wanted us to meet. Nothing happens on its own. Everything is preplanned and destined to happen.

"Wow," I offer as an honest response.

"I agree." Ari places her hands down on top of the table; folding them together and interlocking all of her perfectly manicured fingers. "I know you have a girlfriend, or at least, I'm assuming so by what Olive said that day at the gardens. It is not my intention to cause any issues or ripples in your life and I hope I haven't done so by asking you to meet me here tonight." I don't think it's necessary to admit the trouble this has actually caused because I'm sitting across from Ellie's beating heart.

"I do have a girlfriend, but that has nothing to do with us," I admit. She smiles at this and I'm not sure I understand why.

"I'm glad you are happy. It takes a little more of the guilt off of me."

I don't understand how she could feel guilt. Ellie died and was noble enough to think of what would happen in life once she was gone. "You should never feel guilty. This moment right here, right now, shows me how wonderful of a person Ellie was to think ahead and want to save a life if hers were to end. It makes me love her even more."

"She was a great woman," Ari says, once more stealing the breath from my lungs.

"Can I take your order or do you need a few more minutes?" The waitress interrupts this incredibly important discussion, and Ari uses it to her advantage.

"Could I have the garden salad with oil and vinegar, topped with the grilled chicken, please?"

Losing track of the fact that I'm sitting on top of a mile-high roller coaster waiting for the brakes to release, I look at her, dumbfounded. "Salad? Are you serious?"

She places her hand over her chest. "Gotta keep this ticking."

"She'll have a burger and fries." I know that was rude and she could be a vegetarian or a vegan or something but Ellie would want her to have a burger and fries. If there was one thing Ellie did right, it was eat, and she did it as if she were going to die the next day. Which she did—she had an entire Cheese pizza and two orders of fries the night before Olive was born. She knew they weren't going to let her eat anything at the hospital and early labor had already started. It was her last pre-mommy wish. The woman got what she wanted and it made her night; thankfully, since it was her last. Talk about a last meal.

"Hey," she croaks out.

"Are you a vegetarian?" I ask pointedly.

"No," she laughs.

"Burger and fries it is, then. Same for me, please." This helps the waitress speed up the process, leaving us back at the top of the roller coaster. "You knew Ellie? I know you made mention of it in one of your last letters, but hearing it out loud stuns me again."

She avoids my gaze as tears pool in her eyes. I give her the moment she must need as I watch her fingers weave tightly together, forcing the whites of her knuckles to glowing under the hanging table light.

When she refocuses her attention on my face, there's a reflection in her flooding tears, showing a disfigured version of my facial features. I wonder what the look on my face is right now. I feel so many different things, none of which I've ever felt before. "I was her student teacher two years before she passed."

"Student teacher?" I'm not sure why I'm asking this since I knew she had several of them over the course of the four years she taught but she never mentioned any of them in particular to me. "I don't understand," what one thing has to do with another.

"I was dying," she says as the tears dry. Her words sound sour coming from her mouth, but also rehearsed as if she was forced to look in the mirror and tell herself over and over again that she was dying.

"From what?" I should assume. I am assuming. But I need to hear it all.

"Congenital Heart Failure. I wasn't supposed to make it past twenty, but I did," she explains. Her explanation makes my breath catch in my throat. Ellie was always one to come home and share heart-breaking stories with me. She always had an idea on how she could fix the world single-handedly. It was never a matter of explaining a person's situation with pity. She always had a solution. Why she never mentioned Ari to me is baffling. "She wanted to help me."

"That was Ellie. She considered becoming a nurse but she has—had—an aversion to blood and a teacher was the next best thing when it came to helping people, so that's what she did. She also had a thing for little kids—born to be a mother, I always thought."

Ari pulls in a quivered breath as her lips curve into a small smile. "She told me if it was meant to be, I would receive my heart—meaning if her heart were to outlive her brain before I passed away, I would be pretty damn lucky. The kindness of Ellie is something that has been infused within me; it has remained in her heart. But her telling me I would be lucky didn't seem so clear until I found out the heart was going to be mine. I wouldn't consider her death in exchange for my survival to be very lucky."

I wanted to hear every last word Ari just said but my mind is hooked on one particular statement that I can't move past. "I'm sorry," I shake my head. "What were you saying about her heart surviving her brain?"

Paleness encompasses her cheeks. "That's what she said to me," Ari simplifies.

"But why would she consider that possibility?" A cold sweat is creeping up the back of my neck and it's making me dizzy and weak to the point where I just want to put my head down and rest for a minute. Instead, I try to hold my ground and ask the questions that need to be asked. "You must know why she would say something so random?" I hear my voice becoming louder and more aggressive, but as much as I want to tame my outburst, I can't figure out how to. Ari looks taken aback—slightly frightened even. It feels as if the restaurant is closing in around me, closing me into this hollow bubble where everyone is looking in at me, talking about me in whispers as if I can't hear them, which I can't. I can only hear the thoughts in my own head, fighting with each other, battling it out for one simple understanding.

Ari looks to the side, taking in the staring gazes from the tables surrounding us. I should feel bad for making her uncomfortable but instead, I'm concerned about imploding.

"She said it was her destiny to give life. It was God's plan for her," Ari offers.

"No. There was more," I reply, doing my best to keep my volume down.

"This is not my place," she says. "I don't feel right about this, which is exactly why I have kept my distance over the years. I didn't come here tonight to tell you things Ellie confided in me. I came here to end the pain I've presumably been causing you, which is evident now." Ari looks down to the bench she's seated on and gathers her purse and coat, scooping them up into her arms. "This was a terrible idea."

She's leaving. No way. She can't leave. Not after all of this. I grip her arm as she passes by, holding her in place, not allowing her the freedom she deserves. "Don't leave me," I stammer.

"Let go, Hunter." She pulls her arm from my loose grip and continues for the door.

I reach into my back pocket and pull out a fifty-dollar bill. I toss it onto the table and grab my coat, slipping out of the booth to follow her. I expect to find her locked in her car by the time I make it outside but she's sitting down on the curb in front of the restaurant, slouched over, holding herself tightly.

For a moment, everything inside of me eases, but I'm not sure if it's because I'm temporarily not afraid of losing control or if I'm overly hopeful for a confession that I deserve to know.

"Ellie and I kept in contact over the years. I knew when you found out you were pregnant with Olive. I knew when she went into labor. I knew when she died. In fact, I saw you in the lobby of the hospital," she explains delicately.

"How did you know who I was?" I take a seat beside her on the curb, instinctively placing my arm around her as a peace offering, trying my hardest to understand that I'm not the only one who has felt pain, regardless of my confusion surrounding Ari's friendship with Ellie. Why had I never heard of her? I truly thought Ellie told me everything.

Ari combs her fingers through her hair again, a habit I have been noticing over the past few times I've seen her. She exposes the profile of her beautiful face, which is now glowing under the orange street light and the creamy moon. She sniffles softly and pulls her hands up to her chest, shivering against the cold breeze. "She loved you so much," she says through a soft breath. "Like more than I've ever seen anyone love a person. She would show me pictures at school, like stupid insignificant pictures to an outsider, but she wanted to show off a certain smile you had when you were painting a room or the look you had after you just burnt a meal you spent three hours making." None of this rings a bell to me, but I want to hear more.

"Ellie was madly, senselessly, in love with you," Ari continues. "Every decision she made somehow revolved around your life, and while I never met you in person, I felt as though I knew you from the amount she spoke of you." My heart aches with contentment, listening to her words, her explanations for a reason I may never fully understand. I needed to hear this. I've needed this so badly.

"I knew it was she who died when I was called about the donation. I was told to come to the hospital immediately. I was filled with a combination of heartache, despair, and hope. I had never felt so many intense feelings at one time. Selfish luck was one of those feelings, the one I'm most ashamed of. I wanted to pretend Ellie wasn't the donor and she didn't lose her life, in turn giving me a future I wasn't meant to have. I tried my hardest to put it out of my mind as I walked into the hospital that day."

Ari stands up, still clutching her hands over her chest. Walking into the middle of the parking lot and up to her blue hybrid, she stops to lean against the back of her car. "I saw you the second I walked into the hospital. I thought my heart was going to give out before I had a chance to accept the donation. You were propped up against a wall beneath a payphone, your knees were pulled into your chest and your eyes were inflamed, your cheeks were red and stained with a constant flow of tears. You don't usually see the moment a person breaks down or loses the love of his life." She breathes heavily from her overflow of words. "But if you did, you would feel sorry for him or her, regardless of knowing their story. And I knew your story. The guilt that found me in that one particular moment has remained frozen within my head."

"You saw me that day, that moment?" I clarify.

"I stood and watched you for five minutes until my mother forced me to continue walking. I could hardly hold myself up from the weak state my body was in, but I felt it was the repercussion I needed before I went in and took your wife's heart."

"Did Ellie know she was going to die?" I need to know and I will continue to beg her for information until I no longer have the opportunity to do so.

"Hunter, would you want me to tell you something that she told me in confidence?"

CHAPTER FOURTEEN

MY FIST IS growing weak as I continue knocking on Charlotte's door. I know she's home. I'm also aware it's close to midnight. I pull out my phone and send another text, pleading for her to answer.

I'm not giving up until she does. I need to talk to her. I've been trying to avoid calling her in case her volume is up since I don't want to wake Lana this late at night, but she's leaving me no choice.

My finger hovers over the call button just as I see the hall light illuminate through the foggy glass. I hear footsteps. Please don't be Lana. The door opens sluggishly and Charlotte is standing in front of me in a ratty white robe, her hair tousled everywhere and her eyes half-lidded and also full of confusion. She hasn't yet given me the opportunity to see her without make-up and now I don't understand why. Every one of her features is lighter, more natural, flushed—beautiful.

"Hunter, it's midnight," she yawns.

"I know, but I need to talk to you," I state the obvious.

"Can't it wait until morning? I was asleep," she says, slowly coming to the realization of what she looks like. Her fingers press through the roots of her hair, smoothing out the snarls as she pulls her robe closed a little tighter across her chest.

I step forward, forcing her to step back, allowing me in. "She knew Ellie. Ellie promised her the heart. The woman from the letters was the woman I ran into at the gardens. That's crazy, right?"

"What?" Charlotte says through a hazy groan. "I don't follow." Annoyance sets in, as I need her to keep up right now. I need her to help me figure this all out.

"She knew her, Charlotte. I didn't know her, but Ellie knew her. Ellie told her she would give this woman her heart if it survived her brain. What sense does that make?" My voice is growing in volume and Charlotte's attention locks on the stairwell.

"Please keep your voice down so Lana doesn't wake up." Her words come out in soft caws. I shouldn't have woken her. I need to get a grip.

"I'm sorry," is all I can offer. With my voice lowered, I calmly explain everything again—Ari being the heart recipient and also the woman in the gardens. As I'm explaining, I keep wondering if Ellie wanted Ari and me to meet. None of this can be coincidental. I don't believe in that crap, especially since Ellie can't send me any of those soul-gripping whimsical messages through the wind and shit. There has to be more than what Ari admitted to me. I need to know the rest.

Charlotte's hand reaches for my arm and she pulls me toward the couch as we both sit down. "You have to calm down." Her hand rests on my back as she traces her fingertips in small circles below my shoulder.

I take a deep breath, one I've needed to take for hours. "I know this all sounds ridiculous," I explain.

"It's not ridiculous. I would want to know who she is if I were in your shoes, too," she says.

"You would?" I look up at her, needing the validation in her eyes, telling me I'm not completely insane.

"Of course," she says, but there is no validation in her eyes. Instead, there's a distant look. "Hunter…"

"I shouldn't have woken you. I just—you're the one I wanted to talk to."

"You're making this so damn hard," she says, sinking farther into the couch. "Hunt, this really isn't the best time to have this conversation but since you're here…"

"What?" I ask, my voice sounding as worn out as I feel. What is she about to say?

"I don't know if I can follow you on this path you're heading down. I do want to be here for you, understand you, and support you, but this is incredibly difficult with your fluctuating moods and behavior. I mean, you couldn't even tell me you were going to meet this woman tonight. I feel hurt by that, I guess." It completely slipped my mind between all of my racing thoughts of Ari that I didn't tell Charlotte I was meeting her tonight. Nice move, Hunter. "Whether this is innocent or not with her, I just wish you had been honest with me today—tonight." She drops her head into her hands, releasing a heavy sigh, a non-forgiving sigh. I fucked up tonight. I deserve this. "I just—I'm not sure what you need from me right now, but I don't know if I can handle it. I've been through my fair share of crap—nothing compared to you—but I don't want things to be like this. So confusing, hard."

"I didn't mean to make things hard on you," I tell her. She is the last person I would want to make things hard for.

"I know." Her elbows fall to her knees and she hunches over, clearly exhausted. I watch, waiting for her thoughts to subside. "Hunt, I just don't think your heart and/or mind are in the right place for us right now," she says with tears filling her eyes.

She's breaking up with me and I can't think of anything to say. I do want this—her. Things have hardly had a chance to begin with us and now they're ending and it's my fault. "So that's it. You're done with me?"

"Things have been really fun. I love being with you, and Olive of course, but something feels like it's missing. There's a void—and it's starting to hurt me. I can only imagine it will get harder—worse over time—as I fall for you more than I already have. So this is me protecting myself." She places her hand over my bouncing knee and squeezes gently. "I don't want it to be like this, but you need to figure some things out."

"Charlotte, I want to be with you. I need to be with you." The words come out far easier now than they did a month or two ago. I've really grown attached to her, to the point where she feels like a crucial part of my life, a part that feels normal with her in it. I didn't even know I could find anything remotely close to normal before I met her, and I don't want to lose that. "I should have been honest with you today. I was wrong and I messed up," I tell her, wrapping my arm around her shoulders. "Please don't do this."

"Hunt, you made it clear that you need to explore this newfound part of your life and I want you to be able to do that. You clearly have a connection to this woman and for the chance that you want to explore that after reading her letters for five years, I want you to have that freedom. Olive has told me about the look in your eyes when you read one of her letters. She told me you have a special smile just for this woman's words." I want to argue with her and tell her she's completely wrong but I'd be lying if I said I felt nothing toward Ari. And Charlotte's right—it isn't fair to her. "Take some time and figure out what you want. If by chance, you realize it's me, I'll be here. And if it's her, I understand completely."

"Charlotte, I do want you!" But I want to know more about Ari, too, and I'm seeing right now that I can't have it both ways. I didn't ask for things to be like this. It isn't fair.

"Then that's the way things will end up."

"Don't throw this fate shit at me, please," I tell her. While I'm saying this, I hear Ari's argumentative words about our predestined paths in life. I don't know how the hell I'm going to figure out if Charlotte is my less chosen path...my road not taken, or if Ari is.

"I don't believe in fate, Hunter. I believe in choices."

I stand up, as this conversation has a defined end mark that I am trying to step over. "I'm sorry for waking you up so late." This fucking sucks. I'm thirty years old and I'm being dumped by the first person I've allowed myself to have feelings for besides Ellie.

"Anytime, really. We're friends, we're neighbors, and our daughters are connected at the hip. We're stuck with each other." Kiss of death words. Her voice rattles with an uncomfortable laugh as she tugs at her robe again. "Hunt, we're adults; we can work through this. I don't want there to be awkwardness, okay?"

"I've seen you naked," I add with a teasing smile, testing the waters.

"And I've seen you naked," she says.

"Whatever."

"If whatever is meant to be, it will be," she responds.

I leave the conversation at that, quietly slipping out the door, unwilling to turn and look back at whatever emotion is written across her face. I know I'm the cause of her pain and confusion, and now mine, as well.

Thank God. Mom is asleep in the guest room and Olive is snoring away. I quietly pad across the floor barefoot, heading up the stairs, avoiding the spots that creak. Once inside my bedroom, I flip on the lights and slide open the closet doors, reaching up for the large brown box with Ellie's name inked across the top.

I rest the box on my bed and open the flaps, exposing all of Ellie's belongings that I could squeeze into this thing. I reach my hand down the right side until I touch the bottom, feeling around for the book I'm looking for. The moleskin fabric comes into contact with my fingertips and I slip it out carefully.

I've skimmed through her journal many times before, selfishly ruining whatever privacy she wanted while she was alive, but most everything I read were things I already knew, which is why I only skimmed the pages. The memories always seemed to hurt more than help. Now, though, I need to look harder for the parts of Ellie's life she kept secret.

I get it. We all have secrets. We all have demons and we all have moments so personal that we can't share them. I just never considered the parts she left out.

Turning page after page, I drag my finger down the center of Ellie's beautiful words, the penmanship I always admired. I teased her that she was born to be a teacher, with her perfect handwriting. It's the kind of script that is so clean and crisp no one would ever struggle to read it like most cursive writings.

As I begin to read, the words sink in and memories join them. I haven't done this in a while so it feels fresh, as if the words were nightcaps to a perfect day I experienced only hours before. Ellie wrote in this journal once a month, recapping every important detail for the prior thirtyish days. She started this new journal the day we got married. She said it was a new chapter and deserved a new book.

My cheeks burn as I read her memories on the first night of our honeymoon, the inner thoughts she had while we commenced our marriage in Puerto Vallarta in front of our open porch doors, which overlooked nothing but the water, stars, and moon. The warmth around us felt like a cocoon shielding us from everything and everyone. It was only us that night, and I would give everything I have to be back in that moment with her.

The way she looked at me, as if all of her dreams had finally come true, made me understand the true meaning of life's plan. Men don't typically dream about their wedding day, but since the moment my hormones replaced the thoughts of Ellie only being a friend in my life, I had dreamt of that moment, in that bed, in that hotel room, on that night with her. Even though we had plenty of prior practice, that night felt like the first time all over again.

Flipping to the next page, I continue to read her poetic thoughts, stumbling over a certain line I know I never read before.

If only God had placed me on this earth to serve more purpose than just making a man slowly fall in love with me for seventeen years, I could promise him seventeen more years. 'Till Death Do Us Part' is a truth I will give my soul to for eternity, wherever that may be.

Ellie always had a way of talking in circles when she wrote, words that seemed to make little sense to me, though I knew there was always a deeper meaning behind what was delicately rolling off of her tongue via the tip of a pen. These written words, however, make sense to me now, but were her thoughts intuition or a secret? That's what I don't understand.

I skip forward several pages, finding another indented quote centered in the middle of the page.

A gift doesn't always have to be tangible

It doesn't always have to be enfolded with a bow
Occasionally it's protected in blood and arrives without a label
While full of soul-rendering love, it can also produce sorrow
I offer this bequest
In the remains of my shadow
A gift that will surpass my last breath

I read the poem over and over, doing my best to make sense of it—the gift she's speaking of—a gift covered in blood. Ellie, my Ellie, the one with a smile always carved into her perfect, rosy lips, never expressed a morbid thought. I want to be in denial of the thought that she might have known of an expiration date. Her parents would have known, and yet they have never shared a hint of expecting her untimely death. Would she have kept something like this to herself?

I'm afraid to read more. I'm afraid to search for more insightful rhymes that I can't make sense of. I close the journal, hugging it against my chest tightly. "Ellie, what were you keeping from me?" I ask as I lie back against my pillow. Being alone in this cold bed that I have occupied myself for so long, it feels extra empty tonight.

Peering over to the nightstand, I see that it's two in the morning, and the gears in my head are working harder than they do in the middle of the day. My pain has always been about missing her, sadness for what she lost and what Olive and I have lost out on, but now there's a pain from wondering about what I never knew—what secrets she was keeping from me.

I don't remember falling asleep, but when the bed shifts, I know it's morning. After an endless night, the daylight is painful, filling my body with slight flu-like symptoms. Exhaustion has me pinned to the bed, unable to move other than lifting my eyelids as far as they will go.

Sunshine is filtering through my half-closed blinds and glowing through Olive's blond curls. I take the moment to look in her eyes, admiring how blue they appear surrounded by the youthful bright whites encircling them. Why does my heart sometimes hurt when I look at her? A father should never feel pain when he looks at his daughter, but I do so often that I feel guilty.

"Are you okay?" Olive asks me softly while running her small hand across my forehead. "You don't feel warm." She lifts the covers and pulls them up to her neck, regardless of already being completely dressed from head to toe for school. "Grammy is taking me to the bus stop. She said you aren't feeling well. Why are you still in your clothes from yesterday, Daddy?" I continue to watch her face move as she asks me all of her questions. "Why aren't you answering me? Is something wrong with you?"

I pull my heavy arm out from behind my head and wrap it around her shoulders. "I'm just fine, Olive. I'm tired, that's all."

"Grammy said you aren't well," she continues. "I don't want you to be sick, Daddy. I can ask Grammy to make you soup. Why do you look so sad?" Olive's question falls short as her chin trembles and a tear falls from her eye. "Please don't be sad." Why is it I'm only good at making people cry?

I pull her against my chest, still having no words to make her feel better. I kiss her head and inhale the sweet scent of her watermelon shampoo. "I'm okay and I love you more than anything in this whole world. Do you understand that?"

"I love you more than the sun, the sky, the grass, the moon, and the stars. I love you so much it hurts, Daddy." Her mature words sting my nerves, making me wonder how much she understands of what she said. It's as if Ellie's whirlwind lyrical thoughts were genetically laced within Olive's DNA.

"I don't want you to ever feel pain, Olive."

"But sometimes—" she pauses, looking down at a piece of lint on the sheet, "When I look at you, I feel your pain." Oh, God, what have I done?

"Do you want to stay home with me today?" I ask her.

She nods her head slightly as a small smile touches her lips and she lies down in the crook of my arm, nuzzling her head against my chest.

"Olive, we have to go," Mom says from the hall.

"I'm keeping her home with me today," I respond.

Mom walks into my room, her hands on her hips and an unsettled look on her face. "Hunter, you can't keep her home for no reason. The school frowns upon that." I squeeze Olive a little tighter. "Hunter, did something happen?"

I can only offer her a weak, pitiful smile. "What's wrong with me, Mom?"

"Olive, sweetie, go downstairs and turn on the TV for a bit. I'll let the school know you'll be staying home today," Mom directs her.

Normally, Olive would be elated to find out she's staying home, but she's upset, and it's because of me. She takes her time climbing out of the bed and brushes by Mom at the door without another word.

Mom comes closer, sitting down at the edge of the bed. "I am very concerned about you," she begins. "We need to find you some help."

"That doesn't answer my question," I remind her. "What the hell is wrong with me? It has been five years and I'm no better today than I was that day at the hospital and now things are pretty much over with Charlotte, too."

Mom runs the back of her fingers down the side of my face, making me realize this conversation is not one a grown adult has with his mother. I'm not a grown adult at this moment, though. I'm her little boy again. I'm losing it. I've lost it—my mind is gone. "Oh, sweetie," Mom exhales. "They say it takes the same amount of time to get over a person as it took to fall in love with a person. You loved Ellie since you were five years old. That's what's wrong with you."

"You're saying I'm going to feel like this for another fifteen years?"

"Not this amount of pain, but some pain. For now, though, you need to talk to someone. This is affecting Olive now that she's old enough to understand. We've had these talks, Hunter. You just keep pushing us away, and we can't do anything to help you if you don't want our help."

Everything she is saying is true. I've acknowledged it all before but have ignored it for a long time. "Ellie was keeping a secret from me."

Mom snaps up straight, her brows pulling in toward one another. "What on earth are you talking about?"

"Ellie knew she was going to die. She told the woman from the letters—the woman I met last night. She knew Ellie, and Ellie had promised her heart to this woman."

Mom looks as baffled as I felt last night. "I thought you were meeting with a client last night?"

"I lied."

"You met that woman?" She closes her eyes and shakes her head, probably trying to clarify everything I'm saying. "She knew Ellie? Ellie knew she was going to die? Hunter, that makes no sense at all." Redness webs across her cheeks as she stares through me. "I speak to Ellie's parents all of the time and not once have they ever hinted at knowing this could have happened. Don't you think that's something they would have shared with us—with you?"

I shrug because I don't have a good response. I'm questioning a lot right now and I wouldn't put any kind of secret past Ellie's parents.

"If this is true, they didn't know, Hunter. I can tell you that much," she continues. "Did that woman tell you any more than what you just said?"

"No, she said she didn't feel right sharing Ellie's secret."

"Oh my."

CHAPTER FIFTEEN

MARCH
-ONE MONTH LATER-

YOU KNOW YOU'RE on a downward spiral to nowhere good when you cancel jobs to get out of working. AJ is pissed at me, or I'll assume he's pissed at me because I haven't called him back in an entire week and I don't even know if he went to get a paternity test he had scheduled or how that all worked out. I've been a shitty brother, as well as a shitty co-worker, and yet part of me doesn't care, which is even shittier.

I can look in the mirror and tell myself I have a problem and I need help. I just haven't gotten to the point where I've picked up the phone to get help. Everything hurts all of the time whether I'm awake or asleep. I have spent every day these past few weeks sitting on the frozen ground in front of mine and Ellie's tree. It's fucking cold out here but this pain is only skin deep and it hurts far less than everything in my stomach and chest.

"You fucking dickwad," his voice echoes between the snow banks. "How many jobs are you going to make us lose? Get your head out of the clouds and get your ass in the truck." AJ rounds the slight corner from the stone stairs, holding his arms tightly around his body, shivering against the frigid temperatures.

"What are you doing here?" I ask, wondering why after sitting here for at least an hour I feel far less cold than he looks.

"Looking for you, jackass. Why haven't you returned any of my calls? Or Charlotte's? What the hell is going on with you? First it was the unusual silence and now you've just been completely MIA. I've seen this before, Hunter. You've been down this road already. You aren't going back down it again. I won't let you."

I can only stare back at him because I have no good response, as usual.

"Get up and get in the truck, Hunter," he demands. "I've let this go on long enough."

Instead of moving, I relax my head against the tree and close my eyes, lifting my chin toward the sky. Flakes of snow are feathering down over me as particles of ice rest on the tip of my nose. While inhaling the painful air, AJ yanks me from the ground and pins me to the tree. With my back scraping against the engraved letters I once carved, anger floods through me, and the desire to swing at my brother is nearly irresistible. Exercising restraint, I grit my teeth as AJ's face stops only inches from mine. "Get in the truck, now," he says again.

I didn't agree or disagree but he's dragging me up the stairs and I'm complying with little effort. Suddenly, I'm freezing and my muscles are aching below my numb skin. The steps become a blur and I don't regain my strength until my back is pressed up against AJ's truck. The passenger door opens and AJ shoves me inside. Never in our lives has he been stronger than I am. I've always been the bigger of the two of us but right now I don't have the energy to fight back.

He slams the door and makes his way around to his side, sliding in and slamming his door in the same fashion. His fists drop against the steering wheel as he releases a brash growl. "I've had it, Hunt. We've all had it."

I let him talk because it doesn't matter what I say, it won't make a difference and it won't diminish his anger. That's AJ. He wears himself out until the steam goes away. He starts up the truck and peels out of the lot. The snow is coming down harder now, making visibility tough as we continue down this road. I glance down at my watch, noting the time. It's only noon but if the snow is going to continue like this, they might dismiss Olive earlier than normal. "Where are you taking me?"

"Don't worry about it," he mumbles through a shiver. Reaching over to the center console, he turns the heat all the way to the max and then does the same with the volume knob, allowing the sound of the heater to mix with the harsh tones of Metal Rock.

I turn both down, glaring at the side of his face, waiting for him to tell me where the hell he's taking me because at this point I know it sure as hell isn't home. "AJ, don't be a dick."

He laughs and looks out his window as if he doesn't want to acknowledge my statement. "The baby isn't mine. I've contacted a lawyer to draft up the papers and at the end of this week, I'm checking out of the hotel I've been crashing at and I'm staying with you." All of my answers in one simple sentence. Regardless, I should have called him, especially since I thought he had already sort of moved in with me and yet he didn't come home this past week. Part of me just assumed he was working things out with Alexa but I should have asked. I get it.

"What the hell were you doing at a hotel all week?" I ask.

He shrugs and looks over at me with defined anger staining his eyes. "If you had answered any of my calls, you would have known but when you nicely ignored my tenth call, I figured you didn't want me crashing at your place. Then Mom filled me in on your bullshit behavior."

"Of course she did."

"Dude, you fucking need help. This isn't okay and it isn't fair to Olive."

"Don't you dare bring her into this," I snap back.

"Yeah, no, see, I am bringing her into this because this is all about her. She is the only thing that matters and should matter in your life and yet you can't even get your ass to work right now so you can continue to support her. So as Olive's God-dad, I'm here to step in and get you the help you need to give that little girl as normal of a life as she can have without a mother." His words stun me, they taser me, holding me hostage along with the truth I would rather deny.

As I'm considering everything he said, the truck jerks around and we pull into a nearly empty lot against a small house-looking structure. "What is this?"

"Let's go," he says, stepping out of the truck. He's out of his mind if he thinks I'm following him into whatever this place is.

"Tell me what this is, AJ," I demand as he opens my door. "Quit it with the bullshit." I'm losing steam and I can see he's only gaining more of it.

"We can do this the easy way or the hard way. Choice is yours," he says, folding his arms over his chest.

"Yeah, I'm not walking into some deserted building just because you want to threaten me."

I remain seated in the truck as he smashes his fist down on the roof. "Fine." He pushes off of the truck and walks off and into the building, leaving me sitting here watching and waiting for him to come back out. I glance around, looking for a sign or a hint of where we might be, but there's nothing.

Since he took the keys with him, I close the door, trying to lock in some of the remaining heat. This is stupid. Yanking my phone out of my coat pocket, I check it to make sure I haven't gotten any messages from the school about an early dismissal.

Nothing yet.

With my phone blaring in my face, I tap on the text message app and thumb in a quick note, hoping for a response this time.

Me: Ari, I really need to talk to you.

The message falls below the last five messages I sent over the past few weeks. I'm beginning to assume she gave me a bogus phone number just to shut me up. I'm not sure she was planning to offer me her number, but I asked. She definitely battled with a moment of internal debate before finally offering it up.

I hold my focus on the message I sent, waiting to see a delivered note pop up. As I'm waiting, my door reopens, bringing along a drift of snow. A woman stands behind AJ, draped by a down jacket and a black ski hat with her salt-and-pepper-colored hair hanging loosely over her coat. She doesn't appear cold, annoyed, or uncomfortable while standing behind AJ as he presses his finger against my chest. "Don't be an asshole."

AJ moves to the side, allowing the woman into the opening of my door. "Hunter, I'm Amy Torris and I'm a therapist who specializes in helping widowers such as yourself. Your family seems quite concerned with your well-being and I'd love to offer some guidance if you're open to it." Does it look like I'm open to it?

He brought me to a goddamn shrink. He out of all people brought me to this chick. Un-fucking-believable. "You don't have to answer any questions or even talk," Amy continues. "Maybe you could just come inside for a few? I have a fresh pot of coffee brewing." Is she trying to lure me in like a creep offering a child candy? Not working.

"You've hit rock bottom, Hunt," AJ chimes in. "Do this for Olive." Olive. Her name could put me in a hypnotic trance and he knows I will do anything for her. If he's telling me I'm hurting her, I will do what it takes to undo that. I unclick my seatbelt and step out of the truck, going against everything I want to do in this moment. Passing by the therapist and AJ, I make my way up to the front door of this ratty looking building.

I let myself inside, looking in each direction for which way I should continue walking in. Before I approach the gold-plaque directory on the wall, Amy's voice interrupts my question. "Take a left and it's the first door on the right."

Rather than walking ahead, I allow her to lead the way and AJ follows behind me. Her office looks nothing like the outside of the building. In here, it's warm, swathed with a bright yellow paint and cream-colored furniture. Magazines line the small tables between each chair and it smells like fresh coffee, just as she promised. "I don't need therapy," I warn them both. But maybe I do.

"This doesn't have to be considered therapy, Hunter. It can be two friends chatting." Her words are ridiculous, and the meaning behind them is even more ridiculous. People don't become friends after two minutes, especially when one is forced to meet the other. "Hunter, if you don't want to talk, you can leave. You have to walk in at your own will."

161

"Do it for Olive, Hunt," AJ says again.

I groan silently and follow Amy through a wooden door that squeaks a melody when opened. AJ remains in the waiting area, leaving me alone with this woman I met ninety seconds ago. As we enter her office, a new scent, which accompanies the roasted coffee, fills my nose. Lavender mixed with lilac, likely aromatherapy oil. Ellie was obsessed with those in the winter since it was as close as she could get to the scent of a flower in the cold months.

It takes me a moment to look around the room noticing the decor is similar to the waiting area, but with the addition of psychiatry degree plaques lining the wall behind her desk. I take a seat on the couch, trying to make myself comfortable, but I notice a box of tissues on the oak coffee table in front of me. Is this woman's job to make people cry? Maybe I should be a therapist. I make people cry.

"Your family is very worried about you," Amy begins. "Normally, I don't work in this fashion since it trifles with the line of patient confidentiality but oftentimes I find that men and women in your situation need a little shove in the right direction."

"Look, I appreciate you going along with my family's concerns, but maybe they left out the fact that my wife died over five years ago. This isn't a new life for me and I'm not crying for help." A thin line stretches across her mouth. I want to say it's a condescending look but it's probably not. "Really, I'm fine." I wonder if I could send less convincing.

"To be defined as fine is all relative to each person's thoughts. Would you have considered yourself fine if you looked ahead and saw yourself in this moment ten years ago?" This is a trap. Of course I can't say yes to this question, which by process of elimination suggests her accusation is true. "Why don't we go this route? Your willingness to speak with me only for the sake of your daughter tells me that you will do just about anything for her, so we can focus on that?"

While her words float in through my ears and out of the top of my head, I hold my focus on the box of tissues, wondering how many widowers she has spoken to here, how many of them have sat on this couch crying so hard their organs hurt. Widowers know that organs do in fact hurt because our hearts get tired of enduring all of the pain and eventually allow it to spread elsewhere to ease some of the weight.

"I'm not going to pour my heart out to you and tell you all about my daughter and then tell you how sad my life has been for the past five years. I'm not even going to tell you why I've been so miserable for the past week. I internalize my thoughts and while it might not be the healthiest method of dealing with problems, it works for me." I will admit I'm a little shocked to see she isn't writing down my every word. I've been to therapists before, even ones who specialize in widowers. Typically, they start with a pen and paper and jot down every mentionable moment of my life up until the current day. So I'll give Amy that respect, she's truly soaking it in rather than creating parts of a research paper on the inner workings of a fucked-up man.

"You don't have to tell me anything at all," she says. "Do you have a picture of your daughter on you? AJ told me how adorable she is and now I just need to see for myself." I know this is another trap but I can never stop myself from showing off Olive. I slip my wallet out of my back pocket and open the flap to pull out the picture I have of her. I lean forward, holding it between my two fingers for Amy to take.

She meets me halfway and slides the photo out of my loose grip. Studying it for a moment, another smile finds her lips. "She looks just like you. I take it your wife must have had the blond hair, though," she laughs. She laughs because my hair is jet black and Olive's is so blond it's nearly white.

"Yes, she's all Ellie, right down to the words she uses and the way in which she says them."

"That must be nice," she offers simply. Again, I expected a: "And how does that make you feel?" but she doesn't say that.

"It's a great reminder," I add in.

"Does Olive enjoy the snow?"

"Not really. She is one of the very few children who would rather sit inside and sip hot cocoa than get all bundled up to go out and make a snowman. She prefers the warm weather." And just like that, I'm yapping like a fool. Clearly, this woman knows exactly how to get me to talk.

Amy leans forward, pressing her elbows into her thighs. "I don't think there is anything wrong with you, Hunter. It sounds to me like you're a doting father and just a little lonely without Ellie. That doesn't exactly define the word crazy. I know that's why you must think you're here right now, but most of the time, I just listen to things no one else wants to hear you say over and over."

I lower my head in debate. I know I need this but I also know what happens every time I cave to the idea of therapy. It opens old wounds and I end up exactly where I am right now. "I don't know," I tell her.

"And that's fine," she says, pressing her lips together. "Take all of the time you need. Amy reaches to her desk and retrieves a business card from a little marble tray. "If you decide you need someone to listen to you, call me."

I take the card from her fingers and slip it into my coat pocket. "Thank you," I mutter. I'm glad she didn't ask me to make an appointment or make me feel guilty for not making one. I'm thankful she isn't pushy and is honestly allowing the decision to be mine, unlike AJ and I'm guessing Mom, who is likely hiding behind AJ.

As I stand from the chair, I feel a vibration in my back pocket. Without considering the thought of being rude as Amy is reciting the hours in which she can be reached, I look down at the screen of my phone, seeing the notification of a new text message. I press read.

Ari: I'm here.

I quickly thumb the keys to ask:

Me: Where?
Ari: My shop. 250 Main Street.

I peer up at Amy, who is now watching with a curious expression. "Is everything okay?" she asks.

"Yes, it's great." It's more than great.

Her brows knit together with confusion. "Whatever that message was, it certainly changed your mood pretty fast."

"It's—" I hesitate before unveiling more information about my life. She seems more interested than anyone else I would share this with, though. "It's Ari, the woman who has Ellie's heart."

"I don't understand," she presses.

Elation is bubbling in my stomach and I just want to leave but I remember now that AJ is waiting in the lobby for me, and I'll have to explain to him why I have walked in and out of here in ten minutes.

I look back down at my phone, pondering for a moment before typing in my next message.

Me: Will you be there in ninety minutes?"
Ari: Yes, I will be here until five today.

I glance up at the clock and sit back down in the seat, removing my coat to make myself more comfortable. I interlace my fingers and rest them on my knees as I lean forward. "Ellie died giving birth to our daughter, Olive. To my surprise, beyond her death, she had a private agreement outside of our joint will that stated she would donate her heart if the situation were to arise. Since she died from an aneurysm, her request was fulfilled. Weeks after Ellie's death, I began receiving letters from the recipient. They were all anonymous. Five years have gone by, and last week, for the first time, the woman with Ellie's heart asked to meet me."

Amy looks intrigued—beyond intrigued, really. There's a passion filling the question in her eyes. She must love what she does...hearing the stories, then trying to place the puzzle pieces back into the perfect picture she never saw in the first place. Without direction or an image to copy, it must be difficult. "It turns out I have met this woman a few times before. She's wonderful and captivating, and she knows secrets about my wife that Ellie never cared to share with me. This has all come to a culmination in the past week and it feels as if my mind is imploding."

Amy laughs quietly. Not a mimicking type of laugh, a sympathetic and commiserating type of sound. "We just got through about five sessions worth of information in three minutes," she says, leaning back in her leather chair, which whines against her weight. "People don't always keep secrets to hurt others. Sometimes they keep secrets to protect the ones they love. I'm curious, though, you said Ellie and this woman knew each other?"

"I guess so; though, I'm just learning this now," I tell her.

"How interesting," Amy says. "Are you going to continue searching for the answer?"

"How can I not?" I respond. The constant thoughts of Ellie keeping secrets from me have consumed me and caused ripples in the life I have tried so hard to put back together. "Yes, I need to see this woman again."

"Do you think you are happy to see this woman because she owns this secret or because she has a piece of Ellie alive within her?"

"Both," I tell her. Of course, it's both.

"Do you have feelings for this woman?" she continues.

Flashes of Ari's eyes seep into my mind as I consider this answer. "I'm not sure. I was in the beginning of a nice relationship with a woman who happens to live across the street from me, but she isn't exactly interested in being with me as I figure out my feelings for Ari, the woman with Ellie's heart." The answers are so simple, yet the resolution is so difficult. I'm not sure anything will ever be resolved and I could end up in the same situation I was in before I met Charlotte. Alone. If I never find another woman to be with again, it will be fair, though. Most people aren't lucky enough to have an Ellie in their life for as long as I did and then live on to experience anything even remotely close again. I've come to terms with living out the rest of my life focused only on Olive, but it seems lately that a part of me wants to be selfish, as well.

"Your mind must be aching from the number of thoughts coming and going each minute of the day," Amy says. "I do think you're going about this the correct way. You're sparing the woman you were with any discontent and you're being fair to yourself to learn what your feelings are for this other woman." Amy uncrosses her legs and scoots toward the edge of her chair, reaching over to my hands. "For a person whose family thinks he is a mess, you have yourself put together quite well."

My focus locks on Amy's hand resting on mine. By the looks of her rippled skin, I'm guessing she is around Mom's age, which tells me that she's not only speaking from wisdom and knowledge but life experience, as well. It's a bit comforting, I suppose.

"I want to come back and talk with you again," I tell her, looking up into her hazy light eyes.

"You tell me when and I'll be here." She pulls out a planner and opens the front cover while she leans toward her desk to retrieve a pencil.

"Next week, same time?" I ask, feeling a slight weight lifting from my shoulders.

She jots my name down into the appropriate box in her planner and reaches to her desk once more for a card. She writes the time and day down on the back of it and hands it to me. "I'm looking forward to hearing what happens with Ari," she says with a lopsided grin. "Good luck, Hunter." Amy reaches out to shake my hand and I return the gesture. As I stand once more, replacing my jacket over my shoulders, I feel more space inside of my lungs, like it suddenly became a little easier to breathe.

While walking from the office door, my phone buzzes in my pocket again. I slide it out and see the school's number calling. Shit.

I answer the phone, pressing it against my ear, listening to the pre-recorded message telling us that the bus will be bringing the children home an hour early to due to the impending blizzard. A blizzard at the end of March? Awesome.

I press through the wooden door, finding AJ comfortable on one of the chairs, thumbing through Better Homes and Gardens. The sight of him reading that particular magazine makes me laugh. We are carpenters, but it ends with the floors, especially for AJ, who has no color coordinating abilities considering he's color-blind.

"Shit, that woman is magic, huh? A smile and everything," AJ says, placing the magazine down on the side table while standing up.

"Thank you," I tell him, feeling a twitch in my chest and twinge of pain behind my eyes. Maybe I've been blind to it and Amy possibly enlightened me just a touch, but I realize it's nice to know I have people who love me and care about my well-being while I work through this mess. Even my jackass brother who is going through his own shit right now.

"We have to get home. School let out early and Olive's going to be back in forty-five minutes."

"Dude, have you seen it outside?" AJ asks. "You might want to call Charlotte to see if she can get her."

And just like that, irritation seeps back in. Not at anyone but at the thought of missing my opportunity to talk to Ari today. "I'll call her when we get into the truck."

The moment we step outside, I see that AJ isn't exaggerating. Three inches must have fallen in the past half hour we have been in here. I pull the sleeve of my coat over my hand and brush the snow off the windshield on the passenger side before sliding in. This sucks.

We pull out onto the road, going less than ten miles an hour, as it's almost impossible to see out of the window with how hard the snow is falling.

I dial Charlotte's number and listen to the three rings before she answers, sounding out of breath. "You okay?" I ask her.

"Yep, just shoveling now before it gets too heavy," she says.

"I'll clean your driveway off when it stops. You're going to pull your back out again."

"It's fine, Hunt, really, but thanks. Do you need something?" Our conversations sound so friend-zone, but I do care about her as more than a friend and there are many moments where I wish our timing was different.

"AJ was nice enough to drag me to a therapist beyond my willingness to go on my own. I just got the call from the school and we're trying to get back but there's a line of brake lights in front of us right now. I'm worried we won't get there on time."

A huff of air creates a loud scratching sound in my ear. "You went to talk to someone?" she asks, a hint of hope filling her voice, telling me she was likely in on this intervention, too. "Hearing that makes me really happy."

"I'm glad," I tell her softly, almost intimately, speaking nearly under my breath to avoid the looks from AJ. Although, with how hard he is focusing on the road, I don't think he even realizes I'm on the phone.

"I'll get Olive and bring her back here until you're home. Don't rush, just be careful, okay?"

"I will," I tell her.

"Is AJ driving slow?" she asks.

"Yes, Mom," I tease.

"Hunter, don't start. We both know how AJ drives."

I'm smiling at her anger but she would normally have a valid point. Today, though, AJ isn't even hitting ten miles per hour. "I'll see you when I get home."

I can hear a smile on her lips as she says, "Whatever."

CHAPTER SIXTEEN

THE TRAFFIC HAS cleared, or the three accidents, I should say. People in New England seem to think they're superheroes in the snow with their front-wheel-drive cars. AJ's truck is a little skittish but it's only because his pick-up bed is empty—thanks to me canceling our job for the day. We pull down the street of the bus stop just as we see the bus slowly creeping down the hill. Olive is probably upset right now. She doesn't like when things change or are out of order. It makes her nervous. I step out of the truck just as the bus comes to a stop. The snow is thick and heavy as it covers my head. I pull my hood on and step up beside Charlotte, who looks like an Eskimo.

"You under there?" I nudge my shoulder into hers.

She tugs on the hood of her coat, allowing only a little opening for her eyes to show. "Are the roads bad?" she asks.

"They're not good."

The door of the bus squeaks open and Olive jumps off the bottom step right into a mound of snow. Her lip curls as she tiptoes around the big piles that haven't been plowed yet. "It's cold!" she shouts, making her way over to me. I wrap my arms around her, doing my best to warm her up.

"Hey, as much as I hate this damsel in distress crap, my washer is leaking and I have a week's worth of laundry to do. Any chance you can take a look at it tonight?" The last of her question is cut off with a loud heave as Lana swings her arms around Charlotte.

"I lost another toof, Mom!" Lana points to the big gap in the front of her mouth.

"My goodness, you have no more front teeth!" Charlotte says through laughter.

"Do you think the toof fairy will make it in the snow?" Lana asks.

"Yes, she's magical and strong. She can make it through anything," Charlotte explains, squatting down in front of her.

"Just like you, Mom. You're magical and strong and you tell me all the time you can make it through everything. Remember you said it last night when you were crying on the phone?"

Taking in the conversation between Lana and Charlotte, I'm filled with questions as I wonder why she was crying last night and who she was on the phone with. Not that it's any of my business but I hope she's okay.

"Lana, start walking with Olive," she says, standing back up and brushing the snow from her knees.

Charlotte looks over at me, her eyes wide. I'm guessing she's either hoping I ask or hoping I don't ask. "Spill it," I say.

"It's nothing," she responds, taking a few steps backward and turning to head home.

I look over to AJ in the truck, waving at him to get his attention. He cracks the window and I shout over, "I'm going to walk home. I'll see you in a few." The window closes and the gears grind as he turns the truck around to go down the street.

"Hunter, you don't have to play this role, remember?" Charlotte says through a shiver.

"Don't make me beg, Charlotte. What's going on? And I'm not playing any kind of role. I care about you a lot. You're the one who doesn't want to be with me right now..."

She looks at me like I did something wrong or just said something stupid, which seems to be the norm lately. I question if anything intelligent ever comes out of my mouth these days. "And I care about you a lot, but I don't want to get into it—" She exhales with exaggeration.

"Why were you crying last night?" I ask again.

"You just asked me that..."

"I'm persistent. So, why were you crying last night?" I ask in a softer voice as we catch up to the girls.

"Because that jackass took away my goddamn child support," Lana says in a mock-adult-Charlotte voice.

Jesus.

"Lana," Charlotte snaps. "What did I tell you about eavesdropping, and what did I tell you about repeating things you hear me say in the house?"

A strong pout pulls across Lana's lips, a bad fake pout, "I forgot," she says. Then, she yells, "Olive! Look!" And the girls run ahead until they reach a snow bank created by a plow. Olive stops and watches as Lana climbs up and then slides down into the street. "Come on, Olive!"

Olive contemplates for a long second, knowing her aversion to the cold snow, but I think she notices the amount of fun Lana is having and decides to join her. Without snow pants, the two girls instantly become soaked from the makeshift slide. Normally, Olive would have a fit about being wet, but evidently neither of them feels it, or they're having so much fun, they don't care. If only life as an adult could be so carefree.

Charlotte drops her gloved hands into her deep pockets, walking one step ahead of me. "Are you okay?" I ask.

Her head shakes under her hood and snow dusts off of the material. "Can you fight this in court?" I ask. I don't know much about divorces or how they work but I can't imagine whatever is happening isn't fair.

"He took a job for an underground contractor. He's being paid illegally and isn't reporting any income. To the court, it looks like he doesn't have a job or money so they can't force him to pay child support," she says. I'm having a hard time hearing her with the snow blowing and the kids screeching so I take her arm and force her to turn around, keeping my eye on the kids at the same time.

"How did you find this out?" I ask.

"My lawyer called."

"What's next?"

"I don't know, Hunter. Please, I don't want to talk about it."

"I can't help you unless you give me the details." I realize she didn't ask for help but she clearly needs someone to at least talk to.

"I didn't ask for your help. There's nothing you can do for me," she says. "All that matters is I'm going to lose my house if I don't figure this out." Sadness tears through my chest as I consider the thought of Charlotte and Lana not living across from us anymore.

"I won't let that happen to you," is the only thing that comes out of my mouth. I'm not sure how I can promise that but it seems like the only thing to say and the only thing I want to say. "We both know I have plenty of space in my house, so just know you have that as your backup."

"Hunter, how could you offer such a thing?" How could I not?

"Charlotte, how are you still questioning how much I care about you and Lana?"

"I'm not questioning that. I'm questioning every other part," she says, pulling her hood back down so it hides her eyes. She turns around and continues walking as she pulls her phone out of her pocket. It's lit up and ringing a soft tone. I take a step closer as she studies the name on the phone and intentionally brings it in front of her so it's out of my sight. It doesn't matter though because I already saw it. Someone by the name of Lance. Lance. Who the hell is Lance? I've never heard her mention a Lance, and why wouldn't she pick up the call? Although she has taken her glove off and is now texting someone—Lance, I assume. Is she seeing some guy named Lance? I am still the one she asked to look at her washing machine. Is that a good thing?

I give Charlotte the space I'm guessing she wants and grab the two girls, one under each arm, as I shuffle down the snow-covered street. The girls are hitting me and shaking their snow covered fists at me through laughter. I love how much these two love each other and it's just another reason I would be heartbroken if Charlotte moved.

As we approach our driveways, I assumed the lack of conversation might get awkward but there is zero awkwardness as Charlotte takes Lana by the arm and leads her up their driveway without so much as saying goodbye.

"Is Charlotte mad?" Olive asks. Obviously, it isn't in my head if Olive is noticing it, too.

"Not sure," I tell her, tugging her into the house. "I need you to go change your pants because we have to go out for a few minutes."

"Where are you going?" AJ asks from the other room. "It's horrible out there."

"Yeah, where are we going, Daddy?"

"The store," I answer.

"We have food," AJ responds. "Dude, you shouldn't be going back out in that."

I'm looking back and forth between AJ and Olive, both looking back at me. I take my phone from my pocket and thumb in another text to Ari.

Me: Are you still there?

A minute passes before the three little dots flicker beneath my text.

Ari: Unfortunately. I don't think I'm going anywhere tonight.

I replace my phone in my pocket and glance over to Olive. "Do you want to come with me or stay here with Uncle AJ?"

AJ is glaring at me and crosses his arms over his chest. "Olive, why don't you stay here and help me make something yummy for dinner."

Olive covers her mouth and giggles. "Uncle, you can't even make Lucky Charms."

I laugh along with Olive because it's true. AJ lunges for her and flips her over his shoulder. "Oh yeah, little girl?" Giggle fits erupt as he tickles her until she's breathless. "That's why I need you to stay here and help me."

"Okay, okay," she agrees. "Daddy, I should stay here with Uncle so he doesn't ruin the food."

"Where are you really going, Hunt?" AJ asks. I look at Olive, now realizing that bringing her with me wouldn't have been a good idea, nor do I think she should know where I'm going. Allowing her to get attached to any other woman in my life right now isn't healthy for her. Not yet, anyway.

"Go upstairs and change your pants," I tell Olive. "You're soaked."

She skips up the stairs, followed by her door closing.

"Ari is stuck at her shop and she agreed to talk to me. The sooner I can figure all of this out, the sooner I can stop debating my life decisions," I explain.

"For the fact that you are acting partially normal this second, I won't give you shit for trekking out into a blizzard for some chick—not that it's normal to do that."

She isn't some chick. AJ knows this but that's how he sees her. Arguing this won't help anything, it'll just waste more time. "Do you mind watching Olive for a bit? I'll try to keep it under two hours."

"Dude, it'll probably take you two hours to get there in this crap."

"I'll keep you updated," I tell him. I look out the window, watching a plow fly by. "I'll be fine."

Olive comes flying back down the stairs in sweatpants and t-shirt with her dress-up apron on. "Ready!"

"When I get home, I want to hear more about what happened with Alexa," I tell him. I do feel guilty for completely ignoring his life issues.

"Not much to tell," he says. "In fact, I'd like to forget her name all together."

"Understood," I say, slipping on my jacket.

"Make sure you're home in time for dinner, Daddy," Olive shouts from the kitchen.

"Yes, Ma'am." Another giggle floats through the air. "Love you, Olive."

"Love you!"

Two hours. Pft. Try twenty minutes. I followed a salting truck half of the way, which sort of worked out perfectly. At least they're keeping up with the roads. As I'm driving, I realize I never responded to Charlotte's request to fix her washing machine. Well, she'll just have to wait or let Lance take care of it.

When I pull up to the flower shop, I create a spot for myself along the sidewalk. I'm sure I shouldn't be parking here right now since the plows are trying to get by but there's nowhere else to park. Plus, Ari's car is buried right in front of me.

I kick through the foot of snow and make a narrow path up to the glass door of the flower shop. I'm guessing this might be why she isn't going anywhere tonight. Besides the fact that her car is pretty much stuck, thanks to the drifts, the door is also snowed in.

I walk back to my truck and grab a shovel out of the bed. Clearing a path, I remove the snow so the door can move freely, but as I pull on the handle, the door doesn't budge. I knock a few times, rubbing away a coat of frost on the window so I can see inside.

Through the blur, it only takes a few seconds before Ari appears in the door with a smile. She unlocks the deadbolt and pushes on the door. "You were stuck in here and felt the need to lock the door?" I ask with amusement.

"You never know who is crazy enough to have a shovel and dig me out so they can break in and abduct me," she says with a cunning grin. Her soft laughter fills the air as she brushes a few strands of hair away from her cheek. At the same moment I'm watching her, the mixed scent of different flowers hits me all at once, nearly making my knees weak. So many of the scents remind me of Ellie. She always had a new flower obsession and each flower had its moment in the spotlight under the skylight in our family room. The aroma from the flowers always filled the house.

"Have you always been into flowers?" I ask Ari.

She bobs her head from side to side as if her answer is neither here nor there. She lifts a planter from one of the stands and places it down on the glass counter. "Actually, no, but because my parents are gardeners, I was always around plants and flowers. You know, too much of anything can sometimes be more than enough."

"Yeah, I can understand that." Kind of.

"Anyway, once I recovered from the transplant, I sort of needed a fresh start. I considered going back to teaching but they made me take a year off for liability reasons and I wasn't about to waste precious days of my life sitting in front of the TV. My parents were friends with the guy that owned this place and he was getting ready to retire. A month later, I was running the shop. Crazy, right?"

"I guess everything happens for a reason," I tell her. "Ellie would have loved this shop. She lived and breathed for flowers. It was just a hobby but it was her greatest passion."

"I know," she says. "She told me many times." Ari moves the planter to the back counter and I follow. "Knowing that definitely helped with my decision to manage this shop. I think it's a nice tribute to her." She turns around, finding me probably a little too close. "I know it's silly but I sometimes wonder if she can sense me being in the shop here—you know if she really is connected to me and stuff."

"I'd like to think that," I tell her. Her words are enticing, soul-filling, wonderful and similar to the thoughts I don't share with anyone. Why does that make me want to tell this woman I love her? Why do I want to kiss her and press my hand up against her heart and never separate from her existence again? I do not know her. This is wrong.

If I'm wrong, though, why is she looking at me like I'm right? My heart is pounding so hard I can feel it in my head and in my arms and legs. I just need to... I shouldn't. There's Charlotte. And Ellie, but part of Ellie is inside of her. I have to...I think...

The struggle is short lived and I act on an un-thought-out whim, cupping my hands firmly around her face as I press my lips against hers. I startle her, as well as me, and she falls heavily against the back counter, her hands moving back and forth from my waist to the counter behind her, as if she can't make up her mind on the right or wrong of this situation. I'm kissing a complete stranger who I might soulfully know the most in this world. My chest is against hers and holy shit, I can feel her heart pounding. My cheeks are burning and I squeeze my eyes shut tightly, avoiding tears that would destroy this moment before it had a chance to unravel. I can feel her heart. Ellie's heart. It's beating against mine again. It's beating against me. I can feel it. I can feel her. Ellie. Ellie. It's pounding so hard, just like mine. It feels everything mine feels, just like it always had before. She's in there.

As our lips part, I realize I didn't even consider the sensation of her mouth against mine; my only thoughts were focused on her heart. That's all I can feel. Still. I can feel it against my chest even though there is space between us now.

"Hunter," she says between heavy breaths. "Is this wrong?" Yes. Completely wrong. My mind is spinning between Charlotte and Ellie and now Ari, and why would I throw myself into a mess like this?

"I don't know."

"Don't you have a girlfriend?" she asks. "Oh my God, you do. This should not be happening. I shouldn't have done that...Ellie. God, I don't know what I'm thinking right now. This isn't right. This definitely isn't right. This, us, we are not supposed to be doing this."

I agree with everything she just said. I shouldn't be kissing her when I feel the way I do about Charlotte, but my lips against hers make Ellie's heart beat faster. This attraction is a connection, one I am so desperate for that I can't tell her I'm sorry for what I just did. "Charlotte broke things off with me so I could figure out what I want," I tell her. "Meeting you has added a whole lot of confusion into my life." Maybe that's too honest.

"Oh," she says. We're staring into each other's eyes and all I want to do is see Ellie's soul within her beautiful gaze. But souls cannot be seen, they can only be felt and I feel it. I'm at a loss for words. I don't know what to say to her. "Why did you kiss me if I'm adding confusion to your life?"

The answer shouldn't be complicated. How do I tell her I fell for the words on every typewritten note she gave me? How do I tell her I want to be near her because it's like being near Ellie? It makes some sort of screwed up sense in my head, but I'm not sure it would make much sense to anyone else. "I wanted to," I say simply.

"I don't think you want to get involved with me, Hunter."

Not that I can decide whether it's a good idea to get involved with her or not, but why would she just spit that out? Clearly the kiss didn't bother her since she didn't stop me. "Why?" I should be asking myself the same question. Because of Charlotte.

She smiles at me and touches her finger to her lips before slipping out of reach. Grabbing the broom from the corner of the showroom, she begins sweeping around me. I place my hand on the broomstick and stop her. "Why?" I ask again.

"I'd fall for you," she says.

"You don't have to," I tell her as if it would be that easy.

"I know, but I would."

"So what if you did?" What am I saying? Love? I can't love anyone else...I don't think. I should be telling her she doesn't want to be with me. I might only want to be with her for what's inside of her body.

"You'd end up hurt," she finishes the back and forth with this stabbing statement.

"How could you be so sure?" I push for a deeper explanation, one I don't quite need but curiosity is stabbing at my brain.

Ari stares coldly into my eyes and I swear I see her thoughts assembling within her gaze. "Hunter," she begins, though it sounds more like a prolonged pause.

"What is it?" I ask, gripping my hands around her slim shoulders. The sensation of touching her is foreign, considering I jumped from every other stage of getting to know someone right to kissing her.

Her focus breaks from my face and she looks down between us. I want to press my finger under her chin so she looks back up at me but I give her the time she needs, hoping she decides to divulge.

"Ellie's doctor told her she had an unruptured aneurysm. They discovered it when they did a CT scan after the car accident you were both in." Her words are soft, almost hard to hear, but the meaning of what she is saying is louder than a piercing foghorn. "The doctors told her that operating on it would only result in a fifty percent chance of survival. They also told her that by not operating on it, she would only have a fifty percent chance of survival. Because of where the aneurysm was located, it could rupture with any intense activity or trauma. The doctors advised her not to pursue a pregnancy."

My knees literally give out and I'm on the ground, leaning up against the counter, staring blankly out the glass door. Everything I thought I knew was not accurate. Ellie was hiding the world from me behind her truth-filled eyes.

"She wanted a baby so badly," I say out loud to myself. "We tried to conceive Olive for three years. If I had known—"

"You wouldn't have Olive," she interrupts me with sternness laced into her voice.

I could never respond to that with what first comes to mind because I would never give Olive up for anything in the world, but I should have known. "She kept this from me," I say. Ari slides down against the counter, the clamminess of her hands scrape down the glass as she places herself close to my side. "I thought I knew everything about her, down to the order she put her make-up on in the morning. We didn't keep things from one another, and now I know she kept everything from me."

"This isn't everything," Ari says. "This is one secret that she kept from you."

"This one secret is everything."

"I asked her once what you thought about her condition and I'll never forget the look that swept across her face at that moment. I had never seen that look before, not that I've known Ellie my entire life or anything but she was my mentor and we spent a lot of time together." Ari reaches up and sweeps the back of her hand under her eye. "She told me it was something she couldn't figure out how to tell you and she hadn't decided if she wanted to ruin your life by telling you. Even her parents didn't know. She knew the chances of surviving were poor and the last thing she wanted was to be treated differently because of it. Especially by you."

"I don't understand why she would want a baby so badly if this is all true." How could this all be true? I was with her at the hospital after the accident—she never said a word. The doctor we saw for the pregnancy, he would have had to know, too. This information had to be in her files somewhere. Why would no one tell me?

"She wanted to leave her mark in this world, and Olive was the way for her to do that," Ari says, placing her hand on mine.

"She left me purposely, leaving me with a little girl who I'm raising alone." She did this deliberately and I don't know how to accept this fact. How could she ever assume I would want to be left without her, and as a single parent?

"You were left with a part of Ellie," Ari says, as if she can hear my thoughts.

"Why the hell would she tell you all of this? You were a student to her—student teacher, whatever. Why the hell you instead of me?" I stand up, doing little to conceal my growing rage. Why Ari and not fucking me? I deserved to know. I was her life. I was the one pushing her closer to her death every month we tried to get pregnant, and nothing in her head made her think we weren't meant to have a baby so she could live. Nothing made her think that. We could have lived a relaxing life and kept her safe against extraneous activity. It didn't have to be this way. She could have lived.

Pacing from the door to the middle of the shop and back, I notice Ari out of the corner of my eye, hugging herself in the back of the shop, looking a bit frightened. I shouldn't be blaming her. I should be blaming Ellie. All of these years I have refused to feel any resentment or anger toward Ellie, even if I felt it sometimes on the nights when Olive wouldn't sleep and the days she was sick and I had no idea what to do to help her. I wanted to scream so loudly in hopes of Ellie hearing me so she knew how angry I was about having to raise our little girl alone. What did I know about raising a kid? Nothing. I was supposed to have a partner in this life. Olive was supposed to have a mother.

Olive was supposed to have a mother.

Olive was never meant to have a mother. She was only meant to have me.

"A car accident, even a fender-bender could have killed her," Ari says through a whisper. "Then you would have been left with nothing." I don't want to listen to Ari and her thought-out words. I don't want to hear the truth or any more lies. Now I know why Ari didn't want to tell me and I can pretty much assume why Ellie didn't tell me. I would have talked her out of it. I would have put her in a bubble and cared for her. She didn't give me that option, though. "Instead, she left parts of her behind." Ari places her hand on her heart, clutching at the material over her chest. "Olive has so many parts of Ellie."

"You don't even know her," I remind Ari. I know it's an asshole comment but it's true. Unless she knows Olive, too, and just decided not to share that with me either.

"You're right, but it takes two people to create another human being; therefore she is, in fact, half Ellie."

"Okay," she says. With nothing left to argue about, Ari wraps her hand around mine and pulls it toward her body. Placing the palm of my hand flat against her chest, she holds it there firmly. I close my eyes and focus on the thumping rhythm. "It's her." Ari's gentle voice vibrates through her chest.

I focus solely on the beat of Ellie's heart, trying to remember a time where I listened to her heartbeat. There's only one time that I can remember, though. The first heart doppler check we got at the beginning of her pregnancy. We thought the heartbeat was Olive's but it was really Ellie's. It had taken a minute before we heard a similar sound, just softer and more delicate. I didn't consider how badly I would want to remember that sound. Does it sound the same in Ari's chest? Does it work that way?

"When the doctor told me there was a heart waiting for me, I knew," Ari says. "The doctors told me there was little to no chance of finding a heart donor with the same blood type. So I knew it was Ellie. Excitement, relief, and gratefulness never set in when I heard the words come from my doctor's mouth. I had less than a month to live at that moment. I was deteriorating by the day and we were at the point of looking for hospices since it was becoming too difficult for my parents to care for me themselves."

"You weren't happy that you were getting a heart?" I ask, clarifying what she's explaining.

She presses her lips together as an uneasy smile threatens to show through the evident pain. "Like I said, I knew it was Ellie. I knew she had died. I knew she was due to have Olive, and I knew the likelihood of her surviving labor and delivery."

I want to tell her this isn't fair, that she knew and I had my life ripped out from beneath me but I'm still focused on feeling her heart beating beneath my hand. I know why Ellie named Olive before she was born now. She knew it was over. "I don't know whether to be angry or grateful for her actions, but I'm hurt. Incredibly hurt."

"I can imagine," she says, releasing my hand from hers. "But you can't be angry with her. She didn't want to die, but sometimes in life we don't get to choose the path we want, sometimes we're only left with shitty options and she chose the less shitty one in her mind." How can I agree with that? "She didn't deceive you to hurt you...she made the choices she did because she loved you so much. She wanted to leave something behind that belonged to both you and her. That something was someone...Olive."

As much as I need space right now, my hand isn't moving, so I close my eyes, trying to piece everything together. My head hurts. The thoughts coming and going are in a jumbled mess. How did things end up like this?

"Why aren't you teaching now? Your year off has come and gone. Why didn't you go back?" I ask her, wondering why she would spend all of that time being mentored by Ellie and now not be doing what she wanted to do.

"In order to maintain my license the year following my surgery, I would have needed to get my MBA. I decided against it," she says.

"Why, though?"

"For the same reason you shouldn't consider getting involved with me, Hunter." A struggling grin tugs at the corner of her lips and she cups her soft hand around my cheek. "I'm not good for you. I'm simply the soul carrier of Ellie's heart. If our paths were to have crossed in different circumstances, we might feel different, but that's not the case."

This confuses me. I didn't know who she was when we first met in the gardens and yet I was pulled to her—I was attracted to her and her expressive way of speaking since it sounded so much like the way Ellie spoke. "That's not true," I argue.

"I was at the gardens because I visit Ellie on a regular basis to thank her for her generous life-giving gift. That's why we met. If it wasn't for Ellie's heart, we wouldn't have met," she says.

That's a ridiculous statement, especially for someone who seems as intelligent as she is. "Unless you're God, I'm not sure you can truly know that for sure." She removes her hand from my face and stands up to walk toward the front door, forcing space between my hand and Ellie's heart. She peers out through the glass. "What is the real reason you didn't get your MBA, and what is the real reason why I would end up hurt by you?"

"The snow has stopped," she says.

I stand up too and move up behind her, placing my hands on her shoulders. "Why?"

She turns around, her hair flying into my face as she faces me. "We all have our secrets, Hunter. Mine is my reason for everything."

Without an understanding as to why her words don't drive me utterly mad, I take her face back into my hands and kiss her gently, focusing on the texture of her lips and the warmth her skin offers mine. Her arms wrap around my back, squeezing me gently but tightly. I slide my hand between us, pressing it up against her chest, feeling the heavy thuds of her heart as our lips remain connected. Needing a more intense reaction, I slip my tongue into her mouth, immediately noticing the effect on her heart, the increase of beats, the speed in which it's racing. I still have an effect on this heart.

Ari pulls away breathlessly, looking at me with wonder in her eyes. "What did you feel?" she asks, dragging her tongue along her bottom lip before biting down on it.

"Your heart," I tell her.

"And I feel her heart." By the look of expression on her face, it wasn't the right response. I don't know what a right response would consist of though. Should I tell her she's hot and an amazing kisser? Is that what women really want to hear? Because I've always seemed to think differently. "You're in love with this heart, that's all this is."

"Ari, that's ridiculous," I argue, but maybe she's right...

She huffs a quiet chuckle and lightly presses her fingers against my mouth. "The flowers, the scents, the truths, this heart—it's her, not me, Hunter. You don't know me."

"I do know you. I know every word you have written to me over the past five years. I have learned about your desires, wants, needs, and passions. You're appreciative of everything you have and you live as if you are caring for the most prized possession this world has ever had. Your stories and updates on how you are caring for Ellie's heart are what made me know you. The only thing I didn't know was your name and where you lived."

She creates space between us, seemingly struggling with my words, struggling with this moment. "Everything you have said means a great deal to me, knowing you read every word I wrote, knowing you appreciated the thoughts behind each letter. Writing became my inspiration to heal from the guilt attached to this borrowed heart, but the letters were never intended to make you fall for me because I know I am not the path for you. Please understand that. And those words, they were words to describe what Ellie's heart was feeling, so I understand why you felt connected. I came to realize I was doing you more harm than good by sending you those letters, that's why I put a stop to it. It wasn't so I could make you fall for me."

Her explanation of why I should not think anything more of her than the recipient of Ellie's heart dumps me into a new level of confusion. "What are you saying?"

Her eyebrows pucker as she presses her hand to her throat as if she's feeling strangled. "I don't know," she cries softly as she throws her arms around my neck and places her head against my chest. Her body trembles within my hold and her breaths are shallow and uneven. If I'm confused, so is she. The weakness within her decisions is making my chest ache.

I take her by the hand and bring her into the back room where I find a couch. As we both sit down, she looks at me with tears clouding her eyes. "This is wrong," she says. "I do like you, Hunter...but I think it could be for the wrong reasons." Ari brushes the back side of her hand under her eyes, wiping away the fallen tears. "I don't know if what I feel is because of Ellie's heart or if it's because I selfishly needed to know you. I just wanted to make sure your life wasn't destroyed after Ellie's sacrifice for me. The pain I felt for you that day in the hospital made me want to help you the way Ellie helped me. I won't ever be able to know the answer to my own question; therefore, this could never work."

"But what if I only want to be with you because of Ellie's heart? Doesn't it make our confusion even?" What am I saying? Why am I saying this out loud? It's ridiculous...I think. She is a person, too, not just placed on this earth to carry around Ellie's heart—which is how I have imagined her for five years. That's terrible.

"Maybe it makes us even, but you have to understand, I might be good at being part of your present, but I will never be part of your future. I think we're meant to be in each other's lives for a different reason. A reason that makes sense to me and that I'm not sure I can explain."

"You should never assume what our future will hold," I say. Regardless, she has summed up my self-confusion in only a breath full of words. I just need her in my life, in any capacity, simple as it may be. "Though, you make everything make sense."

CHAPTER SEVENTEEN

MAY
- TWO MONTHS LATER -

"HEY, ARE YOU ready?" I shout into the kitchen. "If you don't want to come, you can wait here."

She grabs her sweater from the closet. "Yup, I'm good. I just wanted to get the frosting on the cake."

I poke my head into the kitchen, looking at the cake she made. "It's pretty awesome."

"Yeah, I'm not that bad in the kitchen," she says, playfully punching me in the shoulder as she walks past me. "You're sticking around tonight, right?"

"Yeah, about that, I was going to see if you were okay with Ari joining us tonight. She wants to meet you and Lana and spend some time with Olive." The oddness of my relationship with Ari is something that's hard to explain. It isn't your typical boyfriend/girlfriend thing. I can only explain what we have as a connection I can't imagine breaking away from. I feel like I need to be around her and she feels the same way. I love being with her, learning everything about her. It's the strangest relationship I've ever had, but it feels right to me.

"Of course. As long as you don't mind if Lance joins us, too," Charlotte says. That's a whole other story. Charlotte has actually moved on. Boyfriend label and all. I can't blame her. My mind is in ten places and she deserves to be the one and only focus in a man's life. She kind of knows the gist of my relationship with Ari, but it baffles her at the same time. From what I can tell, Lance can offer her a simple, non-confusing relationship. I want Charlotte to be happy, but I'd be lying if I said it didn't suck to hear about him.

"Of course not," I laugh. "I love Lance-a-lot. Get it?"

"You're an ass," she says, opening the front door.

"Yeah, an ass who lets your cute butt live here." It's been a little over a month since Charlotte and Lana moved in. With no child support coming in, Charlotte was going to have to move out and rent her house to make ends meet. It seemed like the right thing to do...letting Lana and her move in with Olive and me. I told myself that's why I did it. That, and so Olive and Lana wouldn't be separated. But the truth is, I didn't want Charlotte to move away. I like having her around, even if we're not "together" anymore.

"You're not allowed to talk about my butt," she sings, walking down the driveway. I pull the door closed and jog up to Charlotte's side. "You sure you're going to be cool with meeting Lance tonight?" she asks. I knew this meeting was inevitable at some point since she's kept things private until now. The only thing I've seen of Lance is his stupid ass haircut from the car when he picks her up.

"Of course. He makes you happy, so that makes me happy," I lie.

"Right," she laughs quietly, which blends into an awkward silence.

We walk side by side past several houses as the quiet between us starts to burn. Things between Charlotte and I have been fine. Just fine. It's been a little awkward at times, but overall it's worked out pretty well. We don't ask and we don't tell. It took her weeks to actually admit that she was dating Lance, but it was easy to make the assumption based on the extra perfume she was dousing herself with before leaving at night.

Regardless of our two separate lives veering off in different directions right now, I like having Charlotte and Lana around. My lonely house that Olive and I felt so small in just a few months ago is now full. It's nice.

"Are you getting nervous about your court date?" I ask Charlotte, breaking the silence.

"Very," she sighs. "My lawyer thinks she has enough evidence to at least open the case back up but we won't know for sure until things get started."

"It's a gamble, I guess." I can't imagine how she must feel. I have a pit in my stomach just thinking about her situation.

"Why, are you eager to get rid of me?" she asks, peering over at me.

I cup my hand around her elbow, stopping her in her steps, and force her to turn toward me. "I don't want you to leave, Charlotte." Wanting what's best for her, I want her to get the case opened back up. At the same time, the thought of her moving out fills me with dread.

"How can you say that?" she asks, pulling her arm from my grip. "You're in a relationship, or whatever you want to call it, with someone and so am I." She has a point, and to tell the truth, even though it's hard living with her while she's dating Lance, the thought of not having her in my life at all would feel way worse.

"I say it because it's how I feel," I admit.

She pulls in a sharp breath and clears her throat, then changes the subject. "I got more milk and Lucky Charms this morning. Olive told me she ran out. I tried to explain to her that she doesn't need to fill the bowl up to the rim since she only eats about half of it," she says.

"Good luck with getting her to go along with that. Olive likes things in a certain way. Or else," I laugh. "But thank you for doing that, though. You didn't have to. I could have gotten her more cereal."

"It's no big deal," Charlotte replies. "I needed a couple of things at the store anyway."

We reach the bottom of the hill and take a seat on the bench. "Are you heading back to your job site for a bit before dinner?" Charlotte asks. "I noticed AJ has been gone since six this morning."

"Yeah, I have to help him finish up after I grab Olive. It was a quick in and out job today."

"Is he doing okay?" Charlotte asks, crossing her legs and leaning back into the bench.

"Yeah, I guess so. I think he's gone on a few dates over the past month but nothing serious. He might still be bent out of shape over Alexa. I couldn't blame him."

"Maybe," she agrees. "She definitely gave him good reason."

Our conversation fizzles when the bus pulls up. "It's today," Olive shouts, jumping off the bus. "It's toooodayyyy."

"What's today?" Charlotte asks her with a grin. I'm sure she suspects Olive's exuberance is associated with Lana's birthday party tonight.

Olive stops singing her words and directs her body toward me. "Oops," she says. "I forgot."

I wrap my arm around her and pull her in to my side, giving her a quick kiss on the top of her head.

"Oh," Charlotte says. "Are you excited to see Ari tonight?" I'm not sure how Charlotte put two and two together so fast, but she did. I had told Olive about Ari before I asked Charlotte if it was okay to bring her to Lana's birthday dinner tonight. I've wanted them to meet but Charlotte has come up with excuses each time I've tried to make plans. She would never admit to being jealous, especially since she's with Lance, so I really don't get it.

"Yeah," Olive whispers, "but only a little. It's just because she looks like a princess, you know." While I know Olive was trying to downplay her uber excitement, I don't think she realizes that she just hammered that nail in a little harder.

"Well, I can't wait to meet this princess," Charlotte says, playing along, giving me an indecipherable look. I scrunch my nose and shake my head, trying to tell her that Olive's description is mildly off. Except it's not. Ari does look like some fairytale princess. But that's not the reason I want to be so close to her.

"We get to meet Mr. Lance tonight, too," Lana pipes in. Okay, so I feel a little better knowing that Charlotte had already made this plan even though she just asked me if I was okay with it. It's almost worse that she invited him over without talking to me than it was for me to invite Ari over without talking to her. It's my house.

We're even. I think we can just leave it at that.

"Olive, we have to go help Uncle finish a job."

"Oh," she says, kicking a small pile of dirt. "I thought I was going to help Charlotte cook."

"She can stay with me," Charlotte says while yanking Lana's backpack off.

"Yes!" Lana shrieks, yelling so loudly her birthday crown flies off of her head and spirals into a gust of wind. I run to catch it, grabbing it mid-air. "Thank you, Hunter," Lana shouts, running over and wrapping her arms around my leg. "You're the best."

Why does it feel like the four of us have turned into a family? It feels so normal, yet completely abnormal at the same time. I mean, we're not together, yet, I could guess that we're closer than some couples. That right there makes this weird as hell. We're doing this all wrong.

Just to confirm my thoughts, I walk behind Charlotte and the girls, admiring the fact that Charlotte has her arms wrapped around both girls, one on each side as if they were both hers. Maybe we were just meant to find each other so we could be each other's solid rock, the sturdiness we both desperately need in our lives right now. Could that be the reason we were meant to meet?

Once in a while I cave and let Olive stay with Charlotte after school, partially because she gets a chance to do her homework while she's not tired, and she really enjoys the girl time with Charlotte and Lana. It has been hard letting go and making the decision to do what's right for Olive rather than what feels right to me.

Amy—the listener, as I call her—has helped me work through my selfish traits versus what is being mixed up for my love for Olive. It turns out that someone can actually be smothered by love, even a daughter. As a dad, I'm a work in progress, I guess.

We step into the house and the girls run upstairs quickly. Charlotte is standing in front of me with a look I can't figure out. Maybe she's thinking what I'm thinking. "I miss you," I want to tell her. Even though we live together, I miss her. I miss the "us" that was too short lived. It's like our relationship continued to grow even after she ended things with me. It's not supposed to work like that. I step up to her and wrap my arms around her neck. "You look like you need a hug today."

"I do," she whispers.

Driving to the job site, I pull up to the driveway, finding AJ loading up the truck with the tools. As I take only a step out of my door, he shouts, "I just finished up. I wanted to make sure we were home in time for dinner, so I turned up the AC/DC and got that shit done."

"You're awfully chipper about dinner tonight," I say, with a sort of question lingering through my words.

"Uh," he laughs, running the sleeve of his arm across his forehead. "Do you have any idea how much drama is going to take place tonight? And I have front row seats! Yeah, not missing that for the world."

"Drama?"

"Yeah, you both have a date and it isn't each other," he laughs, a gut rolling laugh.

"How the hell did you—?"

"You two are so fucking loud on the phone. You think the walls are soundproof? What did you think was going to happen when you made me move into the room between you two?" he asks, continuing to laugh. Such an ass.

"You're about to move into the basement," I tell him, sliding back into the truck. "Plus, I can't count Ari as a date. I told you, things are just…"

"Fucking weird," he finishes my sentence. "You want to be with a woman who you don't fuck, just so you can be closer to her heart. Does this sound strange when you hear it coming from my mouth? Because it's weird as hell coming from you. You are aware this is the weirdest thing I've ever heard of, right?"

"I wouldn't expect you to understand," I tell him. "Ari and I just get each other and our relationship is something we both desperately need. It's healing."

"So then why aren't you with Charlotte if you and Ari are just friends?" AJ adds in.

"I wasn't the one who broke things off and now she's with someone else, so it is what it is and we're both where we need to be, I guess, plus I never said Ari and I are just friends." In truth, I don't know what Ari and I are.

"Neither one of you are where you should be," he says, climbing into his truck. "You may think I know nothing, but you and Charlotte are supposed to be together. I know that much. No one said you can't be with the person you love and have a friend who owns your wife's heart at the same time." AJ finishes his thought and then steps back out of the truck. "Holy shit, your life is so fucking confusing. Dude...I don't even know." And with his last bit of insightful information, he shakes his head and hops back into his truck. Thank you for the talk, AJ.

Charlotte is putting the garnishes on the turkey and I'm stirring up the gravy as Olive and Lana both shout from the living room. "Someone is here!"

"Ooh, Oh, Oh!" AJ shouts, running down the hall into the living room. Sometimes, I swear he's an eight-year-old trapped in a man's body. I know he's just playing along with the girls, but part of him is teasing both Charlotte and me. My chest tightens and my palms are a bit sweaty. Whether it's Lance or Ari coming in, both are making me feel uneasy right now. This wasn't a great idea, for either of us.

Plus if this situation is difficult for AJ to understand, it is probably confusing the hell out of the girls. We have waited a while before bringing either of these two into this house but we don't have a typical situation. Actually, I wonder how much Lance even knows about Charlotte's living situation.

"Someone else is here, too!" Olive yells. Oh great, they're both here. They're both going to walk up the driveway at the same time and they're both going to wonder who the hell each other is.

I lean back to look out into the living room, seeing AJ manning the door. He opens it and gives them a wave. "Hi there! Come on in, the party is just getting started!" Why does he sound like the biggest tool ever right now? With the way he's talking, he should be wearing a cardigan, Dockers, and penny loafers, rather than a nearly see-through white t-shirt with paint stains and torn jeans.

"Hi," Ari's voice wafts through the house. "I'm Ari, you must be—AJ?" she asks with question, unsure, but assuming, as well.

"That, I am," he says. "You must be Ari," he says in a teasing voice dripping with sarcasm.

I wipe my hands off on the dish rag and place the wooden spoon down on a napkin. "Hey hon," I say, walking toward Ari. "I see you've met AJ. Feel free to ignore him; he's in a particularly obnoxious mood today."

"Hon," I hear Charlotte's voice quietly echo through the kitchen. I don't think she intended for me to hear that, but I did. Irritation noticed.

"How was work?" I ask Ari.

"Good, we did well today. You know, with Mother's Day in a few days, things have been a little crazy." Mother's Day—the day I have hidden Olive and myself from in a dark room as we watch movies from the minute we wake up until the minute we go to bed. I have done my best to avoid her knowing much about Mother's Day. I don't think it's necessary, seeing as it would probably cause her unnecessary sadness. She's aware it's a holiday but she knows it as the day we watch movies together all day. Movies without commercials, I should add.

Ari moves her hand out from behind her back and reaches out with a small bunch of blue jasmines. "Olive, I heard these are your favorite?" she says, leaning down to hand them to her.

Olive runs over to Ari and carefully takes the flowers from her hand. "These are my favorite. My mom's, too. That must be why you drew them on the back of daddy's letter," she giggles.

"It is," Ari says softly.

Olive looks up to me and back at Ari. "Daddy said you knew her?"

A tight-lipped smile touches Ari's mouth, illuminating her deep dimples. "I did know her. She was a beautiful and incredible woman and you look just like her." Ari touches her fingertip to Olive's nose.

"Daddy says that, too," Olive giggles.

"Hi, I'm Charlotte." Charlotte steps out from behind me and offers her hand to Ari. "I—I've heard so much about—you. You—," she laughs uneasily. "It's nice to—this is nice." Her voice sounds friendly enough, although unsure, as she introduces herself.

"Oh my goodness," Ari says gleefully, "I-I" she stutters, sounding similar to the way Charlotte does. "I've heard so much about you, too. Hunter gushes about you all of the time." Gushes? Geez. Didn't know I was going that far. Charlotte's cheeks turn a scarlet hue and she backs away, moving toward the front door where Lance is now standing. Wow, this is awkward.

"Hey babe," he says to Charlotte. Babe. Gross. He gives her a peck on the cheek and runs his hand down to the small of her back. I shouldn't be watching, but I am, and now I know Ari is watching me watching them since she nudges her shoulder into mine before gripping the sleeve of my shirt and pulling me into the kitchen. This was such a bad—no this was a fucking horrible idea.

"Are you okay?" Ari asks me, grabbing the wooden spoon from the counter and stirring the bubbling gravy. "You haven't met Lance before tonight?'

"Yeah, this is a little more stressful than I thought it would be. I'm just glad you came," I tell her, trying to laugh through my words.

"Why? Because your ex-girlfriend invited her new boyfriend over to your house to celebrate her daughter's birthday?" Ari's eyes are squinting from her grin and her teeth are pressed firmly into her bottom lip. I can't tell if she's being sarcastic, or truthful. "Then you add me into the picture, the carrier of your wife's heart, and things can seem a little weird." Her laughter relieves some of my stress. "Relax. Everything is fine. There's a reason there is no instruction manual for life."

"Uh," yup, that's the only thing I can think to say right now because everything she just said is true.

"Hunt, not to make things more stressful, but I do have one question?"

With only a second of breathing freely, my chest tightens back up. "Yeah?"

"I'm pretty sure Charlotte is married to the chief of surgery at Brookhill Hospital. Or was, I should say...I mean, he was the chief of surgery."

"What? She's divorced."

"Oh, well, that makes sense then," Ari retorts.

"But, I didn't think he was a surgeon," I say. Although, I do remember the on-call doctor at the hospital recognizing Charlotte the day Olive fell at school. I never thought to ask how she knew anyone there because I was so wrapped up with Olive. I'm always so wrapped up that I never ask important questions. I also never thought to ask much about her ex-husband. Other than hearing he's an asshole on a daily basis, I didn't see the need to know more about him.

"Was the chief of surgery?" I ask her.

"Yes," she says, her eyes scanning the kitchen, rather than looking at me.

"So, do you know Charlotte?" I ask, holding my focus tightly on her wandering eyes. I realize wives of surgeons aren't typically found in the hospital but I can't help but wonder, after their odd greeting in the living room.

Ari looks down to where her fingers are fidgeting with the hem of her black shirt. "Yeah, I mean, Dr. Don Drake was my doctor for years. He was the best there was and I was dying. I was practically living at the hospital with the amount of testing and episodes I had, and Dr. Drake seemed to always be on an endless shift so Charlotte was around quite a bit. Actually, a few times she brought me flowers. I'm just not sure she remembers me. I'm sure she visited plenty of his patients."

It's like this whole other side of Charlotte I don't know. How could a heart surgeon of his status be consulting underground somewhere now?

"Charlotte!" I shout into the living room. I'm getting to the bottom of this.

"Hunter, what are you doing?" Ari, says, pressing her hands up against my chest. "Stop."

It is several seconds before I even hear Charlotte's feet moving across the floor and I'm guessing her hesitation is playing a part in her speed. "Do you need something?" she asks, walking over to the turkey.

"Hunter," Ari says again.

"Look at her, Charlotte," I tell her.

Charlotte turns on her heels and slips her hands into her back pockets. It takes her a minute but she lifts her chin, forcing eye contact with Ari who now looks incredibly uncomfortable. "Ariella," Charlotte says. "How could I forget you?"

Charlotte places her hand gently on Ari's shoulder. "How's the heart?"

"Did you know about Ellie?" I ask Charlotte. "Your husband, he's the chief of surgery over at Brookhill. Don Drake, is that his name? The surgeon who removed Ellie's heart." My words may be a little harsh considering Ellie died from an aneurysm, but for five years, I have had no one to blame and right now blaming him feels so damn good.

"Ex-husband," she snaps. "And I don't believe Ellie was a patient of Don's," Charlotte says softly, so softly I'm not sure she's being truthful. "He was a heart surgeon and Ellie didn't have heart problems, right?"

"No, she didn't." There is still a lingering explanation somewhere in this room and I don't know who the hell to turn to.

"You know something, don't you?" I take the wooden spoon from the counter and throw it across the kitchen. "Did you know I was the fucking reason Ellie died? Huh? Did you, Charlotte? God," I laugh. You must have. "You fucking knew about Ellie, didn't you? Clearly, HIPAA regulations don't matter in your household. You know all that doctor-patient confidentiality crap. Is that why Don doesn't have a job at the hospital anymore? Because he immorally broke laws?" As the words continue to filter from my unfiltered mouth, I hear Dad's words ringing loudly in my head. You know what assuming does.

Tears are now spilling from Charlotte's eyes, and she's holding herself tightly as Lance steps into the kitchen with his gym-buff air-lats stance. Dude, you don't fucking work out. You look like you just stare in the goddamn mirror all day flexing.

"What's going on in here? Everything okay, babe?" Fuck you and your babe shit.

"Yeah," she says, sniffling. With a hand on his shoulder, she forces a fake, tight-lipped smile and squeezes her hand around him a little more. "Just a misunderstanding. Why don't you go talk to AJ for another minute? I promise I'll be right out."

Without much concern on his part, he places a quick kiss on the top of her head and grabs a beer from the counter before heading back into the living room.

"You have some nerve accusing me of all that," Charlotte says under her breath. "You also have the audacity to upset Ari after she's only been in this house for five minutes. She didn't ask for any of this."

I glance at Ari, who is leaning awkwardly against the wall, hugging her arms around her body with her sleeves curled over her hands. Her teeth are pinched over her bottom lip and her focus is glued to the tiled floor.

I cup my hand around Ari's elbow and tug her into me. "I'm sorry."

She begrudgingly complies with my effort to make her less uncomfortable but she doesn't look at me or say anything.

"I did not know Ellie's history and to be quite honest, I didn't know much about her death. What I do know is that Don lost his job after a hospital-wide malpractice suit following Ariella's transplant. You must have heard about his case; everyone in this state heard about it. It was all over the news, as was Ari." That's why she looked familiar to Dad. Unbelievable.

I feel lost at the other end of her story. I don't remember hearing anything about this doctor. "I wasn't exactly watching the news after Ellie died. I was managing a newborn while mourning."

A sheen of sweat covers Charlotte's forehead as she rakes her fingers through her hair. "Things were kept under very tight wraps when it came down to the details but what the public knew was that Don mishandled the paperwork for the transplant. And I don't know more than that because days after the surgery, he was let go from the hospital. At the same time, he told me he wanted a divorce. I asked him over and over again what had truly happened and he would only tell me there was a misunderstanding and he was wrongfully terminated. That's how our marriage was—need to know basis only."

"Mishandled paperwork? What the hell does that mean?" I bark at her, as I pace back and forth with my hands on my hips. Did he do something to Ellie? I know that sounds absurd but what can be mishandled with organ transplant papers?

She shrugs. "Your guess is as good as mine. Regardless, he now sells scripts underground to international sources, making more money than he did as a surgeon. Except, he doesn't have to file taxes or let anyone know he's making a dime. That is why I'm here, living with you, in case you forgot."

Stunned, at a loss, and trying to piece together this garbled information, Charlotte sweeps by me, grabs the platter of sliced turkey and takes it out into the dining room.

"I know what she's talking about," Ari speaks up after Charlotte is out of hearing distance.

I huff a soft laugh. "What?"

"I didn't know he got fired because of me."

"What are you talking about?" I ask again.

"I shouldn't have gotten Ellie's heart, Hunter."

"Didn't you say she wanted you to have it?" The oxygen left in my lungs feels like it's being sucked out through a tiny straw. "Tell me what you're talking about."

"She did but I guess a living donor can't promise a heart to a particular person. It's against medical ethics or something."

I'm trying to think my words through before they spew off the tip of my tongue, ultimately putting Ari in a corner and emotionally beating her senseless. "Then how did you end up receiving her heart?" The question I form is much better than many of the other thoughts I had to choose from.

"Dr. Drake sort of had a thing for me…"

I can feel my face burning from the inside. I know I'm red. I know I look like steam should be coming from my ears. And I'm not sure I can handle whatever is about to come out of her mouth next. "You can't be serious…"

"I never gave in, Hunter, but he made his feelings pretty clear," she says, breaking her gaze from my face.

"You didn't tell anyone?" I ask, trying to keep calm regardless of how flaming angry I am right now.

"He wanted to save me more than any other doctor. I—"

"I get it," I cut her off.

"When Ellie and I figured out we had the same blood-type, she came with me to meet with him and told him she would only donate her heart if it went to me. She played him, knowing she could easily blackmail him with what I told her about Dr. Drake—the things he had said to me, the moments he tried to..." She sighs and swallows hard. "In any case, it worked. There was no paperwork. Everything was a verbal agreement."

I squeeze my hand around my chin, feeling my head begin to pound. It feels like someone just slapped me upside the head with a frying pan. "Jesus."

"There would have been no other donors—my chances were less than two percent. He didn't even put up a fight. I can only imagine what you're thinking right now, but if you were me, wouldn't you have done questionable things to save your own life?"

Guilt. That is what Ari is surviving with. Owning the heart from my dead wife, being the reason the chief of heart surgery conducted malpractice and subsequently lost his medical license. He should have lost it, regardless. Piece of shit. I wonder if the answer to her last question would be different if she asked herself that right this second. To live or die? I think most people would choose to live, regardless of what the repercussions might be.

"I get it," I tell her. I still don't get why Ellie didn't tell me any of this, though. I would have told her not to get involved.

"I don't expect you to understand. Ellie kept this from you and you have every right to be angry and heartbroken, but I promise you she kept this from you because she loved you." It doesn't matter how many times she says this, the thought of secrets, secrets this fucking big, between us, hurts like hell.

"I need a break from this conversation. My head might explode trying to come to terms with all of this." Ellie was a strong-minded woman. If there was something she wanted to accomplish, nothing was getting in her way. It doesn't come as a surprise that she would bust her way into the chief of surgery's office just to tell him what's what. Only my wife could control what happens to her organs after she dies. The thought brings a proud smile to my face—a foreign feeling when considering the unknown details of Ellie's life I've come to learn in recent months.

What I do know is that she wanted Ari to live. She made that happen.

"We should join everyone. The food is going to get cold," Ari says. I place my arm around her and lead her out to the dining room, pulling out a seat for her.

"I want to sit next to Ari," Olive says breathlessly, as she runs into the dining room. "And Daddy, you can sit on the other side of Ari."

Everyone circled around the table is quiet except AJ, who is chewing his bread obnoxiously loud while taking the time to stare at each one of us for several seconds.

"So," he says, pointing with his butter knife. "You two know each other?" He points back and forth between Charlotte and Ari. "Small world, huh?" The room goes utterly silent. Oh God, AJ. Shut the hell up! I yell, inside my head, while trying to catch his eye.

"I would hardly say we know each other," Ari responds. "Charlotte was just a lovely person who brought me flowers on occasion."

"Did you know Ari received Ellie's heart?" AJ continues with a question to Charlotte, a question I considered asking but decided to hold off on after the way the last conversation ended.

"You and Ellie were friends, right?" Charlotte asks Ari, redirecting from AJ's question.

"We just worked together, but yes, you could call us friends." Keeping my thoughts to myself. Keeping my thoughts to myself. I knew all of Ellie's friends. All of them except Ari. Why did you keep this from me, Ellie?

"And Ellie promised you her heart once she died?" Charlotte continues.

"Well—" Ari stumbles.

"Ah," Charlotte says. "Don made it very clear he was not going to lose you. I assumed the mishandling of papers might have had something to do with your case but I never knew for sure." Charlotte isn't being rude with the way in which she's stating her realization. Instead, her jaw is grinding back and forth, suppressing what looks like a possible grin. "That man was a total a-hole to me and never failed to let me down, but to his patients—some of his patients—he would never let a beautiful girl like yourself down."

"I'm sorry you had to find out like this," Ari says, cautiously.

"It doesn't really matter now," Charlotte says. "It's actually nice to finally have an answer to what happened."

"Nothing happened…" Ari says, sounding on the brink of tears.

Charlotte allows a slight smile to form over her lips, almost as if she's grateful for the answers. "Thank you."

Silence consumes the table and the discomfort grows ten-fold. Lana and Olive are staring at each other with perplexity, and AJ and Lance are probably trying to figure out what the hell everyone is talking about. I never intended for tonight to end up like this. I didn't think tonight through very well, obviously, and we have gotten way off track from celebrating Lana's birthday.

"We have a birthday girl here tonight," I say. "That's why we're all here so let's put everything else aside so we can let Lana enjoy her favorite dinner."

"You started it," Olive says, her nose crunched up and her bottom lip pursed over her top.

Charlotte snorts and mutters something under her breath, which I'm assuming is some type of sarcasm.

"So," Ari says, following my lead, "how old are you today, Lana?"

Lana holds up a hand full of fingers and then two more fingers on her other hand, but doesn't speak up. She's upset. Lana is always talking unless something is bothering her.

"Sweetie, is something wrong?" Charlotte asks her.

"Is Daddy a bad man?" she asks, fingering a hole into the piece of bread in her hand.

Again, we're all silent. Normally, we're careful about what we say out loud but things slip in anger. "No, Lana, your dad is not a bad man." Charlotte closes her eyes and clasps her fingers together. My attention is drawn to her hands, noticing the red polish coating her nails. I have never seen her nails done before tonight. She's a t-shirt and jeans girl. I take a better look at her face and see she's wearing way more makeup than usual, too. Is she trying to impress this dickwad?

"Are you lying?" Lana asks.

"Do I lie to you?" Charlotte snaps back.

"No," Lana replies.

"I want you to tell me what you want for your birthday. What have you been asking me for since September?" Charlotte asks her.

A wide grin unfurls across Lana's lips while her thoughts of her shitty dad melt away. "Ummm, a bike?" she squeals.

"Lance, could you grab Lana's gift?" Charlotte had asked me to help her with the bike and I obviously said yes but when she never followed up, I assumed she went in a different direction. Now, I realize, she just had Lance-a-lot help her. Douche.

"Sure, babe." Is that all he says?

Lance stands up, pressing his chest out to make a show of it, and groans as he pulls his chair away from the table. He points a finger at Lana and winks. "Wait until you see this, little girl." That doesn't sound creepy at all.

Lance slips out the front door and returns a minute later carrying a turquoise bike with a big hot pink ribbon on the handle bar. Lana lets out a shriek that could be confused for a pterodactyl screaming.

Olive looks excited for Lana because I just bought her a bike for her birthday, too, and the two girls have many plans to go bike riding all summer.

"Sweet ride, kid," AJ says in his tough guy voice. "How many different speeds you got on that thing?"

Charlotte thwacks AJ in the chest, forcing him to choke with laughter. "Do you like it, sweetie?"

"I love this so much, mommy!" Lana croons. With her arms flung around Charlotte's chest and Charlotte's head resting over hers, my heart warms up from the past hour of coldness. "Thank you, thank you, thank you." Lana releases her arms from Charlotte and hops over to Lance, giving him the same hug. And that hurts me. It shouldn't. I'm not her father and I'm not her mother's boyfriend, I'm only the person she is staying with right now. But I love her, regardless.

"Olive, you should go get Lana's gift now," I tell her.

"Yay!" Olive shouts while skipping up the steps. I hear her wrestling with the wrapped package in her bedroom before she returns.

"What is it? What is it?" Lana asks, gleefully.

"Two-way radios!" Olive spills the beans before Lana can open the gift but it doesn't seem to take away from the excitement. The two girls have been asking for these for the last couple of months so I thought it might be a nice gift.

After the gifts are opened and the girls have settled back down, we're digging into our cold dinner. Everyone seems content for the moment so I think we're all okay right now.

I scrape up my plate first, looking up at Charlotte just because she's sitting across from me. I catch her looking back at me with a small, almost unrecognizable grin. AJ, Ari, and Lance are all caught up in a conversation about flowers and Ari's shop, the girls are in the living room playing with their radios and Charlotte and I are lost in a staring contest. "I never wanted to cause you any more pain, Hunt," she says softly. "When you first told me Ellie's full name, I did put two and two together but with the amount of pain I saw in your eyes after so many years had passed, I didn't see the purpose of telling you who my ex-husband was. I wasn't withholding the information for any reason other than not causing you more stress."

I want to reach across the table and take her hand but that would be inappropriate right now. I believe what she's saying. "I know," I tell her.

"This town is so small it's hard not to come across someone who you haven't had some degree of connection with."

"Oh," I laugh, "I know."

I stand up from the table and collect as many plates as I can hold at once. Charlotte does the same on her side of the table and we meet in the kitchen.

"This all feels wrong," she says to me, once behind the wall between the kitchen and dining room.

"What does?"

"This whole situation tonight. I don't like Lance and I think I've come to realize that I need to fix some algorithms on my dating site because it matched us together." She looks somewhat embarrassed, and yet, humored at the same time.

"Yeah, you might want to get on that," I say, placing my hand on her shoulder. Charlotte looks over at my hand as if it is strange for me to be touching her at all. Which it is, once again, considering our current status.

"Are things still in limbo with you and Ari?" she asks.

I close my eyes briefly, unsure how to respond. "Yeah, pretty much. But she has Ellie's heart. I'm in love with that heart and I don't know if it has anything to do with Ari but I'm in no shape to push her away after wondering who she was for so long."

Charlotte places her hands on the outsides of my arms and looks up at me. "I get it," she says, her eyes squinting slightly with the sense of understanding. "I really, really get it."

"You do?"

"Yes, just be fair to your heart too, Hunt."

CHAPTER EIGHTEEN

JULY
-TWO MONTHS LATER-

"I THINK I HAVE the last of the boxes, Charlotte."

"It'll be so nice to be home again," she says. "Not that living with you and Olive hasn't been a treat, but I miss my stuff."

The renters across the street took an extra month to move out, which pushed Charlotte's plans back a little. The only thing that matters, though, is that she won the court case and Don is no longer selling scripts to the underground consultants. Proving this fact was a challenge but with Lana's well-being at stake during the very few visitations she has with Don, the judge was easier to convince with the evidence presented to him. I don't know if

Charlotte is over all of this, and I don't think she'll ever trust Don again but her life is slowly falling back into place and that is what is most important.

"Mom, do we really have to move back across the street? I love living here. Plus, Olive and I are like sisters, and you should never separate sisters. Don't you know that?" Lana and Olive have been moping around the house for the past two weeks since we told them the news. It's breaking my heart a little.

"Girls, you will only be a hundred feet away from each other. It's hardly something to be upset about," Charlotte tells them.

"I don't understand. Why are you leaving, though?" Olive asks. "Aren't you and daddy married now? Don't married people live together?"

Olive's questions stun me and a large pit gnarls at my stomach as I kneel down and pull her toward me. "Why do you think Charlotte and I got married, Olive?"

"You live together and you love Lana." Her reasons are so simple, innocent, and true, but yet so far from reality.

"Honey, that doesn't mean two people are married."

"But Daddy, you love Charlotte, too," she says, loud enough that both Charlotte and Lana hear. I can feel Charlotte's gaze burning a hole into my back right now.

My conscience can't handle many more of Olive's intellectual life questions and assumptions. "Ollie, you're six. How do you know what love is?"

A little smile forms over her lips as she closes her eyes and presses her hands into my shoulders. "It's the warmth you feel when you're around someone, like you belong together. Isn't that how you feel when Charlotte and Lana are here?" Her question stabs right through me, as I never assumed she would be so in tune with all of this, and if I had known, I would have been more careful. I'm just not sure how I could have been more careful in this situation.

"What time is Ari coming over today?" Charlotte asks.

"I don't know if she is," I respond.

"What do you mean? It's Friday. Don't you two normally go to the gardens?"

"She's been a little distant lately, but I guess I have been, too."

"How so?" Charlotte pries.

"I don't know." I kind of shrug her off. In truth, I haven't paid much attention to the lack of communication Ari has had with me, mostly because I've had back-to-back jobs for the past two weeks. I'm also a little bummed that Charlotte and Lana are leaving, so I haven't felt too motivated to do much. AJ got his own place last month and for the first time in months, it's just going to be Olive and me again. I'm happy to have our alone time back but this house is going to feel very empty as of tomorrow morning.

"Oh," Charlotte says, seeming a little surprised. She lifts a small box and brings it over to the door to label it. "That's odd."

It is weird. I pull out my phone and send Ari a text message.

Me: It's Friday, are you still coming by today?

Ten minutes pass and there is no response from her. There has been no response to the last several texts I have sent her over the past two weeks—of me checking in and asking her to have a meal with me, or just talk at least.

"Why don't you go talk to Ari at the shop?" Charlotte suggests.

I nod in response, agreeing with her suggestion. "I'm getting the feeling she might not like that but I need to know what's going on, I guess."

"Go ahead; I got the girls. We'll go start unpacking."

"Thanks," I say as I lift Olive up and hug her tightly. "I'll be back in a couple of hours."

She places her small hands against my cheeks. "Mommy's heart isn't mommy."

"Olive," I respond through a hoarse grumble. "I know that."

"It's the truth," she says into my car. "Just remember that."

I place her down and look over at Charlotte, who has her hand flattened against her chest, pulling in a deep breath. "I hope everything is okay," she tells me. "Tell her I say hello."

"You sure you're okay with the two of them while you unpack?"

"Yep, we'll be fine." Charlotte takes the few steps between us and wraps her arms around my neck—a gesture she hasn't offered since the moment she moved in here. "Thank you for saving us when I needed it the most. What you have done is unforgettable and you are truly the most genuine, best friend I have ever had. If that's what I'm lucky enough to walk away from you with, then I am grateful."

"You're talking like you're never going to speak to me again now that you aren't forced to," I respond nervously.

"I didn't say that," she says. Pulling back a bit, she sweeps her thumb across my cheek before placing a small kiss where her thumb was. The touch of her lips sends comforting warmth through my entire body and it was only my cheek that she kissed.

I grab my keys from the side table and step outside into the warm July air. The sun is hot today and the air is dry, making for the perfect summer weather—Ellie's favorite kind of day. Shortly after we got married, we would go to the gardens, find a bench directly in the sun and sit there until it got too hot. We'd hang our heads backward over the top of the bench's back as we allowed the sun to wrap us up in its heat.

Before heading to the flower shop, I take a detour to the gardens, arriving alone for the first time in a couple of months. I take the steps slowly down into the shaded area where our tree is. It's surrounded by the jasmines Ari and I planted here a couple of months ago.

I place my hand over the engraved writing and press my head against the tree. "Am I doing this all wrong, Ell? I feel like that's all I ever ask you. I just wish you could answer me for once." I sigh heavily and drop down into the grass. "I thought I had this all figured out but you know what I can't figure out? I was never supposed to have to make a decision like this. You were supposed to be with me until we were old and gray." Gripping at the sharp blades of new grass, blame filters through me like it often does. "Instead, I was a jackass and got us into a car accident. And you were a jackass and didn't tell me that the car accident shortened your life by seventy years or so. I guess us two jackasses were destined for each other. But now I'm sitting here in front of two paths and I don't know which way to go." I take a deep breath, contemplating the answer to my own question. "Ell, do I follow your heart or mine?"

"You follow yours, Hunter." Ari's voice is soft among the slight breeze. I didn't see her walk down the steps, and I didn't see her car in the lot when I came in but she's come from the path behind me, which means she was here all along.

"Ari," I say, standing up, brushing the dirt from my backside. "Why haven't you returned my texts or calls?"

She places a hand over her heart, Ellie's heart. Looping her other arm around mine, she pulls me toward the bench where we both take a seat.

"Do you remember when I told you I was no good for you, that you would end up hurt because of me?" she asks.

"Yeah, I remember that conversation." I place my hand down on her trembling knee.

"I'm selfish. I've been selfish, Hunter, but please, go along with this—whatever this has been—companionship, friendship, connection, a little more."

I don't understand what she means by that. My eyes strain against the sun as I continue staring at her with wonder. "There is no such thing as selfish, considering the hand you've been dealt."

"I've known all along that you're in love with the heart in my body, and I can't help but feel like I took it for granted—the way you treat me is like no one else has ever treated me. You're a gentleman and perfect in every other way, too. As simple as our relationship has remained, you have still managed to make me feel things I was sure I would never have the opportunity to feel, but mostly, you have made me feel alive."

"Are you saying goodbye to me?" I laugh anxiously, realizing that while I want to think it's a joke, I'm pretty sure it's not.

She looks up to the sky and closes one eye against the brightness. "I saw you and Charlotte at the grocery store last week." She pauses and smiles up at the sun. "You know you two are meant to be together, right?"

"What? Where were you? Why didn't come over to us?"

"I—I can't answer that yet."

"I don't understand where this is all coming from, Ari."

"I know," she says. "Hunter, I know you want to be around me for more reasons than just Ellie's heart. We've gotten really close, but I'm hurting your life right now. You just don't realize it."

I lean down and pick a small, white flower from the ground, holding my focus on it as I digest every word she's saying. "How could you think that?"

"Besides that I feel like I'm preventing you from moving on to have a normal relationship with Charlotte, the one person who will likely be there to grow old with you, there's one fact you have overlooked, or possibly never considered."

A gust of wind blows the small flower from my loose grip, and my heart pounds heavily as I look back over at her. Her pinched lips tell me she is struggling to retain her composure. "I don't know what you're getting at, " I say, tilting my head, and giving her a bewildered look.

"Some people are incredibly lucky and live a long life with their transplant but one out of two heart recipients don't survive for more than ten years."

"Well, you're on the better half of that fifty percent," I tell her, feeling angry that she should consider being on the other end of that half. Ellie's heart is meant to survive. With that, I see a fascinating stone I think Olive would like. Attempting to distract myself from what I'm hearing, I bend down to pick it up, noticing that it is, ironically, heart-shaped—not like a valentine heart, but a real heart.

She shakes her head and sweeps her hair behind her back. "No, I'm not," she says, through a frustrated exhale.

"What? What are you talking about?" I ask, my voice betraying my anger as I chuck the stone as far as I can throw it. "You have no way of knowing that. Ari, you shouldn't talk like that. You need to stay positive. Look how far you've come in the past six years."

"Hunter," she says calmly. "Stop. Just stop."

"Ari, what the hell are you trying to tell me right now?"

She stands up from the bench and wrings her fingers around her wrists as she paces back and forth. "Last Friday afternoon I had my bi-annual heart check-up. The doctor found something we had all been hoping not to find."

"What? Ari, tell me, please," I beg.

"The scans came back showing that I have accelerated coronary artery disease." I don't even know what that means but the word disease and artery give enough away.

"Well, they can fix that. They can give you meds or change your diet, right? Now that they know you have it, they can treat it...surely." I know I sound ridiculous and I have no idea what I'm talking about. "I'm sure they can do something to help you. Again, don't be so negative." I'm nearly yelling at her, scolding her for saying what she's saying. Why is she saying all of this to me? Why does she look like she's about to be sick? Why do I feel like I'm about to be sick? Why the hell do I feel like I might start crying like a goddamn baby here in a minute?

"They gave me a year at most, Hunter," and, just like that, she says the words I was hoping never to hear from her. "I was going to keep this to myself for fear of putting you through something like this after what you have already been through."

I stand up and, without any words to say, I grab her and pull her into me tightly. I squeeze her harder than I should, and I cry harder than I've let anyone see me cry in years. I bury my head in her shoulder, shaking her along with my shuddering body. "No," I cry. "No, no, no…"

She wraps her arms back around me. "I was given six years—a gift from Ellie. It was a gift, Hunter. I was never supposed to make it past twenty and now I'm almost thirty. It's a gift. Please, realize what she did for me. Her heart was supposed to be only for her but she shared it so I could experience just a little bit of a normal adult life. It's all I had wanted since I was diagnosed with heart failure at fifteen. I'm not sad. I'm not scared. I'm so unbelievably grateful for what you and Ellie have given me." What did I give her? I didn't give her Ellie's heart. I would have fought Ellie on giving away her heart if I had known her plans. I wanted to keep her together and whole for my own selfish reasons, which is crazy since she was cremated into a billion pieces, but because she was smart enough not to tell me, Ari was given time because of Ellie. Only Ellie.

"I'm not leaving your side," I tell her.

"Yes, you are," she responds. "You're going to go be with the woman you are in love with, and it will make me happy to know I can leave this world to find Ellie up there and tell her that in return for the gift of her heart, I made sure your heart is happy."

Her sentiment is appreciated but I can't sit here and tell her I'm walking away now because she's dying—because Ellie's heart is dying. "I'm going to do whatever it takes to help you."

"I'll be fine," she says. "My parents are moving in with me next week."

"Is it going to just happen or…"

"I've been through it once before. It'll be a gradual deterioration again, the doctor said."

"What about another donor? Can we find you another donor?" I'm spitting off ideas I'm almost positive she has already considered.

"Hunter," she laughs quietly. "Ellie was my one and only. Trust me. I'm sure you knew she had a rare AB negative blood type."

"Yeah, the rarest of blood types. It wasn't something I ever had to think about, though," I tell her.

"Fate brought Ellie and me together, I believe. Less than one percent of the population has that blood type and to end up finding her, it all just felt like a sign for both of us." Ironic, how we both feel the same way about Ellie—for so long, I considered Ellie to be my one and only. Though, the healing process has recently proven to me that sometimes there is more than one chance for all of us.

"One percent of the world's population is seventy-one million, Ari."

She squeezes me again and rests her head against my shoulder as her hand finds mine and brings it up to her chest, allowing me to feel Ellie's heart beating again. "Now do you understand why I told you I am not your path?"

"Yeah," I breathe, "but your path brought me to where I am right now. You were right about Robert Frost being wrong."

"Take me to Charlotte," she says. "I need to talk to her."

"What? Why?" I ask, pulling away, staring at her with question.

"Just take me to her."

During the ride from the gardens to my house, I feel like I'm stuck in gridlock traffic. I grip the steering until my knuckles are white, my chest is aching, my throat is tight, my head is pounding, and I still feel like I might get sick. I'm trying to understand everything Ari just told me. I'm also trying to find loopholes and ways to spin this in a better direction. No one has ever told me they're dying and now that it has happened, I feel lost in the center of a black tornado, one that's sucking my organs out of my pores. She was right in a way about Robert Frost being full of it. In some aspects there are no paths to choose from, everything is predestined and when a person is meant to die, they die. There are no options.

"Do you feel sick and stuff?" I ask her.

"I've been a little tired, breathless, and nauseous, but I have definitely experienced worse." Of course she has, she was days or weeks from dying when she received Ellie's heart. Now she has to go through this all over again. How cruel is life to do this to someone twice?

"I want to help you," I tell her again. I'm not going to sit back and pretend she doesn't exist until I read her obituary in the paper some day.

"I appreciate that," she says, "but knowing what I will go through over the next several months is not something I want anyone to bear witness to."

"That's selfish," I tell her. "Do you think I care what you look like?"

"Hunter," she says firmly. "I will not put you through this a second time. Losing Ellie was more loss than you should ever have to deal with in one lifetime."

I twist and squeeze my grip around the steering wheel, wanting to say so much but knowing nothing I say will have any effect.

"What about the flower shop?"

I see her shrug out of the corner of my eye. "I'll keep working until it becomes too much."

"And what, you just drop dead one day while you're alone in the shop?" I shouldn't have said that. Her eyes are shooting invisible daggers at the side of my face and she has every right to be looking at me that way.

"My mother calls me every hour. If I don't answer, she will assume I'm dead," she snaps, finally getting angry, herself. Her tone is harsh, her words cold, and full of so much fucking pain, pain that she's been trying to hide.

"Can I visit you?" I ask, attempting to act a little gentler. I feel like I already know the answer to this, considering there are only so many ways I can ask the same question.

"No," she says without much thought.

"But the store is open to the public, isn't it?" Now I just sound childish, which I know won't help but it makes me feel better.

"Hunter," she sighs. "Please don't make this harder than it has to be." Now she sounds like Mom lecturing me. "If you don't think I would like to die some meaningful death beside the man who has become so intricately woven through every facet of my life, then you're wrong. I love that you have chosen to spend so much time with me over the past few months. To know the man who lost his heart the day Ellie gave hers to me has offered me more peace than you could ever imagine. Again, though, that was selfish. I wanted to meet you so I could feel better knowing you weren't still that man folded in half beneath a pay phone at the hospital. I needed to know you were surviving. God gives and God takes. He gave to me and took from you, and I needed to personally thank you because it was the least I could do." Ari sniffles briefly through a pause in her clearly unfinished thoughts. "You're an incredible person, Hunter, and I have cherished the time we have spent together—my guilt isn't as suffocating since I know you're going to be okay. But beyond that, my selfishness ends here. Now, I want to protect you from watching another person in your life—die." She makes it sound like she was using me but I wanted to be near her for a selfish reason, as well. A reason that won't exist for much longer because she's going to die.

Die. Those three letters pack a punch every time I hear them— they symbolize the end of everything. My ears should be numb to that word by now, but they aren't. It takes such a short breath of air to say it and while it seems to always be followed by a period, there is no real need for one because "die" defines completion. The period should be a silent punctuation mark; quietly puncturing it's way through the heart of anyone who witnesses the meaning of this stupid word.

We pull into my driveway and I step out first, watching as Ari stares expressionlessly out through the windshield. I want to know what is going through her mind. I want to know if everything she just told me was a forced lie and that she really does want me to be there for her. But as the thought runs through my mind once more, I remember the last breath I saw Ellie take on her own without a goddamn machine hooked up to her. I remember witnessing her lifeless body only moments after her brain died. The life that was once written across her face relaxed into a smooth surface of plateaued nothingness. I'm not sure I have it in me to live through that again in any form, whether our relationship was based on selfish gains or not, but I would if it meant something to her...I would stand by her side.

I have not fallen in love with Ari in the typical man loves a woman fashion. Instead, I love the person who has taken the time with Ellie's heart to make sure everything her heart has touched has been cared for in some way. I love that a person was able to keep her heart alive, even if only for a short time. Ellie's heart was large and full of so much love, care, and compassion that it deserved to go those extra miles.

I open Ari's door and offer her my hand. "I can get out myself," she says, humbly. "Thank you, though."

Once outside of the truck, Ari leads the way toward my front door but I stop her. "Charlotte moved home today." Ari looks at me for a few long seconds, peering back and forth between my eyes. "She was happy to get her house back."

Ari's brows arch a touch as she processes this tidbit of information. Then she turns and brushes by me, heading down the driveway toward the street. I follow her onto Charlotte's driveway and up to her front door. I still have no clue why she wanted to come here or what she needs to say to Charlotte but we're here now, and I should find out soon why she's doing this.

Charlotte answers the door, looking confused at first. "Ari? Are you okay?" She didn't see me at first glance but now she does and the question grows stronger within her eyes. I give her the same puzzled look back, letting her know I have no idea what this is all about. "Come in," Charlotte says, backing away from the door, allowing us to come inside. Boxes are now scattered, rather than stacked how I left them. Half of them are torn open and the other half are still taped shut. The furniture hasn't been taken out of storage yet but the moving company is supposed to be bringing everything by tomorrow morning. Basically, the house is empty.

I hear the girls singing and dancing in one of the rooms upstairs and the echo of their voices tells me that room is still barren, too. "I'm sorry to intrude on you like this," Ari says, taking in the scene of the empty house. "I'm sure you have a lot to do and you don't need me taking up any of your time but I felt it was necessary to come over here and talk to you. Both of you."

Charlotte's expression has turned into worry, and I can assume she is as in the dark as I am on what this could be about and why Ari wants to be here in Charlotte's house.

"I'm sorry I don't have a seat to offer you," Charlotte says. "You look frazzled. What's going on?" Charlotte looks at me as if the answer might be written across my face or spoken by my eyes but I don't think there's a look to convey that a person in this room is dying.

"Hunter is in love with you," Ari says in between heavy breaths, sounding as though she just climbed a set of stairs. "He talks about you all of the time. His eyes light up when I mention your name. He talks about Lana as if she were equally as much of a daughter to him as Olive. Sharing a home with you for the past few months was a treat for him, something he enjoyed, rather than a person living with a roommate. You moving out is hard on him. You are the family he has wanted since Ellie passed.

The relationship that has existed between Hunter and I has been a glorified friendship, one I have enjoyed more than I could ever explain. I am only the person who carries Ellie's heart, and I'm not the one who should be standing between you two."

"Ari," Charlotte croaks. "Why..."

"I'm saying this because you look at him the same way. You talk about him whenever you and I speak. You love Olive. You have loved living with the two of them and you are only moving out because you think it is what he wants."

"That's not true," Charlotte says with the sound of hesitation woven through every word. "Not all of it is true." I'm not sure it matters what parts are or aren't true. They all essentially mean the same thing.

"Hunter adores me," Ari continues. "He is in love with my heart. He has been a really good companion and he has removed the guilt I was desperate to shed." Ari walks closer, taking Charlotte's hands in her own. "I feel lucky and grateful to have spent this time learning about him, hearing his happiness poke through his words when he talks about you. I have watched him gradually grow happier as the months have gone by and it's fulfilling to me. It has made me love him." Ari laughs softly as a pink blush fills her cheeks. "My heart belongs to Ellie, and Hunter's heart belongs to you, Charlotte."

Charlotte's eyes grow wide as a film of tears underline her lashes. "I don't think I understand why you're saying all of this," Charlotte says.

I feel like I should step in and shield both of them from the pain, but I don't know how to and I don't know what to say. I don't think it's my right to announce Ari's preplanned future.

Ari leans toward the stairwell, presumably making sure the girls are not in hearing range. As she re-straightens her posture, she draws in a sharp, short breath. "There was never a life-long warranty on this heart I have and each transplant turns out differently. Some are lucky and live a long life, while others don't make it through the first six months after surgery. I've had almost six years and I consider it lucky."

"What?" Charlotte asks through a hitched breath.

"I won't make it through this next year," Ari says without wavering a syllable.

Charlotte isn't as strong, however. Tears are barreling down her cheeks; leaving red streaks down the center of her already flushed skin. There are no words to follow Ari's, as I've already learned. Instead of speaking, Charlotte leaps toward Ari and wraps her arms around her neck. I wonder if Charlotte has ever been told by a person that they are dying or if this is a first for her, too. I'm guessing it is. Charlotte's eyes are wide, unblinking, and staring directly at me as if someone just delivered world-shattering news. It definitely shatters our own little world and changes everything.

Ari wraps her arms around Charlotte in return and rests her head on her shoulder. "I'll be there for you," Charlotte says. "Every day. Whatever you need. We'll all be there for you."

Hearing the warm words float from Charlotte's mouth highlights the feelings I have always felt toward her. "That isn't necessary, but thank you for the kind offer," Ari says, pulling away from Charlotte's tight grip.

"You must be out of your mind," Charlotte argues. "I'm your friend and I will do anything I can to be whatever you need from here on out."

I know they have spoken when their paths have crossed but I'm not sure I would have classified them as friends in the awkward situation I created for the three of us. "I don't want to put you through what is about to happen to me," Ari explains. "Especially Hunter."

"Stop worrying about me," I tell Ari.

"Look," Ari says. "I came over here today because I need you two to work things out and be there for each other. I need to let Ellie know that I did what I promised I would do and that is to make sure Hunter is happy. I made this promise to her years ago when she knew her time would come sooner rather than later. I made this promise when neither of us knew who would outlive whom."

Charlotte and I are in a stare off, apparently trying to read each other's minds.

"It might take some time to intertwine your pieces back together," Ari says, looking between the two of us, "but Charlotte is your path, Hunter." Ari holds her focus on Charlotte now. "And Hunter is yours. I've never been surer of anything in my entire life."

"Ari," Charlotte says, but without anything to follow it up with, silence fills the empty room.

With what feels like the longest minute of my life, Olive's footsteps eliminate the icy silence and she runs toward Ari and wraps her arms around her legs. "Did you tell him?" she asks Ari.

Question and heat spread through me rapidly, wondering what Olive knows and what Ari told her. She is my daughter and I will be the one to explain life and death to her. That is my job and my right; one no one should take from me. Though I realize I might be assuming too much, I can't for the life of me imagine what else Olive could be referring to. When would Ari have told her?

"Tell me what, Olive?" I try to keep my voice calm and my breaths tamed but my face is burning and I'm sure it's red.

"I haven't yet, Olive," Ari says.

"Ari has a gift for you," Olive says.

Ari reaches into her purse and pulls out an envelope. "Read this when it's too late to thank me," she says, handing it to me. The coffee filter looking envelope matches all of the others she sent to me over the years. "Promise me."

My words feel lodged in my throat so I do the next best thing and nod a yes.

"I know you're saying your goodbyes right now, Ari, but you haven't seen the last of us," Charlotte says sternly. "You'll have to hire an army to keep us away."

CHAPTER NINETEEN

- DECEMBER 26TH -

I CLIMB INTO bed with Olive, wrapping my arm around her, embracing the warmness her body offers. Her curls are splayed across her pillow in a knotted mess and her cheeks are the perfect shade of pink. It is her birthday, but she is my gift. Seven years, this little girl and I have made it. Seven years. "Happy Birthday, Ollie," I whisper into her ear.

She whips her head, turning over onto her side to face me, leaving me with a face and mouthful of hair. "It's my birthday," she croaks. "I feel so old today." With quiet laughter, she drags herself up against the headboard, pulling the blankets up to her waist. "Ready?"

I smile and stand up to open the blinds. "Now I'm ready," I tell her.

"Happy Birth Day to you," she begins in her soft voice that mimics a soothing lullaby. I join in with her as we continue, "Happy Birth Day to you. Happy Birth Day, dear Mommy, Happy Birth Day to you."

I make it through our yearly tradition without tears this year but only because the happiness pouring from Olive's eyes right now makes it impossible to feel sadness.

"My turn," I tell her.

"Happy Birthday, to you," I sing all the way through. I lean over the side of the bed and pull out her gift, placing it gently on her blanket- covered lap.

"What is it?" she asks, clapping her hands while bouncing up and down.

"Open it, silly."

Olive tears apart the wrapping paper, revealing the box portion of the gift. "You got me Lucky Charms?" she asks with a goofy smile, like she's unsure if I would really give her something like this for her birthday or if it is a trick. I've never questioned her wit but she would never do anything to hurt my feelings, either.

"Maybe there's a lucky charm in the box?" I tell her.

She shakes the box around a little and pulls apart the tabs on the top. Peeking inside first, she then reaches her arm down into the opening, which swallows her arm up to her shoulder. Her hand fishes around for a minute before she pulls it back out holding Ellie's bracelet with three little charms on it. One represents Olive, one for me, and one for Ellie. "It's so pretty," she says, slipping it onto her wrist.

"It was your mom's. I gave this to her when we found out you were going to be a part of our lives. I know it's a little big, but I want you to have it."

"This is the best birthday gift I've ever gotten," she says through only her breath, admiring it. "I love it so much."

"I also got you something else, but I didn't want to bring it upstairs." I have a tendency to go overboard with Olive's birthday, especially with Christmas the day before, but a part of me has always felt like I have to in order to make sure the day is only filled with good memories.

"You did?" she shrieks, ripping the covers off.

Running out of her bedroom and into the hallway, I hear another loud scream of excitement followed by words bubbling from her mouth so loudly that they make no sense. I follow her out into the hall, seeing Charlotte and Lana at the bottom of the steps holding Jasmine, our new puppy.

Surprisingly, Olive makes it down the steps without falling and slows her speed just before reaching her hand out for the little four-pound powder-puff. "What's its name?" she asks.

"Jasmine," I tell her, walking down the steps.

"Like mom's favorite flower?" she asks.

"Yes," I grin.

Charlotte is beaming as she lovingly watches Olive talk to the puppy under her breath.

"You girls play with the puppy and I'm going to finish up breakfast so we can take it to Ari," Charlotte says as she steps out of the front door, giving me a quick wave as she jogs across the street and into her house. I thought she had started cooking here but maybe she's not done getting ready. I did wake her up early, seeing as our Christmas family dinner went until midnight last night.

I take the opportunity to straighten up a bit more but I only get as far as unloading the dishwasher when the front door opens. "It's just me," AJ shouts from the door. "It's birthday girl time!"

"Hey sweetie, Happy Birthday," Tori, AJ's new girlfriend says to Olive. I like Tori. We just met her for the first time a few weeks ago since AJ kept this relationship under his hat for almost three months, which is very unlike him. I get the sense he did it because things were actually going well and he was probably scared to mess it up in any way. Plus, Olive, with her little trade secrets, is not always helpful. She has enough dirt on AJ to destroy any and every future relationship.

After finishing up in the kitchen, I hear Charlotte return. "All set!" she calls out. "Let's get going!"

We pile into Charlotte's SUV and drive the four miles down to Brookside Hospital. Ari is expecting us today since she was excited to see Olive on her birthday, which also happens to be the very same day she was given a second chance at life—a short second chance, but a reason for celebration nonetheless.

Charlotte grips my hand in the elevator, squeezing it tightly. Neither of us likes being in this hospital. Too many people know Charlotte and of her failed marriage to a man who could have buried this places with his unlawful actions; and for me, the smell alone is like sarin gas attacking all of my senses.

We reach the nurses' station on the tenth floor and I wait for one of the nurses to greet me so we can check in. "Hey guys," one of the nurses says. "Right on time. She just woke up."

"Great, thank you!" I say, ushering Olive and Lana ahead.

"Mr. Cole," the nurse says gently, which grabs only my attention as the others are already walking down the hall. "It's getting close. I might keep the visit on the shorter side today."

I clench my jaw, feeling the familiar burn of tears behind my eyes. This is what Ari didn't want me to go through. These words, while foreign, feel way too damn familiar. "Thanks," I tell her.

I meet up with Charlotte, AJ, Tori, and the girls as we continue down the hall. "What was that all about?" AJ asks.

All I can do is give him a look, a look that should say it all without speaking out loud. I've run through my options of either keeping this from Olive or being honest with her. I've debated about whether or not to allow her to see the sight of Ari's declining condition, but Olive and her sixth sense knew something was wrong without me having to tell her. Her words to me were: "We should be there for Ari like we're her family. That's what mommy would want for her heart." Hearing Olive say that made my decision a little easier. She brings happiness to Ari, and Ari has a very special place in Olive's heart—a connection she may never understand.

AJ clears his throat as he comprehends my look and squeezes Tori's hand a little tighter. Charlotte, who must have noticed the look I gave AJ, reaches back for me and takes my hand within hers.

As we approach Ari's room, I squeeze Charlotte's hand a little tighter. It has only been a week but her skin is considerably paler than it was last time and her cheekbones are more prominent. The darkness of her hair washes out her eyes and she looks like...she's dying. She has looked like she's dying for weeks now but today, I'm not sure if there will be time for another visit.

"Hey," she says weakly, forcing as much excitement through her broken voice as she can. "How's the little birthday girl?"

Olive, fearless as always, climbs right up onto her bed and snuggles under her arm. "I feel so old today," Olive says again. "Can you believe I'm seven? That's like," she pops her fingers up as if she were counting. "Three years away from being ten. I mean, I'll be driving soon, which is good since I'll be able to come visit you whenever I want." And just like that, every ounce of understanding I thought Olive had brings me back to the realization that she is only seven and might not grasp this situation as much as I thought.

Ari struggles to lift her arm and runs her fingers through Olive's hair. "Do you know how happy I am that I met you?" Ari says to her.

"Yeah, I'm pretty cool," Olive jokes.

"I have something for you," Ari says, reaching over to take a small gift off of her nightstand.

"What is it?" Olive asks, her eyes wide and full of excitement.

Ari offers a weak smile and watches as Olive tears open the gift. She opens the box and pulls out an old-fashioned, large, fat gold key. I'm wondering what it's for but I'm sure Ari has a reason. "This is really cool," Olive says, admiring both sides of it. "Where does it go?"

"Some day, your dad is going to show you, but right now it's a secret. So for now, I need you to hang on to the key and keep it safe because you are the only one who is allowed to hold it."

"Is it magic?" she asks, totally enamored by Ari's explanation.

"Definitely," Ari says through a struggling laugh. "It brings people together and keeps them surrounded by love for all eternity."

Olive throws her arms around Ari's neck and kisses her cheek.

I'm looking at Ari with question, wondering if she'll let me in on the magical explanation of the key since I know Olive will be asking me what it unlocks until the day I die.

"You'll see," Ari mouths to me.

Thirty minutes filled with corny "you're dying" jokes, cake, and sympathetic looks come and go, and now Charlotte is suggesting that we let Ari rest. She collects the girls, and AJ and Tori follow them out the door after a slew of goodbyes, leaving me standing here staring at Ari.

With just the two of us in the room, I can't help but allow the pain to re-enter my chest. I can sit here and try to believe she's not dying and I'm not actually looking at a person deteriorating by the second, but I can't lie to myself.

Ari's slim smile reappears across her dry lips. "This is it, isn't it?" I ask.

"You never know," she sighs. "A miracle might happen." I can only assume that she's trying to convince herself, but just as I can't lie to myself, I can assume it's the same for her.

Tears fill her foggy eyes and she looks through me as if I were a window. The unbreakable demeanor everyone thinks she has is shattered into millions of pieces right now and this time, there's no way to put them back together. It's the first time I've seen her face shadowed by fear, accompanying the sorrow and sadness. "I guess I can say I'm dying of a broken heart now."

Her statement is not funny; it's hurtful. I don't know if her words have a double entendre but there is guilt brewing within me like I should have done something different—I'm just not sure what that would have been.

"I thought Ellie's heart would survive a longer measure of time when I met you," I tell her.

"Our hearts determine our paths, the distances we'll go, the direction, and the length of our stay," she says.

She reaches for me and I take the couple of steps over to her bedside, giving her my hand. She places it on her chest, over her heart. I feel the rhythm below my palm and the thick scar lining her nearly bare chest. The beat is slower than I remember from the last time I placed my hand on her chest, which was months ago. "I'm sorry," I tell her.

"We both know this is Ellie's heart, and we both know this is why you and I are connected, but what you have failed to realize is that sometimes our hearts walk around on the outside of our bodies."

I feel my forehead crinkle and strain as I let my head fall slightly to the side, waiting for clarification. "What do you mean?"

"Olive is Ellie's true heart," she explains. "Olive is a part of Ellie. She will go on to have kids of her own, who will have kids of their own, and Ellie's heart will go on for infinity. Olive is Ellie's heart. She has a heart made of time that will forever live on."

Her words are like hands reaching into my chest to wring the pain out of my heart. All of these years I have been chasing Ellie's last remaining organ when all along, a part of her was left with me for my forever. "I get it," I tell her.

"Hunter," she says, closing her eyes for a long blink. "I love you for being a part of my life and I love you for sticking by my side when I told you not to."

"I love—"

"Don't," she says. "I don't need to hear it. I don't want to hear it. You didn't have the chance to fall in love with me. I didn't give you a chance and I'm glad I didn't because I'm not the one for you."

"Then how can you say you love me?" I ask.

"When time is borrowed, you live fast, you love hard, and you put everything on the line knowing that tomorrow you might wake up with nothing— or you might not wake up at all."

"I see," I say, pushing a strand of hair out of her face. "Ari. Thank you for caring for her heart, protecting it, and for treating it like it was a gift. Your letters kept me going through those years— like really kept me going, knowing how lucky Ellie's heart was."

"Boy, it sounds like you're saying goodbye," she says, taking my hand and curling her fingers around mine while her gaze burns into me. "I don't care how long you stand here. I'm not dying in front of you." We both laugh and she releases my hand. "Go on so I can die in peace."

My jaw aches from grinding my teeth so hard, trying to prevent any hint of emotion. I have to be strong for her, at least as strong as she's being while saying goodbye to me. "Ari—"

"Say it, Hunter," she says, her voice a little weaker this time.

I pull in a thick, shallow, gulp of air and allow the words to float from my mouth into what seems like oblivion. "Goodbye, Ari."

I listen to the struggle of her breath as she presses her head firmly into her pillow, gently closing her eyes. I remain standing beside her bed, watching her, intently, waiting for I'm not sure what.

"I'm still not going to die in front of you," she whispers through slightly parted lips.

I close my eyes, releasing my weighted breath as I let go of her hand. Flashing a quick wave that she doesn't see, I turn and exit the room. Knowing I'm never going to see her again isn't easy to comprehend or wrap my head around. A heart-stopping period has been placed at the end of this chapter of my life.

CHAPTER TWENTY

- JANUARY -

I ONLY MET Ari's parents a handful of times. At first, they were warm and welcoming but after receiving the news of her failing heart, they both changed. It was as if a dark cloud descended on them. Smiles were nowhere to be seen, their eyes were covered in thin, red veins, and dark bags lined the creases above their cheeks—the evidence of many tears shed. I saw the look before, right after Ellie died. Ellie's parents never looked the same again. Life as they knew it was stolen from them and there was no way to fix it.

With my heart in my throat, I stand toward the back of the enclosed circle, admiring the strength within everyone. Ari's parents are holding hands so tightly the blood is pooling in their fingers. Her mother's eyes are glossed with tears but her chin is held high. Their chests both move in unison—in and out—slowly, suppressing their pain.

Charlotte's hand sweeps up the side of my back as her fingernails draw small circles to soothe what I'm feeling inside.

As the ceremony comes to an end, soft voices grow into sympathetic apologies and well wishes for Ari's parents. At the same time, Charlotte's nails dig a little deeper into my skin when I hear her whisper, "Oh my God."

I turn to face her, finding a ghostly paleness washing over her cheeks. "What's the matter?"

"Don." She points toward Ari's parents. "That's him." We can't hear the conversation between them but Don has his hand pressed against his chest, and his stature is tall and strong as if he's holding in more air than his lungs are capable of carrying. I've never met the man, nor seen a picture but he's a good-looking guy—sharp, well put together. What else would I expect from someone who used to be married to Charlotte? His suit looks like it might have cost more than one of my mortgage payments and by the looks of it, someone shaved his face for him this morning. Regardless of the outer layer, there is something to be said for the despondent look in his eyes.

With his hand on Ari's mom's shoulder, Don's focus transfers from them to Charlotte, and his face registers shock. He definitely wasn't expecting to encounter her here today. When he sees her, he immediately excuses himself from the conversation he was in and makes his way over toward us. I expect Charlotte to remove her hand from my back and separate herself from me, but instead she loops her arm around mine, squeezing it tightly, as if she suddenly needs me to protect her. Charlotte has never been a woman who seems to need protection. She's dominant, fierce, and knows what she wants. I know she has a soft center but at this moment, her outer shell is just as weak. I'm glad to be the one whose arm she clings to in her moment of weakness.

"Charlotte," Don addresses her. "What are you doing here? Did you know Ariella?"

Charlotte looks blankly at him as if she doesn't know how to respond appropriately. "I—ah."

"Charlotte is with me, and Ari was the recipient of my wife's heart," I say sharply.

Don places his hand over his agape mouth, his large, gold ring flashing a plate of diamonds in our face. "My God," he says. "Eleanor Cole."

Hearing her name come from his mouth makes my gut hurt. The only people who referred to Ellie as Eleanor were the doctors. Even Ellie's parents didn't call her that. It was a name only used in life-threatening matters, during the car accident and then the day she passed. "Yes, that's my wife."

He looks between Charlotte and me, apparently trying to understand it all. "Small world, huh?" he asks, obviously flustered by the situation.

"Very," I say coldly, unwilling to ease his discomfort.

"I take it you have the answers you were desperate for?" he asks Charlotte.

"I know everything," Charlotte tells him. "You're a piece of shit, but I'm still grateful you gave Ari a few extra years."

Don looks down, outwardly ashamed. He digs the sole of his freshly shined wing tip shoe into a small pile of dirt. "I'm sorry I caused you to lose the house, Charlotte. I was—" That's all you're sorry for?

"There's no explanation necessary," she says, cutting him off. For the moments of weakness she portrayed as he was walking over here, I'm impressed and proud of the way she's handling herself.

"I was in too deep and I was afraid of getting caught. I'm no longer conducting business in that way. I've acquired a job with a transplant research firm so you and Lana will be taken care of from here on out."

"Just worry about Lana," I bark. "She talks about you daily and misses you more than you clearly deserve. Charlotte, I can take care of." The words about Lana are lies. I don't want him anywhere near Lana, but I won't get between a father and his daughter. I will just fill those holes in Lana's life. I will be there for her and do whatever I can to make sure she never feels like she's missing something.

Don places a hand on my shoulder, and the cologne from his skin burns the inside of my nose. "Thank you for looking after

Lana, and Charlotte is clearly lucky to have you." He sounds strangled, as if the truth is wrapped around his lungs, suffocating him. Everything about him—his voice, his words, and his demeanor—suggest he's realized what he lost and is smart enough to know it's too late to get it back. Nevertheless, I have no sympathy for him; in fact, he still makes me sick.

"Despite the fact that I think you're a poor excuse for a human being, thank you for saving Ari and fulfilling Ellie's wish," I say, the boldness of my honesty surprising even myself.

He pulls in a sharp sigh. "I'm aware that Ellie wanted her request to remain private. She was a strong woman who knew exactly what she wanted. Very convincing—blackmailing, actually. It was hard to deny a gesture such as hers, and Ari had been my patient for years—a patient I spent half of my career trying to help." Help? Is that what he's convinced himself of? Help is an action that doesn't require inappropriate behavior as gratitude.

"Ellie had a way with people," I say, unintentionally snarling at him.

With an increased look of discomfort Don's eyes, he shifts his weight and sucks in a shallow breath. "Well, take care of yourself, Charlotte," he says, closing the conversation. "Maybe we can discuss custody again at some point." I can only imagine what is going through Charlotte's mind right now. I'm not sure custody in any circumstance will be easy for her to agree to after Don made career choices that caused his own daughter to lose her home for months, never mind everything else flagged on his track-record.

"I need more time," Charlotte says. The court will do whatever Charlotte wants, which makes this even harder on her.

"Understood. Tell Lana I miss her." Don reaches out to shake my hand and I offer mine in return, only because I'm a decent human being. The non-decent part of me would like to knock his fake veneers out. Douche. "A pleasure to meet you and I'm sorry for your loss."

As he walks away, I feel Charlotte's chest exhale against my back as her cheek rests against my shoulder, obviously glad to have that conversation over. "I hate him," she says. "Regardless of the fact that he saved Ari, I really hate him."

"Considering the circumstances, I think that's okay," I tell her.

I reach into my suit-coat pocket and pull out the envelope Ari gave me a few months ago, telling me I could not open it until it was too late to thank her. I've kept it sitting on top of my bureau since that day, practically burning a hole through it with my eyes every time I glanced at it. I've held it up to the sun trying to read whatever is inside but she anticipated my move, covering the envelope's contents with a blank piece of paper.

"Oh my gosh, I almost forgot about that," Charlotte says.

My hands tremble as I separate the flap from the body of the envelope. I expect to see a typical typed note, similar to the ones Ari wrote to me for five years, but it isn't like that. Puzzled by what I'm looking at, I unfold the papers, straightening them out to get a better look. With the sun so bright in the sky, though, there's a glare over the center, but it's instantly covered by a shadow. "Ari made this decision six years ago," a voice says from over my shoulder. I turn, finding Ari's dad standing behind me. "Go on, read what it says."

I scan through the words over and over, trying my best to comprehend what I'm looking at. I guess I know what I'm looking at but how could this be? "I don't understand," I tell him.

"My wife and I owned the Hillview Gardens," he says.

I shake my head, bewildered. "What? I—"

"It has been in the family for some time," he continues.

"Did Ellie know?"

He laughs quietly. "Of course she knew. Ellie came to gardens daily, with and without you. I spoke to her many times over the years and she was the one who got Ari the student-teaching job. Ellie has been a blessing in our lives for as long as I can remember."

"Why didn't anyone tell me this?"

"A good person is doing no good if their reasons are anything more than soul-filling. I'm sure you know that Ellie did things out of the kindness of her heart, never wanting anything in return." That is my Ellie. It always has been. This shouldn't be a surprise to me. "When I told Ellie about Ari's condition and her dreams, wishes, and hopes, it was as if Ellie knew what her purpose in life was. Beyond the love she had for you, she wanted to leave her mark in this world. And boy, did she. In fact, we say a prayer for her each night before bed."

I look back down at the papers, reading them once more. "Are you saying...?"

"The Hillview gardens are now in your name." With shock, and more appreciation than I have ever had for anything, I pull him in for a hug, locking my fists tightly around him. Telling him this means the world to me would not do justice to how I truly feel. I had no idea that Ari's family owned the gardens but it's like my life was planned to go down this path...this unexpected path. I don't understand life's plans and the twisted roads accompanying it. I still don't understand Robert Frost and his thought-provoking words but I do understand that while our hearts may dictate the time we spend on this earth, they also direct us down the path we are meant to take, whether it is the one less traveled or not.

My heart led me to Ellie. Her heart led her to Ari. Ari's heart led Charlotte to me. Life is not one straight highway; sometimes it's an offbeat path with no direction, no signs, no warnings, and often with no apparent reason. It is rarely traveled on because there is no conclusive outcome and no defined ending until a person arrives there.

Here I am, at the beginning of a new bend on this endless path I started down at age five when I met Ellie. I never considered a different direction, nor did I wonder where it might have led.

The peace I have sought from the moment Ellie died has found me here, today, with understanding of Ellie's path that veered away from mine. Some day our roads will intersect again but until that day, I will continue walking blindly around new corners and into unchartered territory, unknowing of what lies ahead. I will allow life to unfold around each bend of the road.

CHAPTER TWENTY-ONE

- ONE YEAR LATER -

"IF I HAVE to move these boxes one more time—" I jokingly threaten.

Charlotte's hands sweep up the back of my shirt as she places soft kisses on my chin. "I said, thank you," she whispers against my lips. "What more do you want from me?" she adds, suggestively.

I scoop her up in my arms and carry her up the steps and into my—our bedroom. "Have I told you how much I love you?" I ask her.

"Only twenty times in the past two hours," she says with a wry grin. "But in case you plan to show me, we only have an hour before the girls get home from school."

I yank the sheets down and pull my shirt over my head. "Then don't waste time," I say in a low growl. She hops backward into the center of the bed, slipping off her shirt, pants, and everything else beneath. I climb over her, lowering my body onto hers, embracing her warmth and allowing it to soothe my aching muscles.

I take a moment to stare into her eyes, brushing the hair away from her cheeks. "Do you know how lucky we are?"

"Our crazy, screwed up lives brought us here, so yeah," she laughs softly.

My mind clears as I focus on Charlotte—her heartbeat, her breaths, her skin against mine, the passion I have for only her. I had been holding myself back from these feelings but with Ari's encouragement, I finally let my guard down. Now there is room in my life and my heart for passion, a second chance at love—a place both Charlotte and I are discovering together, somewhere that is new to each other like a first love. Our first loves can't be replaced but they are part of who we both are, and they indirectly played a part in bringing us together, giving us both the gift of a second chance at forever. This second time around is not for replacing memories, love, or a past—it's only for moving forward and building a new life together as a family, allowing our love for each other to heal our brokenness.

I watch the emotion on Charlotte's face as we move together in a heated motion. With the tips of her fingers pressed into my back, her lips melt against my neck, and soft moans escape her throat. "Don't stop," she whimpers.

Her words trigger rougher movement from me, causing her to clutch my arms harder, bringing along an incredibly delicious pain. "Like this?" I growl, teasingly.

She tries to answer but her breaths are too fast and too loud to create intelligible words. Sweat beads between us as I hold her tighter. The pressure builds, our muscles tighten, and then her tremors cease. I unravel as she does, falling a little deeper into a world filled with light and a happiness that I once thought would be impossible to find again.

Unwinding from our tightened grips on each other, I fall heavily beside her, chasing after each one of my missing breaths.

"Are you ready for tomorrow?" I ask her, curling my arm around her neck.

"Tomorrow is just another day," she says. "I already have everything I want."

I press my lips against her forehead. "Our little girls will finally be sisters," I add.

"And they will have everything they want," Charlotte says with a gorgeous, satisfied smile claiming her flushed cheeks.

My phone buzzes on the nightstand and I reach over Charlotte to grab it. I press it up to my ear, waiting to hear the wrath from AJ.

"Dude, I'm not even halfway through this job. You need to get your ass down here."

"I'm coming, I'm coming," I groan.

"You already did," Charlotte mutters below her breath through a silent chuckle.

"You motherfucker," AJ says. "You're in bed right now, aren't you?"

"Um," I laugh.

"You're going on your fucking honeymoon in two days. Can't you keep it in your pants until then?"

"I'd like to say yes but I'm still making up for the lost time of a five-year, self-induced abstinence." Charlotte runs her hand through my hair and kisses my temple as she rolls out of bed. I stare at her lazily while AJ continues chewing my ear off. The glow of her bare body in the sun is preventing any and all cognitive thoughts. I have no idea what AJ is saying…never mind getting up, getting dressed, and driving two miles to the job site.

"Hunter!" AJ snaps, trying to regain my attention. Ignoring him, I hang up the phone and toss it toward the end of the bed.

"I'll have dinner ready when you get home," Charlotte says, pulling her shirt over her head.

"Thank God, my plan worked," I tell her. "Dinner on the table, waiting for me in my own house."

Charlotte throws a pillow at my face and slips her jeans on. "I still have fifteen hours to change my mind about this forever thing."

"Whatever," I say, grinning like a fool.

She bounces back onto the bed and kisses me wildly before leaving me, breathless and naked in the middle of a mess of sheets.

AJ follows me home after cleaning up the job site and I'm not sure why. I didn't invite him back. Maybe he forgot something in my truck? I step out, waiting for him to open his truck door. But as I'm waiting to ask him what he's doing, Mom and Dad's car pull up, too.

AJ finally opens the door with a cocky smirk. "Surprise!"

"Surprise for what? What the hell is going on?"

"I don't know," he says with a shrug. "Charlotte wanted to have the family together tonight. Something about not needing a rehearsal but just a nice dinner."

Mom hops out of the car with her hands clasped together and a look I don't remember seeing on her face in years. She runs up the driveway and plasters her hands on my cheeks, pulling my head down to kiss me. She leans back slightly and looks into my eyes but doesn't say anything for a long second. "Why are you looking at me like this?" I ask her.

"First, who plans a wedding in three days?" she asks.

"Two people who have already been married once?" I respond through laughter.

"Second, you listen to me—" she begins in her motherly advice tone. "I can say this because I am your mother, no matter how old you are..." She pauses for a moment as a smile perches over her lips. "I am so proud of you, Hunter. So damn proud of you."

I don't need to ask what she means by this. I know what I put my family through over the past six years. They have stuck by my side every day, good and bad. I have yelled at them. I have told them to go away. I have begged them to let me die. Still, they all stuck by my side with understanding and patience. They have all helped me raise Olive while standing far enough away to avoid stepping on my toes. Mom has made it clear over the past few years that I'm too young to call it quits. I now realize that there is life after death and it's okay. I shooed away her comments and advice, thinking there was no way I could ever come to terms with what she wanted for me. Turns out, she was right.

She presses her fingers to my heart. "This is yours. It matters, as it always has, and I'm so happy you are being true to it now. Ellie would be proud of you, Hunter. I promise you that." Without the proper words to respond to her statement, I pull her in for a hug, feeling her body shudder slightly as her arms tighten around me.

"I love you, Mom. Thank you for always be being here for me when I need you, even at those times when I don't know I need you." She grabs my face and kisses my cheek, sobbing silently under her breath.

As mom takes my hand, we all filter into the house, finding Olive running around like a little crazy person, full of excitement. She's getting a sister tomorrow and gets to wear a pretty dress— clearly that's all it takes to make a little girl's world complete. "Grammy, do you want to meet my new sister?" Olive says through giggles while spinning Lana in circles.

"I'm pretty sure we've already met, you silly girl," Mom says.

"You know what else?" Olive continues. "I get to use my magical key tomorrow."

Mom looks at me with question, as I'm not sure I ever mentioned this key that Ari gave her. "Oh really?" Mom says.

"Yep, you'll see," Olive says with a smile.

"What key?" Mom asks me.

"You'll see," I echo Olive, giving her a wink.

Mom rolls her eyes and wanders off into the kitchen to help Charlotte. Dad and AJ fall into the couch, chatting about the job site today and Tori walks through the door. AJ is up and over to her side within a second, ushering his very pregnant wife over to the couch. "Two weddings and a baby this year," Dad says with a proud glimmer in his eyes. "And the Cole name continues. It's a good year."

Throughout the evening, within their happiness, I notice a defined switch in the way my family is acting. It's something I've either been too closed off to notice or something I've caused. Regardless, the amount of love in this dining room has brought me a sense of peace, knowing that tomorrow the final piece of my shattered life will fit back together, differently, with some cracks here and there, but together, nonetheless.

Mom has been staring at me all night with this gleam in her eyes. I think seeing me happy again has finally taken away some of her pain. Her elbow is resting on the table and she's gazing at me. I don't ask her why she's looking at me the way she is, but I smile back—a full heart-filled smile. Tears well in her eyes and she looks up toward the ceiling, silently thanking those above.

The house clears out shortly after dinner since we all need to be up rather early tomorrow. The girls are sleeping in their new bunk beds and Charlotte and I are curled up on the couch in front of the TV.

"I never thought I could find something so right," she says, simply, relaxing her head into my chest. My focus drifts to the picture of Ellie hanging on the wall and I find comfort. My heart beats a little harder and I silently thank her for watching over us, making sure that in the shadow of her life, I'm happy.

"I never thought there was something that could feel right again," I mutter against her ear, kissing her softly. "But I was wrong."

Regardless of needing a normal night of sleep, Charlotte and I both wake up in each other's arms on the couch as the sun peeks through the trees outside. Most people spend the night away from each other before their wedding, but I think Charlotte and I spent enough time apart that it feels most appropriate to wake up just like this today.

I find myself standing in the center of the house as the morning creeps by, watching the women in my life run around trying to make sure they look perfect for today. I know it'll only take me twenty minutes to get dressed, so for now, I'd rather just watch the excitement around me. Or until AJ walks through the door.

He's beaming and he's got a bottle of Jack in his hand. "Just one shot since I wasn't allowed to throw you a bachelor party. It'll loosen up your nerves."

"I'm not nervous, though."

"Oh, well, it's still necessary," he says, shoving the bottle into my chest.

"You're supposed to be my best man, not my worst influence," I laugh.

"Dude, I'm a master at being both." This he is. Finally, something we can agree on.

Even though Charlotte was okay with sleeping beside me last night, she isn't okay with me seeing her before it's time for the ceremony so AJ and I are taking the girls and heading to the gardens.

"I'll meet you there," Charlotte says, leaning around the corner, blowing me a kiss.

"Whatever," I say, giving her a quick wink.

With laughter floating through the hallway, I hear Mom calling Charlotte so she can help her finish getting ready.

"Ready, ladies?" AJ says to Olive and Lana, who are both draped in white knee-length dresses, complete with flowers in their hair.

They're spinning around in circles, making their dresses fly high, and the excitement bursting from them is something I will always remember about today.

Giggles fill the truck as we make the short drive over to the gardens, finding the lot empty except for one car. Just how I like it.

AJ and I escort the girls down the steps, making our way up to the tree. Olive runs ahead and wraps her arms around the trunk. "Good morning, Mommy." She cups her hand around her mouth and presses it against the bark. "Daddy is finally happy and it's the best day of my life. Thank you for watching over him."

Her words make my chest shudder so I take a deep breath and look up into the clear blue sky, repeating Olive's words silently on my own.

We continue walking down an unfamiliar path, one that isn't marked well, one that looks untraveled, but I was told it leads to the place where Olive's key works. Ari's dad shared the big secret with me—what lies on the other side of the gated door—and it's where Charlotte and I should begin our united lives. So that is what we're doing.

SHARI J. RYAN

The path comes to an end and we walk up to a wooden gated door between thickly settled trees. It's like nothing I've ever seen before and it's amazing.

"Go ahead, Olive. I know you've been waiting for this." Olive takes the key from her little, white clutch purse that Charlotte bought for her and slowly places it into the tarnished lock.

With hemming and hawing, the door creaks open, revealing a large enclosed garden full of blue jasmines and white hydrangeas, with a small, narrow cobblestone path down the center that leads up to a white gazebo. A sign perched in front of the gazebo reads, "Olive's Secret Garden." The look on her face is one I wish Ari could see as a thank you for the most incredible gift she could have given.

Olive spins around, looking in every corner before she lies down in a patch of flowers. "It's like Mom is here, everywhere," she says. "This is the most amazing place; it must be like heaven."

I lie down next to her, pulling her into my side. "She's always around you, Olive. She's always with us."

We're in dress clothes and we're lying on the ground, and nothing has ever felt so right.

No, wait. Now, nothing has ever felt so right. Charlotte, in her beautiful dress, lies down beside me and Lana joins us, as well. We look ridiculous but I know now, looking back up into the sky, that Ellie and Ari are watching us. I have to believe they planned this.

"Should I just pronounce you husband and wife?" Ari's dad asks, walking in through the gate. When I told him Charlotte and I had decided to get married, which was more than three days ago, he asked me to give him two months and informed me that he was a wedding officiate. I didn't know why he needed so long, but a garden isn't built in a day, I do know that much.

"Please," Charlotte says, twisting her head, bringing her nose close to mine. Her eyes are glimmering under her lashes and her lips are glossed, reflecting the flowers around us. I'm in love with this woman. I am completely head-over-heels in love with her and it feels right—it feels perfect and complete.

Ari's dad spouts off a few lines before commencing our marriage and the connection of our new family.

246

Never in a million years did I foresee my life going in this direction, being with someone other than Ellie, lying in a meadow of blue jasmines while joining my life with Charlotte.

Life is like the center of a blooming flower with each petal lifting over time, slowly exposing our hearts and souls as the motion of life circles around us. I can't change it and I can't stop it but I can watch and take in the beauty of it all. I definitely took the road less traveled, and my God, has it made all the difference.

Robert Frost, you are a brilliant man.

EPILOGUE

- TEN YEARS LATER -

IT'S EIGHT **in** the morning on a Saturday and I sort of figured I would be the only one awake in the house but the sudden onset of wrestling noises in the basement has me wondering who might be up. Maybe Jasmine got down there again. She has a thing for the musky darkness in her old age. For another moment, I continue to listen for more hints and at the same time Charlotte comes down the stairs, groggy and still half asleep. "What's the look for?" she asks, kissing me quickly before grabbing a coffee mug.
"Do you hear that?" I ask.

Charlotte stops to listen. "Oh yeah, I think Olive was looking for something last night and she's probably down there continuing the search."

"What was she looking for?" I ask.

"She didn't say. You know her, when she's trying to figure something out, it's best not to ask questions." I laugh at her explanation. So true. It's something we have all learned well throughout her teenage years. "Has Ashley woken up yet? She has a soccer game at eleven and I almost forgot," Charlotte says.

"Crap, no. I forgot, too. Let me go down and see what's going on with Olive and then I'll go take our little princess to soccer. You said you needed to go check on some things at the office, right?"

"Yeah, I want to make sure the new updates were completed by the developers last night," she says.

"You got it, my big famous CEO," I say, pulling her down to my lap.

"Very funny," she grins. "Oh, and in case you didn't get the memo, your little princess is nine now and will have no part in you calling her a princess. You can thank me for the warning later."

Girls. "I'll just thank you now and get it over with," I say, pressing my lips up against her neck.

"Ugh, gross," Ashley says, pointing her finger into her mouth. "Get a room." Yep. I do not miss this age.

"Excuse me, Princess Ashley," I tease.

"Oh my God, Dad, get a grip. I'm nine," Ashley says, flipping her auburn hair behind her shoulders.

"Good morning to you, too," I grin at her.

Placing my coffee mug down on the kitchen table, I jog down the wooden steps, finding only the corner light on near the back part of the stairs.

"Olive, what are you doing down here?" I ask as I find her rummaging through an old box.

She collapses with frustration, throwing her hands down by her hips. "Ugh, I was looking for a purse to bring with me tonight and I thought maybe Mom would have had something cute I could use." I see now that she's rummaging through one of Ellie's boxes of clothes. I wonder how often she does this, considering this is the first I've seen her doing it. She definitely looks as if she's done this before.

"Oh," I say. "Honestly, I don't know if any of her purses are in there. I didn't really have the heart to go through her stuff and separate it. I just knew I couldn't get rid of it."

She ignores what I say and continues digging around. "I've seen it in here before," she says. I guess that answers my question of whether or not she has searched through Ellie's items in the past.

"What does it look like?"

"I don't know, it's black and—ah, I think I got it." She pulls out a small black bag with a gold chevron pattern embroidered into the leather. I remember now, it was the last thing Ellie grabbed on the way out the door when she went into labor. I remember questioning why she would need a purse while giving birth but I assumed it's one of those questions a man just shouldn't ask a woman.

"I'm glad you found it. I'm sure she would have loved to know you were bringing it to your prom tonight." Olive stands up, her head now up to my shoulder. When did she get this tall? This beautiful. Her long, blonde curls are a mess and she's still in her PJs, looking somewhat like a young girl and somewhat like a girl on the verge of womanhood. "You're up pretty early, thinking about a purse," I tell her.

"I'm just excited for tonight and a little nervous since Lana isn't here to go with me." This whole year has been a difficult transition for Olive with Lana off at her freshman year at college—a preview of what I will go through next year when my little girl leaves me. Lana does come home once a month or so but Olive misses her like crazy and doesn't do much to conceal her true feelings on the matter. Teenage hormones are a warning I wish someone...anyone could have given me.

"You're going to have a great time tonight. I promise," I tell her.

Olive inspects the purse and unzips it to look inside. She sweeps her hand around inside as a weird look flickers through her eyes. There shouldn't be anything in there since I had to remove Ellie's wallet when we were at the hospital, and I don't remember anything being left inside. Olive pulls her hand out of the purse and a note is pinched between her fingers. "What's this?"

I take the note from her hand and unfold it as fast as I can, finding that it unfolds six times before opening up into a full-size sheet of notebook paper.

"Can you hit the main light?" I ask Olive.

My heart is already aching and I can't make out any of the words in the dark. But as the light illuminates the room, the writing becomes clear.

"Is it from Mom?" she asks.

"Yeah," I say, breathlessly. After all these years, this woman still knows how to steal my every breath.

"Read it out loud." Olive's arms wrap around me and her head rests on my arm as I begin to read.

My Hunter,

Okay, so, I don't know when you'll see this note and I'm actually kind of hoping you never do because if you do, it'll mean something has happened to me and I'm probably not with you anymore. It will also mean you're going to be pretty upset with me when you find out some of the secrets I have kept from you, considering I knew something horrible was going to happen and decided to keep it from you. It really does sound worse than it is. I think.

Before I tell you any more, though, I need you to know how much I love you. From the first day of school when you took my hand and walked me onto the bus and dried my tears as I waved good-bye to my parents, to the second day of school when you had to do the same thing, and actually, every single day the entire first year of school. By June of that year, I kind of knew you would forever be my best friend and it's nice to know that my six-year-old-self was right.

Life without you wouldn't make sense. Growing up with the man you want to spend your life with isn't something every girl is lucky enough to experience. But I was lucky. So very lucky—the kind of lucky a girl gets when a guy drags his girl into a garden at night and carves her name into a tree with his.

I suppose this would have been easier if I had told you that my chances of surviving past the age of twenty-five were unlikely. I could have told you all of the things I wanted to tell you—like, please don't stop living your life because I'm gone, and I hope you find a second chance at true love, even if you don't know the woman for twenty years first.

The moment I found out about the aneurysm after our car accident, I was left with two paths to take: I could tell you I wasn't going to make it or I could keep it from you and pretend like everything was going to be okay. Most people might have chosen the more honest route but I couldn't fathom the idea of telling you what my expected outcome was. You would have spent every day worrying about me, caring for me, acting like I were a piece of breakable glass. You would have married me—I know that, but you would never have wanted a child with me if I told you that the one detail in our lives could be the most likely event to cause the aneurysm to rupture.

You know me; I am scared of blood, cuts, bruises, broken bones, illnesses, and germs, which became sort of ironic when the doctor told me my prognosis. From that point on, nothing seemed to scare me anymore. If I fell and hit my head, that could have been the end. But I overcame those silly odds and we did get pregnant and I'm about to give birth to our daughter. I know it sounds terrible to keep this from you and then possibly leave you to care for our child as a single parent, but I've thought this through. For years, actually. I wanted to leave you with a part of me. You can't spend twenty five years with someone and then have nothing to show for it. I considered the fact that you might not agree with this theory but I also think I know you pretty well and you would want some part of me to hang onto because I would want the same if the tables were turned.

I'm sure you will be surprised when you find out I chose to donate my heart, but I can't really see why I shouldn't. A woman I know was dying and I told her if I died before her, I want her to have the part of me that is still alive. She told me the odds are against her when it came to a donor because of her rare blood type—the same blood type I happen to have. That one sign told me it is the right thing to do. I know you don't know this woman or who I'm talking about since I never mentioned her...it was because she knew my truth and you don't. And yes, I realize as I'm writing this how unfair that sounds, but again, it is only because I didn't want to hurt you for longer than you would already be forced to feel pain for. You got to enjoy the years we had together without each day being overshadowed by worry and fear of when something might happen to me, and that makes me happy. My parents don't even know and they don't need to. It would hurt them too much to know I kept this from them.

I've left notes for our daughter in her baby book, which I hope she will read as she gets older. I hope she looks like me and acts like you. I hope she's kind like both of us and loves everything and everyone. If she has my crazy, curly hair, tell her I'm sorry. If she has your intense sky-blue eyes, tell her she's lucky. If she ever asks about me, tell her I'll be listening and she can talk to me whenever she wants. I will always be your angel and hers. I don't exactly know how it all works up there in the big blue but if my heart can live on, so can my soul.

Don't let yourself go like you tend to do when you're upset about something. Don't shut people out. Let your parents help you, let AJ be the uncle he was born to be, and ignore my parents when they blame you for my death because I'm already sure they will. Most importantly, don't you dare blame yourself for the way my life has gone. I know you took the blame for that car accident even though it was not remotely close to being your fault; therefore, I'm sure the Hunter I love and know is currently blaming himself for my death. It is not your fault. This was my path...it just ended sooner than yours.

You know that poem by Robert Frost? The Road Not Taken? I used to teach it to my students, not because it was written by a famous poet but because of the meaning behind it. The meaning, though, depends on how the reader comprehends it. Some will say we have no choices in life. Others will say we do. I personally think we have a little of both. I didn't have a choice on whether you stepped into my life when we were children. I didn't have a choice when I fell in love with you. I did, however, have a choice when you asked me to marry you and when we decided to have a baby. Maybe they weren't choices others would have decided on the same way but I went in the direction I thought I should go, and while both paths would have eventually led to the same end point, I'm glad I traveled down the path I chose because I wouldn't change a thing.

Remember this as you go through life: sometimes we have choices and other times we don't. It's the times that we do when you should always consider the path that might be less traveled by—it might just make all of the difference. Live on the edge, Hunt, live like there's no tomorrow and you won't ever have regrets. Trust me.

Forever yours,
Your Heart—Ellie

HOW TO CONNECT WITH SHARI

NEWSLETTER:
http://sharijryan.com/sign-up
WEBSITE:
http://sharijryan.com
FACEBOOK:
https://www.facebook.com/authorsharijryan
TWITTER:
https://twitter.com/sharijryan
GOODREADS:
https://goodreads.com/shariryan

ABOUT SHARI

International Bestselling Author, Shari J. Ryan, hails from Central Massachusetts where she lives with her husband and two lively little boys. Shari has always had an active imagination and enjoys losing herself in the fictional worlds she creates.

When Shari isn't writing or designing book covers, she can usually be found cleaning toys up off the floor.

OTHER BOOKS BY SHARI

Ravel
No Way Out
Red Nights
TAG
You're It
Schasm
Fissure Free
When Fully Fused

Made in the USA
San Bernardino, CA
22 March 2017